OUR NIG

OUR NIG;

or,

Sketches from the Life of a Free Black,

In A Two-Story White House, North.

SHOWING THAT SLAVERY'S SHADOWS
FALL EVEN THERE.

by "OUR NIG."

VINTAGE BOOKS
A Division of Random House • New York

This edition of
Our Nig
is dedicated to
Pauline Augusta Coleman Gates
and
Henry Louis Gates, Sr.

VINTAGE BOOKS EDITIONS, May 1983, April 2002

Preface and Revised Notes copyright © 2002 by Henry Louis Gates, Jr.
Introduction and Notes copyright © 1983 by Henry Louis Gates, Jr.

Library of Congress Cataloging-in-Publication Data
Wilson, H. E. (Harriet E.), 1808–ca. 1870.
Our nig: or, sketches from the life of a free black,
in a two-story white house, North.
Bibliography: p.
I. Gates, Henry Louis. II. Title.   III. Title:
Sketches from the life of a free black.
PS3334.W39O9 1983   813'.3   82–49197
ISBN 1–4000–3120–6 (pbk.)

WWW.VINTAGEBOOKS.COM

Manufactured in the United States of America
10   9   8   7   6   5   4   3

In Memory

of

Marguerite Elizabeth Howard Coleman,

and

Gertrude Helen Redman Gates

Acknowledgments

Without the support and encouragement of John W. Blassingame, Professor of History at Yale University and Chairman of the Program of Afro-American Studies, I would not have been able to verify Harriet E. Wilson's identity. When one seemingly solid lead would fail, Blassingame suggested others. Only with the enthusiasm generated by our daily discussions about *Our Nig* was I able to persist in my search for this black woman writer. Blassingame's intelligent advice and his generosity are models of scholarly magnanimity, especially for his younger colleagues. This book, in many ways, is John's book.

David A. Curtis, Director of Research for the Yale Black Periodical Fiction project, devoted several weeks in September and October 1982 to archival research in Massachusetts and New Hampshire, research that helped me to confirm and supplement the initial facts about Harriet E. Wilson I had gathered in the summer of 1982. David Curtis's contribution to the rediscovery of *Our Nig* is major.

Excellent research assistants who participated in this project include John W. Blassingame, Jr., Donna Dennis, Alexandra Gleysteen, and Timothy Kirscher. For their invaluable assistance I would also like to thank expressly: Jeanne Wells, Olivia Iannicelli, Lisa Fetchko, Irma Johnson, Paul Johnson, Mike Saperstein, Anthony Appiah, Martha Clarke, Olufemi Euba, Richard Powell, C. Peter Ripley, Nina Baym, Barbara Johnson, Kimberly W. Benston, Jean Fagan Yellin, Robert Farris Thompson, Mr. Wilfred A. Leduc, Mrs. Helen Draper, Mrs. Nancy Schooley, Mrs. Eugene W. Leach, Sr., Elizabeth Alexander, Maria Fernandez-Gimenez, Denise

Hurd, Mrs. Helen Leahy, Rev. David L. Clarke, and Robert Curran. Thirty-five students in my Yale College seminar "Black Women and Their Fictions" combed through forty periodicals, published between 1859 and 1861, for any mention whatsoever of the book or its author.

William French, of the University Place Bookshop, introduced me to *Our Nig* and to the controversy among booksellers about its authorship. An N.E.H. Chairman's Grant, a research grant from the Menil Foundation, and a Prize Fellowship from the John and Catherine MacArthur Foundation facilitated my research. Carl Brandt, my literary agent, offered astute advice regarding the publication of the second edition of *Our Nig*. Steve Kezerian, Associate Director of Public Information at Yale University, helped generate national press coverage of the resurrection of *Our Nig,* and introduced the project to Leslie Bennetts of the *New York Times,* whose sensitive article spread the word about the significance of H. E. Wilson's novel.

I would also like to thank Accelerated Indexing Systems, a project of major scope for scholars in all fields who find themselves dependent upon public documents for verification of their subjects. A.I.S. could well aid in the rescue of other literary figures from oblivion.

Erroll McDonald, my friend and my editor at Random House, made possible the publication of the second edition of *Our Nig*. Gwendolyn Williams and Mariner Carroll typed the various drafts of this manuscript. Sharon Adams and our children, Maggie and Liza, who inspired this search in the first place, kept me in a civil mood on those days when Harriet E. Wilson seemed to have no past at all.

Henry Louis Gates, Jr.
New Haven

CONTENTS

Preface to the Third Edition—Henry Louis Gates, Jr.   vii

Introduction—Henry Louis Gates, Jr.   xi

A Note on the Text   lvii

Preface, Harriet E. Wilson   3

The Text   5

Appendix: Letters   133
Allida
Margaretta Thorn
C.D.S.

Afterword by Barbara A. White   *iii*

Notes to the Text compiled by Henry Louis Gates, Jr.,
David A. Curtis, and Lisa Rivo   *lv*

Chronology of Harriet E. Adams Wilson compiled
by Henry Louis Gates, Jr., David A. Curtis,
and Lisa Rivo   *lxix*

Select Bibliography   *lxxxv*

PREFACE TO THE THIRD EDITION

The authentication of Harriet Adams Wilson as an African American woman and the author of the novel *Our Nig* (1859) generated a surprising amount of interest among both scholars and writers and in the popular press when it was announced in 1982. From *The New York Times* to *People* magazine, a surprising number of people seemed fascinated that a novel could have been written and published by a black woman before the Civil War, ignored almost completely for well over a century, and then, quite by accident, be rediscovered, authenticated, and added to the canon of American literature. Today, twenty years after I discovered Harriet Wilson's identity, *Our Nig* is regularly taught in literature classes, and has been canonized by its inclusion in the *Norton Anthology of African American Literature* as well as other anthologies.

The reaction to the text among black women authors was especially gratifying. Ann Petry, author of *The Street* (1946), one of the signal works of American naturalism, wrote that reading Wilson's novel "affected me to the point of tears. Everyone, everywhere," she continued, "should read *Our Nig*." Alice Walker confessed that she "sat up most the night reading and pondering the enormous significance of Harriet Wilson's novel *Our Nig*. It is as if we'd just discovered Phillis Wheatley—or Langston Hughes." Maya Angelou hailed Wilson's recovery as the literary analogue for black women writers of Alex Haley's quest to find his African "roots." And even

Ralph Ellison, generally skeptical about the role of the slave narratives in the development of the African American novel, was moved to write about Harriet Wilson, pointing to her use of "the conventions of sentimental fiction [to demonstrate] conclusively that fictional forms were at least as important in determining *how* we write, *what* we write as were the slave narratives." Wilson's existence, Ellison continued, "confirms my suspicion that there was more 'free floating' literacy available to Negroes" before the Civil War "than has been assumed."

The curiously broad attention paid to the recovery of *Our Nig* reflected growing interest in the writings of women, generally, and of African American women, more specifically, largely as a result of the then-nascent field of Women's Studies and the growing interest among black and white feminist scholars in this body of work. The mere fact of Wilson's—and her novel's—existence generated further research in nineteenth-century black women's literary history, leading ultimately to the publication of the monumental forty-volume *Schomburg Library of Nineteenth-Century Black Women Writers,* published by Oxford University Press. Over the past two decades, republication of these and other works has led to the publication of a plethora of scholarly essays and books about the lives and works of nineteenth-century black women writers.

Since *Our Nig*'s republication in 1983, new details about Wilson's early life have been brought to light by the scholarship of Barbara A. White. White has identified the fictional Bellmont family, to whom the novel's protagonist was indentured, as the family of Nehemiah Hayward, "an established Milford farming family." I have included the results of White's research as an afterword to this edition. In addition, the scholar R. J. Ellis has identified several of Wilson's epigraphs, which were not identified in the first edition. These have been included in the notes to the text.

Despite a wealth of new research and scholarship in African American women's literary history over the past twenty years, Harriet Wilson's *Our Nig* remains the first novel published by a black woman, and the first novel published in this country by an African American. The recent discovery and authentication of Hannah Crafts' manuscript of her unpublished novel, *The Bondwoman's Narrative,* thought to have been written between 1857 and 1860, continues to confirm Ralph Ellison's suspicion was correct: a remarkable degree of "free floating" literacy was indeed available to more free blacks and former slaves in antebellum America than we once could have imagined. For them, curiously enough, the will to power—the will to be truly free—was, of all things, the will to write, the will to testify that they endured, despite the odds. And among these pre–Civil War testaments to the human spirit, none is more poignant and compelling than is the saga of Harriet Wilson's heroine, Alfrado.

Henry Louis Gates, Jr.
Cambridge, MA
February 4, 2002

INTRODUCTION

Though I've no home to call my own,
My heart shall not repine;
The saint may live on earth unknown,
And yet in glory shine.

When my Redeemer dwelt below,
He chose a lowly lot;
He came unto his own, but lo!
His own received him not.

—HARRIET E. WILSON, CIRCA 1852

I sincerely appeal to my colored brethren
universally for patronage, hoping that they
will not condemn this attempt of their sister
to be erudite, but rally around me a faithful
band of supporters and defenders.

—HARRIET E. WILSON, 1859

On the eighteenth day of August 1859, at the Clerk's office of the District Court of Massachusetts, Mrs. Harriet E. Wilson entered the copyright of her novel, a fictional third-person autobiography entitled *Our Nig; or, Sketches from the Life of a Free Black, In A Two-Story White House, North. Showing That Slavery's Shadows Fall Even There.* Printed for the author by the George C. Rand and Avery company, the novel first appeared on September 5, 1859. In a disarmingly open preface Mrs. Wilson states her purpose for publishing *Our Nig:*

In offering to the public the following pages, the writer confesses her inability to minister to the refined and cultivated, the pleasure supplied by abler pens. It is not for such these crude narrations appear. Deserted by kindred, disabled by failing health, I am forced to some experiment which shall aid me in maintaining myself and child without extinguishing this feeble life.

The experiment undertaken for financial reasons was a book whose central theme is white racism in the North as experienced by a free black indentured servant in antebellum days: a subject that might have been highly controversial among white abolitionists and free blacks who did not wish to antagonize their white benefactors. Nonetheless, Harriet E. Adams Wilson asked her "colored brethren" to "rally around me a faithful band of supporters and defenders," and to purchase her book so that she might support herself and her child.

Just five months and twenty-four days after the publication of *Our Nig*, the Amherst, New Hampshire, *Farmer's Cabinet* dated February 29, 1860, included among its obituaries the following item:

In Milford, 13th inst [ant], George Mason, only son of H. E. Wilson, aged 7 yrs. and 8 mos.

According to his death certificate, George Mason Wilson succumbed to "Fever" on February 15, 1860. Described as the child of Thomas and Harriet E. Wilson, he was probably named in honor of George Mason, the prominent Revolutionary-era Virginia planter and statesman who opposed slavery. The "color" of the child is listed as "Black."

The death certificate of George Mason Wilson establishes that "Mrs. H. E. Wilson"—the name that appears on the copyright page of the first edition of *Our Nig* and in the *Farmer's Cabinet* death notice—was a black woman, apparently the first to publish a novel in English. Ironically, George's death certificate helped to rescue his mother from literary oblivion. His mother wrote a sentimental novel, of all things, so that she might become self-sufficient and regain the right to care for her only son; six months later, her son died of that standard disease, "fever"; the *record* of his death, *alone,* proved sufficient to demonstrate his mother's racial identity and authorship of *Our Nig.* These curious historical events could easily have formed part of the plot of a sentimental novel. That Harriet Wilson, moreover, dared to entitle her text with the most feared and hated epithet by which the very humanity of black people had been demeaned adds to the list of ironies in her endeavor.

With this audacious act of entitlement, Harriet Wilson became most probably the first Afro-American to publish a novel in the United States, the fifth Afro-American to publish fiction in English (after Frederick Douglass, William Wells Brown, Frank J. Webb, and Martin R. Delany), and along with Maria F. dos Reis, who published a novel called *Ursula* in Brazil in 1859, one of the first two black women to publish a novel in any language. Despite their importance to the Afro-American literary tradition, however, Mrs. Wilson and her text seem to have been ignored or overlooked both by her "colored brethren universally" and by even the most scrupulous scholars during the next one hundred and twenty-three years, for reasons as curious and as puzzling as they are elusive, reasons about which we can venture rather little more than informed speculation.

Reconstructing the life and times of Harriet E. Wilson is as challenging as it is frustrating. While there remains no questions as to her race or her authorship of *Our Nig,* we have been able to account for her existence only from 1850 to 1860. Even her birthdate and date of death are unknown.

The first record of the woman who through marriage would become "Mrs. H. E. Wilson" is the 1850 federal census of the state of New Hampshire. This document lists one "Harriet Adams" (H. E. Wilson's maiden name) as living in Milford, New Hampshire. Her age is said to be "22" and her race is described as "Black" (the choices were "White," "Black," and "Mulatto"). Harriet Adams's birthplace is listed simply as "New Hampshire." If these statements are correct, then Miss Adams was born a free black in 1827 or 1828.

This birthplace and birth date, however, are problematic for several reasons. According to the 1860 Boston federal census, Mrs. Harriet E. Wilson was born in Fredericksburg, Virginia, in 1807 or 1808 (if the age of fifty-two recorded by the data collector was accurate). Again, as in the 1850 census, she is described as "Black." We have found no other black women listed in either Hillsborough County, New Hampshire (where Milford is located), or in Boston, where the author of *Our Nig* registered her copyright on August 18, 1859.

A strong reason for pursuing the leads in the 1860 federal census is that the novel itself asserts that its author lived in

Massachusetts at the time it was written, namely 1859, as internal evidence suggests. In the final chapter of *Our Nig*, where the narrator abandons the mask of storyteller, and, in her own voice, appeals to the reader for sympathy and support, the text reads as follows: "She passed into the various towns of the State she lived in, then into Massachusetts."

If Harriet E. Adams Wilson's place and date of birth remain shaky, we are on firmer ground in the decade between 1850 and 1860. Harriet Adams, in 1850, lived with a white family in Milford, New Hampshire, the family of Samuel Boyles. (Boyles, a white fifty-year-old carpenter— according to the 1850 census—is fifty-two in the 1860 census; similarly, his birthplace has shifted from "Vermont" in 1850, to "Massachusetts," suggesting that discrepancies in census data were common even among stable and middle-class white Americans.) Since the Boyleses had four resident adult nonfamily members living with them, according to the 1860 census—three of whom are described as "Spinsters"— we can surmise that they rented rooms to boarders and possibly were remunerated by the county for sheltering the aged and disabled, probably on a regular basis.

One year later, in 1851, according to records at the Milford Town Clerk's Office, Harriet Adams married Thomas Wilson. This information was "returned by the Rev. E. N. Hidden" in April 1852, along with information about a dozen or so other marriages. The Reverend Hidden, a thirty-eight-year-old white Congregational clergyman, according to the 1850 census, dated the marriage as October 6, 1851, at Milford, New Hampshire. Thomas Wilson's "residence" is listed as "Virginia," and Harriet Adams's as

"Milford." Incidentally, the church's marriage records, which could have provided more information, were destroyed by fire.

In late May, or early June 1852, George Mason Wilson was born, the first and apparently only child of Harriet E. Adams and Thomas Wilson. (Of Thomas Wilson, we know no vital statistics. A brief narrative of the escape of a "Tom Wilson" from New Orleans to Liverpool was published in the Liverpool *Inquirer* on February 28, 1858. This narrative, however, does not overlap in any way with *Our Nig* or the three letters in its Appendix.) We know the child's birth date, his race, and his parents' identity from his 1860 death certificate. His birth date was approximately nine months after Thomas and Harriet married.

George Mason Wilson was born in Goffstown, New Hampshire, just a few miles from Milford, where his parents were married. In Goffstown was located the Hillsborough County Farm, which was established in 1849. One of the letters appended to *Our Nig* states that, abandoned by her husband, the author of *Our Nig* was forced—after "days passed; weeks passed"—to go to the "County House," where she gave birth to a child.

The 1855 *Boston City Directory* listed a "Harriet Wilson, Widow," at 7 Robinson Alley. Two "Harriet Wilsons" appeared in the *Boston City Directory* of 1856. One listing designates a "widow," who lived at 4 Webster Avenue, the other a "dressmaker," who lived or worked at 19 Joy Street. These "Harriet Wilsons" may, or may not, be the same person. In each successive *Boston City Directory,* an annual publication similar to contemporary telephone directories, only one Harriet Wilson appeared between 1857 and 1863: the widow who remained at Webster Avenue.

This widow, according to the 1860 Boston census, was born in Fredericksburg, Virginia, and is listed as "52" years of age. The census describes her as "Black," and living in the home of Daniel and Susan Jacobs, ages thirty-eight and thirty-one, respectively. The census lists Mr. Jacobs's profession as "mariner."

Harriet E. Wilson registered the copyright of *Our Nig* at the District Clerk's Office at Boston on August 18, 1859. Because New Hampshire had had its own District Clerk's Office since 1789, and because the office in Boston served most, if not all, of Massachusetts, it is reasonable to assume that Harriet E. Wilson was a resident of Massachusetts by 1859, and was separated from her son, whom she had been forced to foster to another family because of her desperate financial condition. Since the novel was printed for the author, rather than "published" by a commercial house, and since other Massachusetts printers would have been capable of producing *Our Nig,* the fact that she selected the George C. Rand and Avery company of Boston reinforces speculation that by 1859 Mrs. Wilson lived in or near that city.

Many of these facts about H. E. Wilson's life that have been drawn from public documents correspond dramatically to assertions about the life of the author of *Our Nig* that were made by three acquaintances who endorsed her novel, in the seven-page Appendix that follows Chapter XII. When brought together, these facts leave no doubt that the author of *Our Nig,* who signed her copyright as "Mrs. H. E. Wilson," and Harriet E. Adams Wilson, are the same person. But another source of confirmation is the plot of *Our Nig*— described as autobiographical by her supporters—which parallels major events of Mrs. Wilson's life that we have been able to verify.

Let us first analyze the statements found in the text's Appendix.

Margaretta Thorn, whose letter is entitled "To the Friends of Our Dark-Complexioned Brethren and Sisters, This Note Is Intended," is the source of the little that we know about the author's childhood. She has "known the writer of this book for a number of years," she testifies, and therefore is uniquely able to "add my testimony to the truth of her assertions." Harriet Wilson, "the writer of this books," she repeats as she concludes her first paragraph, "has seemed to be a child of misfortune." Harriet's childhood apparently was less than ideal: early on, she was "deprived of her parents, and all those endearing associations to which childhood clings." She was hired out to a family "calling themselves Christians," Margaretta Thorn continues, adding parenthetically that may "the good Lord deliver me from such." This family put her to work "both in the house and in the field," allegedly ruining her health by unduly difficult work. "She was indeed a slave, in every sense of the word," she continues, "and a lonely one, too."

Harriet's health had been impaired since she was "eighteen," Margaretta Thorn continues, and "a great deal of the time has been confined to her room and bed." This protracted illness forced some authorities, she suggests, to take her child to "the county farm, because she could not pay his board every week." Mrs. Wilson, however, was able to place her son in what we would call a foster home, where, Margaretta Thorn tells us, "he is contented and happy, and where he is considered as good as those he is with." From Margaretta Thorn's assertion that this unnamed foster family treated her son as their son and Harriet Wilson "as a daughter," and refused to maintain friendships with neighbors who did not do so as well, we may safely conclude that the foster family was white. She then concludes her pious epistle, as do both Allida and C.D.S., with an exhortation that those who call themselves friends of the blacks should purchase the novel and thereby enable its author to become self-sustaining and to retrieve her child:

> And now I would say, I hope those who call themselves friends of our dark-skinned brethren, will lend a helping hand, and assist our sister, not in giving, but in buying a book; the expense is trifling, and the reward of doing good is great.

The third appended letter, signed simply "C.D.S.," is dated "Milford, July 20th, 1859," two days short of one month before Mrs. Wilson registered her copyright at the District Court at Boston. The 1860 census for Milford, New Hampshire, listed two residents whose first names begin with "C" and whose surnames end in "S," but none is listed with "D" as a middle name or initial: Catherine Shannahan and Charles Shepard. But "C.D.S." was also a *legal* abbreviation for "Colored Indentured Servant." C.D.S.'s epistle is less informative than Margaretta Thorn's or Allida's, claiming only that he has "been acquainted with" the "writer of this book" for "several years" and knows her character to be "worthy the esteem of all friends of humanity; one whose soul is alive to the work to which she puts her hand." Appealing to "the sympathy of all Christians, and those who have a spark of humanity in their breasts," C.D.S. asks his readers to purchase the book, so "that its circulation will be extensive." C.D.S., we can deduce, is either, like Margaretta Thorn, a white citizen—since he adds the customary confirmation that "Although her complexion is a little darker than my own, I esteem it a privilege to associate with her, and assist her whenever an opportunity presents itself"—or a mulatto indentured servant. Closing by "bidding her God speed," the author signs "C.D.S."

Allida's long letter occupies most of the Appendix. It is an especially compelling document not only because of its length, but also because it contains scattered clues and suggestions about *Our Nig*'s author, as well as three subtexts, including an excerpted letter from Harriet to a "Mrs. Walker," in whose household she lived in W——, Massachusetts, where she mastered the fine art of making straw hats; a poem written by Harriet; and a poem probably written by Allida.

Allida asserts that she has known "the author of this book" for "about eight years," or roughly since 1851, so she is able to verify the "truth" of this strange fiction, which she will later label "an Autobiography." The author was "brought to W——, Mass." by "an itinerant colored lecturer," she begins her testimony. This unnamed town, she continues, is "an ancient town," in which "mothers and daughters" work "willingly with their hands" with "straw," which Allida underscores as if to provide a clue to the town's identity. Of the numerous "W——, Massachusetts" towns, three present themselves as likely candidates for Harriet's temporary dwelling place. Walpole was "well-known" for its straw works between 1830 and 1842 or so; the "straw goods" industry began at Ware, Massachusetts, in 1832, and "straw sewing was done largely in the homes about town," just as Allida informs us Harriet did in Mrs. Walker's household. *The History of Westborough, Massachusetts* claims that the straw goods and millinery industries were "for a long time confined to this part of Massachusetts." From these facts we can conclude that Harriet most probably lived in the section of Massachusetts that includes Ware and Walpole, as well as Worcester, which is approximately fifteen miles from Westborough.

In this town Harriet boarded with "the family of Mrs. Walker," who "immediately succeeded in procuring work for her as a 'straw sewer.'" An ideal pupil, Allida continues, Harriet learned quickly "the art of making straw hats," yet was prevented by ill health ("on account of former hard treatment") from continuous employment, a condition that forced Mrs. Walker to nurse her in "a room joining her own chamber." Citing Harriet's direct speech about her maternal feelings toward Mrs. Walker, Allida reveals that Harriet called her "Aunt J——," confirming that the name "Allida" is a pseudonym. After a brief period of bliss, disaster strikes in the form of a black lover.

"One beautiful morning in the early spring of 1842" (surely a printer's error for 1852, since we know the marriage was *registered* in the spring of 1852), Allida's narrative proceeds, Harriet, out for a walk, met the " 'lecturer' " who had brought her to W——, Mass. He was accompanied by "a fugitive slave," whom Allida characterizes as "Young, well-formed and very handsome," a self-described "*house*-servant, which seemed to account," she concludes, "in some measure for his gentlemanly manners and pleasing address." This "entirely accidental" meeting, Allida laments, "was a sad occurrence for poor Alfrado," the protagonist of *Our Nig* and the author herself: "Suffice it to say, an acquaintance and attachment was formed, which, in due time, resulted in marriage."

It must have been love at first sight because "in a few days, the couple left W——, and *all* her home comforts, and took up her abode in New Hampshire." After a blissful respite, Harriet's husband "left his young and trusting wife, and embarked for sea." Her husband failed to return, and Harriet's "heart failed her." Unable to sustain herself, with no friends other than "that class who are poor in the things of earth," Harriet was forced to seek refuge in "the 'County House;' *go she must.*" We recall that the Hillsborough County House, in Goffstown, New Hampshire, was George Mason Wilson's birthplace. Precisely at this point in her narrative Allida inserts a letter that Harriet purportedly wrote to "her mother Walker" about "her feelings on her way thither, and after her arrival," which, Allida assures us, "can be given better in her own language" than reported indirectly.

Harriet's letter serves as a confirmation of the fictional narrative's style, subtly reinforcing Allida's assertion of the veracity of the storyteller and her tale, as well as of her solitary authorship. Quite unlike the instance of Harriet Jacobs's *Incidents in the Life of a Slave Girl* (1861), whose prefatory authenticator, Lydia Maria Child, admits minimal "revision," "condensation," and "arrangement," not one of the three letters appended to *Our Nig* ever questions that Harriet Wilson wrote all the words in the text in their exact order. Her accomplishment is all the more astonishing because *Our Nig* reads so much more fluidly and its plot seems so much less contrived than *The Heroic Slave* (1853), *Clotel* (1853), *The Garies and Their Friends* (1857), or *Blake; or, The Huts of America* (partially serialized in 1859, then probably serialized fully in 1861), the fictions published before *Our Nig* in the Afro-American tradition; particularly since the authors of two of those novels, William Wells Brown and Martin R. Delany traveled widely, published extensively, lectured regularly, and educated themselves diligently. Delany even studied medicine at Harvard.

Nevertheless, the "autobiographical" consistencies between the fragments of Harriet Wilson's life and the depiction of the calamities of Frado, the heroine of *Our Nig*, would suggest that Mrs. Wilson was able to gain control over her materials more readily than her fellow black novelists of that decade precisely by adhering closely to the painful details of suffering that were part of her experience. On "the portable inkstand, pens and paper" that Mrs. Walker and her friends at W—— presented to Harriet as wedding or farewell presents, Harriet wrote an epistle of lament to Mrs. Walker, which Allida quotes at length, including a five-stanza poem. Harriet's poetry is similar to the religious, sentimental stuff of the period; her letter, however, although suffused with melodrama, is characterized by the same attention to detail and event as is the text of *Our Nig*.

Her letter reads in part:

> . . . just before nightfall, we halted at the institution, prepared for the *homeless*. With cold civility the matron received me, and bade one of the inmates shew me my room. She did so; and I followed up two flights of stairs. I crept as I was able; and when she said, 'Go in there,' I obeyed, asking for my trunk, which was soon placed by me. My room was furnished some like the 'prophet's chamber,' except there was no 'candlestick;' so when I could creep down I begged for a light, and it was granted. Then I flung myself on the bed and cried, until I could cry no longer.

George Plummer Hadley, in his *History of the Town of Goffstown, 1773–1920*, states that the Hillsborough County Farm was purchased in 1849 to house "the county poor, which at that time numbered eighty-eight." The "Farm" consisted of a large farm house, a barn, a "small dwelling-house near the oak tree," and some smaller buildings. The "paupers," as Hadley calls them, were "scattered through different buildings, which were heated by wood fires." Conditions there apparently were horrid: in 1853, some of the inmates "were stricken with smallpox, and it was necessary to build a pesthouse" for their proper isolation and care. As Hadley concludes, "What tales of sorrow could some of the unfortunates unfold."

Allida proceeds to inform her readers that Harriet remained in this desolate institution "until after the birth of her babe," until both were rescued by the return of "her faithless husband," who "took her to some town in New

Hampshire," where, to his credit, he supported his family "decently well." Then, he left again "as before—sudden and unexpectedly, and she saw him no more." Only "for a time" could Mrs. Wilson support herself and her son, then "her struggles with poverty and sickness were severe." Harriet and her infant escaped disaster only through the agency of "a kind gentleman and lady," who "took her little boy into their own family," providing for him well "without the hope of remuneration."

And what of the child's mother? Allida tells us: "As for the afflicted mother, she too has been remembered." Incredibly, "a stranger," one "moved by compassion," "bestowed a recipe upon her for restoring gray hair to its former color." The ingenious Harriet, who promptly "availed herself of this great help," apparently proved to be "quite successful" at this unusual trade, until her health, once again, failed her. Confined to bed, "she has felt herself obliged to resort to another method of procuring her bread —that of writing an Autobiography." Following a paragraph asking the reader to "purchase a volume," Allida ends her narrative of Harriet Wilson's life with an eight-stanza poem, "I will help thee, saith the Lord."

Mrs. Wilson's Preface to *Our Nig*, as unusual as it reads today, adds little to our reconstruction of the life of the author. Harriet Wilson's Preface begins with the expected apologia for all deficiencies in her text. "In offering to the public the following pages, the writer confesses her inability," Mrs. Wilson writes, "to minister to the refined and cultivated, the pleasure supplied by abler pens. It is not for such," she concludes with triumph and impressive control, "these crude narrations appear." She has been "forced to some experiment," she quickly adds, to maintain "myself and child without extinguishing this feeble life." The "experiment," of course, was the act of writing a fiction of her life. Here follows the attempt to anticipate the criticisms that such a book, published by a black one month before John Brown's raid on Harpers Ferry, might engender among those who had a vested interest in preserving the fiction that the stereotypic oppositions between North and South, freedom and slavery, black, as it were, and white allowed for no qualifications, no exceptions. For here, Harriet Wilson admits that her intention in writing this novel was to indict racism, whether it is found in the South or in the North.

> I would not from these motives even palliate slavery at the South, by disclosures of its appurtenances North. My mistress was wholly imbued with *southern* principles. I do not pretend to divulge every transaction in my own life, which the unprejudiced would declare unfavorable in comparison with treatment of legal bondmen; I have purposely omitted what would most provoke shame in our good anti-slavery friends at home.

Concluding that her "humble position" and "frank confession of errors" might possibly "shield me from severe criticism," Harriet Wilson then launches an appeal directly to "my colored brethren universally," asking of them their "patronage, hoping they will not condemn this attempt of their sister to be erudite, but rally around me a faithful band of supporters and defenders."

Although the direct appeal, for sympathy, patience, and financial support, was a standard feature of the apologia, not one other black author before Harriet Wilson felt compelled to anticipate the "severe" criticisms of even the Northern abolitionists. Mrs. Wilson, however, did, and wisely so. For Allida's letter erroneously, but rather self-consciously, attempts to direct the reader's attention away from the central subject of this novel, which is the brutality of a white woman racist who, against the wishes of all other members of her household—with the significant exception of the wicked mother's equally wicked daughter—enslaves the protagonist, Frado, in a prolonged indenture as brutal as any depicted in the autobiographical slave narratives. Lest the point of the narrative be mistaken, Mrs. Wilson's long subtitle of *Our Nig* confirms it:

> Sketches from the Life of a Free Black,
> In A Two-Story White House, North.
> Showing That Slavery's Shadows Fall Even There.
> By "Our Nig."

The boldness and cleverness in the ironic use of "Nig" as title and pseudonym is, to say the least, impressive, standing certainly as one of the black tradition's earliest recorded usages. And if Allida's letter suggests that "Alfrado's tale" is that of love-betrayed, a glance at the text suggests the contrary. The subplot of love, marriage, childbirth, and betrayal only appears in the text's final chapter, Chapter XII, "The Winding Up of the Matter," which unfolds in scarcely five pages of a one-hundred-and-thirty-one-page novel. The chapter, headed by an epigraph from Solomon—"Nothing new under the sun"—recapitulates, almost as does a coda in a musical score, the themes of the text. It is this encounter with the racism of the white *petite bourgeoisie* of the North that Harriet Wilson squarely confronts. Frado's deserting husband, Samuel, dies an anonymous death of yellow fever in New Orleans; Frado's oppressor, Mrs. Bellmont, dies the slow, excruciatingly painful death that her sins, at least in the sentimental novel, have earned for her.

Perhaps another explanation for the obscurity of *Our Nig* was its unabashed representation of an interracial marriage, a liaison from which the novel's protagonist was an offspring. That relationship, which other writers in the decade of the 1850s called "amalgamation," had, it is true, been the subject of a few novels published before *Our Nig;* never, however, was miscegenation depicted with any degree of normality before *Our Nig.* The general attitude toward this controversial social matter was perhaps best articulated by Mrs. Mary Howard Schoolcraft in her novel, *The Black Gauntlet* (1860): "I believe a refined Anglo-Saxon lady would sooner be burned at the stake, than married to one of these black descendants of Ham."

Novels such as *The Ebony Idol* (1860) or *A Sojourn in the City of Amalgamation in the Year of Our Lord 19—* (1835) made the subject an object of bitter, racist satire. Interracial marriage, it is fair to say, was not a popular subject for representation in either antislavery or proslavery novels. As the omniscient narrator of *Our Nig* editorializes about the marriage of Jim, a black man, to "lonely Mag Smith":

> He prevailed; they married. You can philosophize, gentle reader, upon the impropriety of such unions, and preach dozens of sermons on the evils of amalgamation. Want is a more powerful philosopher and preacher. Poor Mag. She has sundered

another bond which held her to her fellows. She has descended another step down the ladder of infamy.

Even this representation, obviously, was not without its ironies, and even demeaning aspects; Jim's proposal is not exactly rendered from a position of strength or from a sense of equality:

> "Well, Mag," said Jim, after a short pause "you's down low enough. I do n't see but I've got to take care of ye. 'Sposin' we marry!"
>
> Mag raised her eyes, full of amazement, and uttered a sonorous "What?"
>
> Jim felt abashed for a moment. He knew well what were her objections.
>
> "You's had trial of white folks, any how. They run off an left ye, and now none of 'em come near ye to see if you's dead or alive. I's black outside, I know, but I's got a white heart inside. Which you rather have, a black heart in a white skin, or a white heart in a black one?"

Despite this less than noble stance, however, Jim and his reluctant bride, Mag Smith, live peacefully, productively, and fairly happily for three years, until Jim dies. Surely this "unproblematical" relationship, at least in the stereotypical social sense of that term, did nothing to aid the book's circulation in the North or the South.

We are free to speculate whether the oblivion into which Harriet Wilson disappeared for well over a century resulted from the boldness of her themes and from turning to that hated epithet, "nigger," both for title and authorial, if pseudonymous, identity. We can, unfortunately, only risk the most tentative speculation. But we can say that a syste-

matic search of all extant copies of black and reform newspapers and magazines in circulation contemporaneously
with the publication of *Our Nig* yielded not one notice or
review, nor did searches through the Boston, Massachusetts,
dailies and the Amherst, New Hampshire, *Farmer's Cabinet.*

How were other contemporary black novels reviewed?
Clotel (1853), William Wells Brown's first novel of four, was
reviewed in 1853 in the London *Eastern Star* (reprinted in
the *National Anti-Slavery Standard* December 31), and in
the Hereford (England) *Times* on December 17 (reprinted
in the *Liberator* on January 20, 1854). On February 3, 1854,
the *Liberator* reviewed *Clotel* itself. The serialized publication of Martin R. Delany's *Blake* was reviewed in the
Liberator on April 15, 1859, as part of an advertisement. But
neither Floyd J. Miller, in his edition of *Blake* (1970), nor
Curtis W. Ellison and E. W. Metcalf, Jr., in their thorough
reference guide, *William Wells Brown and Martin R.
Delany,* could locate any other periodical reviews. Unlike
the slave's narratives, we can see, black fiction was not
popularly reviewed, but it was reviewed on occasion.

That such a significant novel, the very first written by a
black woman, would remain unnoticed in Boston in 1859,
a veritable center of abolitionist reform and passion, and
by a growing black press eager to celebrate all black
achievement in the arts and sciences, remains one of the
troubling enigmas of Afro-American literary history. Encountering *Our Nig* anew, I can only offer the thematic
"explanations" rendered above, as difficult as even I find
them to accept or believe. To suppress a text by ignoring it
because it depicts a "successful" interracial marriage, or a

black man pretending to be an "escaped slave," only reinforces what the tradition must understand as the *difficulty*
of reconstituting an act of language in its own milieu.

It is curious to trace the disappearance and reappearance
of Harriet Wilson and her novel, *Our Nig*. It would be
easier to imagine her presence in the tradition if we could
identify some nineteenth-century reference to her, even an
obscure reference, which then was overlooked or doubted;
but we have found none. She does not even appear in
Samuel May, Jr.'s 1863 *Catalogue of Anti-Slavery Publications in America, 1750–1863,* published just four years after
Mrs. Wilson published *Our Nig*. Neither does she appear in
the U.S. Bureau of Education Report of 1893–1894, which
includes as its third section "Works by Negro Authors," nor
in Robert M. Adger's *Catalogue of Rare Books and
Pamphlets . . . upon Subjects relating to the Past Condition
of the Colored Race and the Slavery Agitation in this
Country* (1894) or his *Catalogue of Rare Books on Slavery
and Negro Authors on Science, History, Poetry, Religion,
Biography, etc.* (1904). Du Bois did not mention her in his
three important bibliographies, published as part of his
Atlanta University Studies, in 1900, 1905, and 1910. Daniel
P. Murray, an Assistant Librarian at the Library of Congress, did not mention Mrs. Wilson or *Our Nig* in either
his *Preliminary List of Books and Pamphlets by Negro
Authors,* which he compiled for the American Negro Exhibit
at the Paris Exhibition of 1900, or in the six-thousand-item
bibliography that was to have been published as part of
Murrays Historical and Biographical Encyclopedia of the

Colored Race throughout the World. Nor was she unearthed in any of the late nineteenth and early twentieth-century black biographical dictionaries, such as W. J. Simmons's *Men of Mark* (1887) or J. L. Nichols and William H. Crogman's *Progress of a Race; or the Remarkable Advancement of the American Negro* (1920).

If the historians, bibliophiles, and bibliographers overlooked Harriet Wilson, then the literary historians fared only a bit better. Benjamin Brawley, a diligent scholar and critic, does not mention text or author in *The Negro in Literature and Art in the United States* (1918; 1930), *Early Negro Amreican Writers* (1935), or in *The Negro Genius* (1937). Vernon Loggins, whose literary history remains the most complete to date, makes no mention of her in *The Negro Author: His Development in America to 1900* (1931). Neither does Sterling A. Brown refer to her in his critically sophisticated *The Negro in American Fiction* (1937). Harriet E. Wilson's name is absent in Barbara Christian's *Black Women Novelists: The Development of a Tradition, 1892–1976* (1980); in Arlene A. Elder's *The "Hindered Hand": Cultural Implications of Early African-American Fiction* (1978); in Addison Gayle, Jr.'s *The Way of the New World: The Black Novel in America* (1976); Richard Alan Yarborough's "The Depiction of Blacks in the Early Afro-American Novel" (Ph.D. Dissertation, 1980); Nina Baym's *Woman's Fiction: A Guide to Novels by and about Women in America, 1820–1870* (1978); and Bert James Loewenberg and Ruth Bogin's *Black Women in Nineteenth-Century American Life* (1976). The most complete bibliography of the Afro-American novel, *Afro-American Fiction, 1853–1976,* edited by Edward Margolies and David Bakish, does not include Mrs. Wilson; nor do Theressa Gunnels Rush, Carol Fairbanks Myers, and Esther Spring Arata in their thorough *Black American Writers, Past and Present: A Biographical and Bibliographical Dictionary* (1975), or M. Thomas Inge, Maurice Duke, and Jackson R. Bryer in *Black American Writers: Bibliographical Essays* (1978). Roger Whitlow's *Black American Literature: A Critical History* (1974) and Maxwell Whiteman's *A Century of Fiction by American Negroes, 1853–1952* (1955) are both silent about Mrs. Wilson's existence. And so on.

I have, however, found five references to *Our Nig*. John Herbert Nelson mentions in passing only the title in his 1926 study, *The Negro Character in American Literature*. Herbert Ross Brown, in *The Sentimental Novel in America, 1789–1860* (1940), implies that H. E. Wilson is a white male, and says that this novel is unusual within its genre because "The author of *Our Nig* dared to treat with sympathetic understanding the marriage of Jim, a black, to a white woman who had been seduced and deserted," an observation about one of the themes of *Our Nig* that simply did not occur to me on a first reading. Monroe N. Work, in his monumental compilation, *A Bibliography of the Negro in Africa and America* (1928), does indeed list both author and title, but under the category "Novels by White Authors Relating to the Negro." James Joseph McKinney's "The Theme of Miscegenation in the American Novel to World War I," a 1972 Ph.D. dissertation, discusses the novel's plot and suggests that the fiction is autobiographical. Both Mrs. Wilson and her novel are listed in Geraldine Matthews's bibliogra-

phy, *Black Writers, 1773–1949* (1975), and in Carol Fairbanks and Eugene A. Engeldinger's *Black American Fiction:
A Bibliography* (1978), but with no information beyond that
found in the second volume of Lyle Wright's three-volume
listing of American fiction (Wright II—2767). Curiously
enough, the most complete entry for the title was made in a
1980 catalogue of the Howard S. Mott Company of Sheffield,
Massachusetts, a company well-regarded among antiquarians.
The listing, prepared by Daniel Mott, asserted that Mrs.
H. E. Wilson's novel was the first by an Afro-American
woman. Mott says he decided that Wilson was black because
of the evidence presented in the text's appended letters. Perhaps it is appropriate that this second edition of *Our Nig*
has been reprinted from Mott's extraordinarily rare first
edition.

Let us, at last, read closely Harriet Wilson's novel. I propose, in the remainder of this essay, to describe the text's
own mode of presentation, to gloss its echoes, to establish
its plot structure and compare this to those details that we
have been able to glean of Mrs. Wilson's biographical
"facts," then to compare these elements of the plot of *Our
Nig* to a typology of "Woman's Fiction" published in this
country between 1820 and 1870, which Nina Baym has so
carefully devised.

Harriet E. Wilson's Preface to *Our Nig*, as I have suggested, is an extraordinary document in the Afro-American
literary tradition; it is, if not unique, certainly one of the
rare instances in which a black author has openly anticipated
a hostile reaction to her text from "our good anti-slavery

friends at home." The author, moreover, confirms here both that her fiction is autobiographical, and that it has been crafted to minimize the potentially deleterious effects such a searing indictment of slavery's "appurtenances north" might well have upon the antislavery cause.

> I do not pretend to divulge every transaction in my own life, which the unprejudiced would declare unfavorable in comparison with treatment of legal bondmen; I have purposely omitted what would most provoke shame in our good anti-slavery friends at home.

There are darker horrors to my tale than even these I set forward here, Mrs. Wilson claims; these she has decided against drawing upon in her fiction for fear of wounding the fight against slavery, since these would be seen to be "unfavorable" even when compared to the treatment of the slave. Hers is not meant to be an attack on Northern whites at all; rather, "My mistress was imbued with *southern* principles."

Let us consider further this matter of the text's silences and lacunae. We may consider Mrs. Wilson's Preface and the three appended letters to comprise the documentary-biographical subsection of the text, while the novel itself comprises the text's fictional representation of Mrs. Wilson's experiences as an indentured servant in a Northern white household before 1850. What is curious about the relationship between these nonfictional and the fictional discourses, which together form the text of *Our Nig,* is this: the "closer" that the novel approaches the appended biographies, the less distance there is between "fact" and romance, between (auto)biography and fiction. This is one of the more curious aspects of this curious text: the fiction, or the *guise* of her fictional account of her life, tends to fall away the nearer her novel approaches its own ending, and the ending of her text, the composite biography written by Mrs. Wilson's friends. It is of considerable interest to outline the manner in which one discursive field "collapses," as it were, into quite another, of a different status than the other.

To be sure, there are tensions between autobiography and fiction early in the novel. This tension is evident in chapter titles. Chapter I, for example, Mrs. Wilson calls "Mag Smith, My Mother." The first-person pronoun would lead the reader to assume that the novel is narrated in the first person; it is not. Rather, a third-person narrator observes and interprets the thoughts and actions of all concerned. Clearly, however, the narrator is telling Frado's tale, a tale of abuse, neglect, betrayal, suffering consciousness, and certain death from that inevitable visitor of the sentimental novel, the dreaded "fever." These stock devices, employed with melodrama, direct appeal to the reader, and a certain florid, stilted diction in speech and thought, nevertheless function to reveal Frado's saga. But Frado's story, as these lapses into the first person would suggest, is Harriet E. Adams Wilson's tale as well. Chapter II, "My Father's Death," and Chapter III, "A New Home For Me," include other instances of the first-person shift. With Chapter IV and after, however, the chapter titles employ the third person, but are more often abstractions. These titles, in order, follow: "A Friend For Nig," "Departures," "Varieties," "Spiritual Condition of Nig," "Visitor and Departure,"

"Death," "Perplexities—Another Death," "Marriage Again,"
and "The Winding Up of the Matter."

What are we to make of the first-person lapses in the chapter titles? We can conclude, with Allida, that the novel is
indeed "an Autobiography," of sorts, an autobiographical
novel. Whether the lapses are the sign of an inexperienced
author struggling with or *against* the received conventions
of her form, or the result of the imposition of a life on the
desires of a text to achieve the status of fiction, these first-
person traces point to the complexities and tensions of
basing fictional events upon the lived experiences of an
author. The latter chapters of *Our Nig* contain events that
parallel remarkably closely those experiences of Harriet
Wilson's that we are able to document. Curiously enough,
the first-person proprietary consciousness evinced in the
titles of the early chapters does not parallel events that we
have been able to document and that we probably shall not
be able to document. Since these early chapters describe
events far removed from the author's experiences closest in
time to the period of writing, the first-person presences
perhaps reveal the author's anxiety about identifying with
events in the text that she cannot claim to recollect clearly,
and some of which she cannot recollect at all, such as the
courtship and marriage of her mother, and the protagonist's
ultimate abandonment by her widowed parent. In later
chapters Mrs. Wilson had no need to demonstrate or claim
the direct relation between author and protagonist, since,
as our research reveals, these two sets of events, the fictional
and the biographical, overlap nicely. In Chapter XII, however, the narrator slips into the first person, in her first sen-

tence, as if to reinforce the connection between narrator and protagonist.

In her Preface Mrs. Wilson explains away the text's lacunae, its silences and reticences, as does the disembodied narrative voice in the novel's final chapter. In the Preface, as I have suggested, Harriet Wilson argues that she has remained silent about those events in her life which, if depicted, could well result in an adverse reaction against Northern whites, and could thereby do harm to the anti-slavery movement. The novel's penultimate paragraph repeats that claim, but with a difference. This difference consists of a direct appeal to the reader to grant the author "your sympathy," rather than withholding it simply because more, critical details are not depicted in the text:

> Still an invalid, she asks your sympathy, gentle reader. Refuse not, because some part of her history is unknown, save by the Omnipresent God. Enough has been unrolled to demand your sympathy and aid.

She has revealed quite enough, the narrator tells us, for her readers to be convinced of the author's merit of their "sympathy and aid." To ask of her even more would be to ask too much. While the scholar wishes for more details of the life to have been named in the novel, details ideally transpiring between 1850 and 1860 in the author's life (Chapter XII of the text), even he must remain content to grant the author her plea.

What do we find in this ultimate chapter in the very space where these absent details of the author's life "should" be? We read, instead, one of the novel's few direct attacks upon white Northern racism:

> She passed into the various towns of the State [New Hampshire] she lived in, then into Massachusetts. Watched by kidnappers, maltreated by professed abolitionists, who did n't want slaves at the South, nor niggers in their own houses, North. Faugh! to lodge one; to eat with one; to admit one through the front door; to sit next one; awful!

It is clear that Harriet Wilson's anxieties about offending her Northern readers were not the idle uneasiness most authors feel about their "ideal" constituencies.

It is equally clear that the author of *Our Nig* was a broadly read constituent of nineteenth-century American and English literature. The text's epigraphs alone encourage speculation about the author's experiences with books. True, the structure of the novel would suggest that Mrs. Wilson not only read a number of popular, sentimental American novels but also patterned her fiction largely within the received confines of that once popular form. *Our Nig*'s plot even repeats a few crucial events found in Mattie Griffiths's novel, *The Autobiography of a Female Slave*, suggesting more than a passing acquaintance on H. E. Wilson's part with Griffiths's book. But *Our Nig*'s epigraphs, placed at the head of each of its twelve chapters and on its title page, reflect a certain eclecticism in Mrs. Wilson's reading habits, perhaps an eclecticism that reflects contact with the arbitrary titles to be found in a small middle-class American library, the "library" that might consist of one shelf of titles, or perhaps two. Josiah Gilbert Holland, Thomas Moore, Percy Bysshe Shelley, Eliza Cook, Lord Byron, Martin Farquhar Tupper, Henry Kirke White, perhaps Charlotte Elliott, and Solomon, are among the authors whom Harriet Wilson felt comfortable enough to quote.

Each epigraph is well-chosen, and each illustrates the predominant sentiment of the following chapter. Most, above all else, appeal directly to the sympathies of the reader, for love betrayed, hope trampled, dreams frustrated, or desire unconsummated. The epigraph to Chapter II, taken from Shelley's "Misery," is representative of Mrs. Wilson's tastes in poetry:

> Misery! we have known each other,
> Like a sister and a brother,
> Living in the same lone home
> Many years—we must live some
> Hours or ages to come.

The range of citation of American and English authors found in *Our Nig* is much greater than that generally found in the slave narratives or in other black nineteenth-century novels. Occasionally, however, we encounter belabored erudition and echoing in *Our Nig*. The five epigraphs that we have not been able to identify could well have been composed by Mrs. Wilson herself, especially since they often read like pastiches of other authors, or like lines from common Protestant hymns. At the least, we know that Harriet Wilson read rather widely and eclectically, and that she preferred the pious, direct appeal to the subtle or the ambiguous.

It is a rewarding exercise to compare the plot structure of *Our Nig* to the "overplot" of nineteenth-century women's fiction identified by Nina Baym in her study, *Woman's Fiction: A Guide to Novels by and about Women in America, 1820–1870*. Baym's overplot consists, in part, of the following characteristics:

1. The device of pairing heroines, or pairing a heroine and a villainess, is a central component of "some exemplary organizing principle in all this woman's fiction."
2. The heroine is initially "a poor and friendless child" who is either an orphan, or who "only thinks herself to be one, or has by necessity been separated from her parents for an indefinite time."
3. The heroine, at the conclusion of her story, "is no longer an underdog." Her "success in life [is] entirely a function of her own efforts and character."
4. There are two kinds of heroine in this kind of novel, the flawless and the flawed.
5. The self is depicted to be "a social product, firmly and irrevocably embedded in a social construct that could destroy it but that also shaped it, constrained it, encouraged it, and ultimately fulfilled it."
6. The heroine, as a child, is abused by those who have authority over her. In the realistic tradition of this kind of novel, a series of events represents "the daily wearing down of neglected and overworked orphans." The heroine's authority figures "exploit or neglect her," rather than "love and nurture her." The heroine's principal challenge "is to endure until she comes of age and at the same time to grow so that when she comes of age she will be able to leave the unfriendly environment and succeed on her own." The heroine must "strike a balance between total submission, . . . and an equally suicidal defiance."

7. The heroine is abused by one of several characters who "are the administrators or owners of the space within which the child is legally constrained. Least guilty are the mothers; often it is the loss of the mother that initiates the heroine's woes, and the memory of her mother that permits her to endure them. Most guilty are aunts, . . . with whom many orphaned heroines are sent to live."

8. The heroine encounters people in her community who "support, advise, and befriend her," precisely as she is abandoned by her own family. They comprise a surrogate family.

9. The heroine's ultimate "domesticity" is not defined by her relations to her own children but to her surrogate family members; and, "although children may be necessary for a woman's happiness, they are not necessary for her identity —nor is a husband."

    A concluding, often happy, marriage "represents the institutionalizing of such families, for the heroine's new home includes not only her husband but all her other intimates as well."

10. The plot of woman's fiction has a tripartite structure: an unhappy childhood, "an interlude during which she must earn her own living," and the conclusion.

    Within this "interlude," the heroine's life is often influenced by strong, magnanimous, unmarried women, who mother her at a period when the heroine is unmarried and not being courted, and whose presence reinforces the idea that "relations with their own sex constituted the texture" of women's lives primarily.

11. In encounters "with a man, economic considerations predominated for these women. The women authors created stories in which, ultimately, male control and the money economy are simultaneously terminated."

12. Husbands and would-be lovers are less important to the heroine than "fathers, guardians, and brothers." The

heroine "is canny in her judgment of men, and generally immune to the appeal of a dissolute suitor. When she feels such an attraction, she resists it."

13. The path to the Christian religion is unmediated by men, so that "faith is thus pried out of its patriarchal social setting."

14. The "woman's novel" contains "much explicit and implicit social commentary." Principal targets of this commentary were "the predominance of marketplace values in every area of American life," oppositions between the city and the country, and "the class divisions in American society." Slavery and intemperance also are themes, but secondary themes.

15. The novelists "abhorred and feared poverty."

Nina Baym's extraordinarily perceptive overplot, as I have summarized it here, enables us to compare the plot of *Our Nig* with that of the tradition into which Harriet E. Wilson's novel falls. Many of these fifteen elements of the overplot of woman's fiction occur almost exactly in *Our Nig*. Frado, our heroine, most certainly is oppressed by her paired opposite, the evil Mrs. Bellmont. Also, Frado has been orphaned twice, once by the death of her loving, black father, then again as she is abandoned by her desperate, yet unsympathetic, white mother, who has now become the lover of her late husband's friend and business partner.

Now left in the home of a white, lower middle-class family, the young mulatto child begins an extended period of harsh indenture. Her two torturers are the evil female head of the household, and her daughter, equally evil, but in miniature. *Our Nig*, too, shares the tripartite structure of other women's novels, including an unhappy childhood, a seemingly endless period of indenture, and the conclusion. During her interlude of abuse, one white woman character, true to the received form, heavily influences Frado, comforts her, and becomes her only true confidant. Just as her torture is defined largely by two women, so, too, is her principal source of succor afforded by her relationship with this principal surrogate maternal figure, and a second, unnamed maternal figure who expands her consciousness with books.

Our Nig does indeed share the "woman's novel's" use of fictional forms to indict social injustice. As we might expect, racism, as visited upon the heroine by another woman whose relationship to the heroine is defined *principally* by an economic bond, is this novel's central concern. Curiously enough, it is the complex interaction of race-*and*-class relationships, depicted in Frado's relation to Mrs. Bellmont as inextricably intertwined, which *Our Nig* critiques for the first time in American fiction. By dividing her white characters, of the same family and the same class, into absolute categories of evil and good, Harriet E. Wilson was allowing for more complexity in her analysis of the nature of oppression than generally did, or perhaps could have, those novelists who wrote either to defend or to attack the institution of slavery.

In a sense, this narrative strategy can be read as a complex response to Harriet Beecher Stowe's *Uncle Tom's Cabin*. Caroline E. Rush's response, for example, was to attempt to enlist the new class of proslavery women writers to turn away from slavery as subject and begin to write about "white, wearied, wornout" women protagonists. Rush, prime propagandist for the peculiar institution, is a dubious source of proto-feminist urgings. Writing in her novel, *North and South, or Slavery and Its Contrasts* (1852), Rush first commands her readers to cease crying for Uncle Tom—"a hardy, strong and powerful Negro"—and start crying for pitiful, destitute children—"of the same color as yourself." The freed blacks, of Philadelphia for example, Rush continues, lack any "elegant degree of refinement and cultivation," thereby demonstrating implicitly that blacks are incapable of "elevation," enslaved or free. Eschew the profit motive, she concludes, and find a new subject:

> Fine, profitable speculation may be made from negro fiction. Wrought up into touching pictures, they may, under the spell of genius, look like truth and have the semblance of reality, but where is the genius to paint the scenes that exist in our own cities?—to awaken a sympathy that shall give strength to the white, wearied, wornout daughters of toil?

It was to address this task, precisely seven years later, that Harriet E. Wilson published her novel, *Our Nig,* a novel written to demonstrate the suffering of a black, wearied, wornout daughter of toil. We see this clearly in the novel's characterization of men and women.

All the men in *Our Nig* befriend the heroine, except for one; all the principal women in this novel victimize the heroine, except for one. The exceptional male is a ne'er-do-well black "fugitive slave," who meets the heroine, seduces her, marries her, impregnates her, disappears, returns, disappears again, and succumbs to "Yellow Fever, in New Orleans," all in the novel's final six-page chapter, as if such matters deserved only an appendix. The great evil in this book is not love-betrayed, however, or the evils of the flesh; rather, it is poverty, both the desperation it inflicts as well as the evils it implicitly sanctions, which is *Our Nig*'s focus for social commentary. Even the six-page account of love, betrayal, deceit, and abandonment serves more to allow the text's narrator to appeal directly to the reader to purchase this book and to explain its writing than it does to develop the plot.

This treatment of the protagonist's marriage is an odd aspect of *Our Nig,* and is one of the crucial ways in which the plot structure of *Our Nig* diverges fundamentally from the overplot that Nina Baym so precisely defines as shared, repeated structures of white women's fiction in the mid-nineteenth century. These significant discrepancies of plot development suggest that the author of *Our Nig* created a novel that partakes of the received structure of American women's fiction, but often inverts that same structure, ironically enough, precisely at its most crucial points. Harriet E. Wilson used the plot structure of her contemporary white female novelists, yet abandoned that structure when it failed to satisfy the needs of her well-crafted tale. Mrs. Wilson, in other words, revised significantly the "white woman's novel," and thereby made the form her own. By this act of formal revision, she *created* the black woman's novel, not merely because she was the first black woman to write a novel in English, but because she *invented* her own plot structure through which to narrate the saga of her orphaned mulatto heroine. In this important way, therefore, Harriet Wilson's novel inaugurates the Afro-American literary tradition in a manner more fundamentally *formal* than did either William Wells Brown or Frank J. Webb, the two black Americans who published complete novels before her.

One major departure that *Our Nig* makes from the received structure of the fiction written by women is its conclusion. *Our Nig*'s tale ends ambiguously, if it ends at all; the third-person narrator asks her readers directly for "your sympathy, gentle reader" for, the narrator continues, Frado remains "still an invalid," as she has remained since being abandoned by her mother. Although by the novel's conclusion, the villain, Mrs. Bellmont, has suffered "an agony in death unspeakable," and the good Aunt Abby has "entered heaven," the protagonist's status remains indeterminate, precisely because she has placed the conclusion of her "story," the burden of closure, upon her readers, who must purchase her book if the author-protagonist is to become self-sufficient. This "ending" is an anomalous one, and reinforces the "autobiographical" nature of the novel if only because the protagonist, the author, and the novel's narrator all merge explicitly into one voice to launch the text's advertisement for itself, for its status as a "worthy" fiction that should be purchased.

Our Nig does not share the respect for mothers that Baym identifies to be an important aspect in her overplot. While Frado's tale of sorrow and woe stems directly from her mother's absence, as is true of much of the contemporaneous woman's fiction, Mag Smith's absence is self-willed, and irresponsible. *Our Nig* questions profoundly the innocence of the mother-daughter relationship not only in Mag Smith and her daughter, but in Mrs. Bellmont's relation of identity with her evil daughter, both of whom conspire to make life miserable for their mulatto indentured servant. Only Aunt Abby relieves *Our Nig*'s searching depictions of its principal white women characters.

Our Nig does not end either with a happy marriage or with the institutional consolidation, through this marriage, of the forces of good—Frado's surrogate family and the protagonist. On the contrary, *Our Nig* concludes with a marriage that ends in desertion and that forces the heroine to abandon her successful work as a milliner, and her first, and apparently liberating, encounters with books. The key members of the heroine's surrogate family are dead at the novel's conclusion, so her marriage to "Samuel" is an ironic, false resolution, one that exacerbates the heroine's condition and leaves her homeless with a newborn child. The desertion of her husband opens, rather than ends, the text, preventing the sort of closure we expect in this genre of the sentimental novel. Indeed, one of the few exercises of free will and desire by the heroine ends ironically and tragically. Frado's marriage to Samuel both obliterates the only independent, peaceful, relatively prosperous phase of her life, and serves as the incident that negates the novel's closure and forces the author of *Our Nig* to write, then attempt to sell, her story.

Similarly, the heroine's encounters with men depart significantly from her sister heroine's encounters in other novels written by women. Frado's relations with (white) men are remarkably free of economic considerations. Rather, the men of the Bellmont household, all of whom ultimately die or move away, are sympathetic to Frado's sufferings and even conspire at times to help her to fight against Mrs. Bellmont's tyrannies. Frado's complex relationship to James, which intensifies as he lies slowly dying, is a curious blend of religion and displaced sexual desire. His economic status, however, does not come to bear directly upon his relations with Frado; however, Frado's dormant passion for religion initially awakes only insofar as she is able to associate being near to God with remaining near to James. While Aunt Abby and the local pastor seek to encourage her religious development, Frado's road to heaven is paved by her toils for James. Indeed, Frado never truly undergoes a religious transformation, merely the *appearance* of one; as the text emphasizes, "a devout and Christian exterior invited confidence from the villagers." Frado's innate innocence, outside of the respectability of the church, is one of the most subtle contrasts and social critiques of *Our Nig*. When the evil daughter, Mary, dies, well after Frado has "resolved to give over all thought of the future world" because "she did not wish to go" to a heaven that would allow Mrs. Bellmont entrance, Frado's innocent joy signifies her ironic rejection of Christian religion. Later, the narrator tells us that "It seemed a thanksgiving to Frado." As Frado tells Aunt Abby:

> "She got into the *river* again, Aunt Abby, did n't she; the Jordan is a big one to tumble into, any how. S'posen she goes to hell, she'll be as black as I am. Would n't mistress be mad to see her a nigger!" and others of a similar stamp, not at all acceptable to the pious, sympathetic dame; but she could not evade them.

This inversion of blackness and evil and good and whiteness is only one example of three, including Frado's lover, Samuel, and *Our Nig*'s title.

Frado, unlike most of her sister characters in other novels, succumbs to her attraction to a dissolute lover, a union that destroys her only period of independence and happiness. As the narrator relates, "There was a silent sympathy which Frado felt attracted her, and she opened her heart to the presence of love—that arbitrary and inexorable tyrant." Then, one paragraph later, "Here were Frado's first feelings of trust and repose on human arm. She realized, for the first time, the relief of looking to another for comfortable support. Occasionally," the narrator concludes anxiously, "he would leave her to 'lecture.' " Accordingly, husband Samuel

> left her to her fate—embarked at sea, with the disclosure that he had never seen the South, and that his illiterate harangues were humbugs for hungry abolitionists. Once more alone! Yet not alone.

Not alone, because husband Samuel leaves Frado in the early phase of a troubled pregnancy. The birth of the son, we know, motivates the author's creation of a text to contain her story and to provide sustenance for mother and child. This "professed fugitive from slavery," one of four black male characters in *Our Nig*, is the evil negation of Frado's father, Jim, "a kind-hearted African," a man she barely knew, since he died within "a few years" of marriage to "his treasure,—a white wife." He is also the negation of the long-suffering James. If *Our Nig* was a simple tale, or if it just conformed to the generic expectations of the sentimen-

1

tal, then black husband Samuel's portrayal would not have been so unremittingly negative, even if it had remained so brief.

Our Nig makes an even more important statement about the symbolic connotations of blackness in mid-nineteenth century America, and more especially of the epithet, "nigger." The book's title derives from the term of abuse that the heroine's antagonists "rename her," calling her "Our Nig," or simply "Nig." Harriet E. Wilson allows these racist characters to name her heroine, only to *invert* such racism by employing the name, in inverted commas, as her pseudonym of authorship. "By 'Our Nig' " forms in its entirety the last line of the book's title; its inverted commas underscore the use as an ironic one, one intended to reverse the power relation implicit in renaming-rituals which are primarily extensions of material relations. Transformed into an *object* of abuse and scorn by her enemies, the "object," the heroine of *Our Nig,* reverses this relationship by *renaming herself* not Our Nig but "Our Nig," thereby transforming herself into a *subject.*

She is now a subject who writes her own thinly veiled fictional account of her life in which *she* transforms her tormentors into objects, the stock, stereotypical objects of the sentimental novel. This, surely, is the most brilliant rhetorical strategy in black fiction before Charles Chesnutt's considerable talent manifests itself at the turn of the century. We may think of Mrs. Wilson's rhetorical strategy as a clever and subtle use of the trope of chiasmus, the trope which also is at the center of Frederick Douglass's rhetorical strategy in his *Narrative of the Life of Frederick Douglass,*

Written by Himself (1845). Though related to Douglass's purposes, however, Harriet Wilson's employment of this device is unparalleled in representations of self-development in Afro-American fiction.

Wilson's achievement is that she combines the received conventions of the sentimental novel with certain key conventions of the slave narratives, then combines the two into *one new form,* of which *Our Nig* is the unique example. Had subsequent black authors had this text to draw upon, perhaps the black literary tradition would have developed more quickly and more resolutely than it did. For the subtleties of presentation of character are often lost in the fictions of Wilson's contemporaries, such as Frances E. W. Harper, whose short story "The Two Offers" was also published in September 1859, and in the works of her literary "heirs."

Our Nig stands as a "missing link," as it were, between the sustained and well-developed tradition of black autobiography and the slow emergence of a distinctive black voice in fiction. That two black women published in the same month the first novel and short story in the black woman's literary tradition attests to larger shared cultural presuppositions at work within the black community than scholars have admitted before. The speaking black subject emerged on the printed page to declare himself or herself to be a human being of capacities equal to the whites. Writing, for black authors, was a mode of being, of self-creation with words. Harriet E. Wilson depicts this scene of instruction, central to the slave narratives, as the moment that Frado defies Mrs. Bellmont to hit her. The text reads:

"Stop!" shouted Frado, "strike me, and I'll never work a mite more for you;" and throwing down what she had gathered, stood like one who feels the stirring of free and independent thoughts.

As had Frederick Douglass in his major battle with overseer Covey, Frado at last finds a voice with which to define her space. A physical space of one's own signifies the presence of a more subtle, if equally real, "metaphysical" space, within which one's thoughts are one's own. This space Frado finds by speaking, just as surely as Frances E. W. Harper's character, Chloe, finds hers while "Learning to Read":

> So I got a pair of glasses,
>   And straight to work I went,
> And never stopped till I could read
>   The hymns and Testament.
> Then I got a little cabin,
>   A place to call my own—
> And I felt as independent
>   As the queen upon her throne.

Reading, too, proved to be a major event in Frado's life. Shortly after finding her voice, Frado decided to recommence her early encounter with books, turning frequently, the text tells us, "from toil to soul refreshment":

Frado had merged into womanhood, and, retaining what she had learned, in spite of the few privileges enjoyed formerly, was striving to enrich her mind. Her school-books were her constant companions, and every leisure moment was applied to them. Susan was delighted to witness her progress, and some little book from her was a reward sufficient for any task imposed, however difficult. She had her book always fastened open near her, where she could glance from toil to soul refreshment.

In the penultimate chapter of *Our Nig*, the narrator tells us that along with mastering the needle, Frado learns to master the word:

> Expert with the needle, Frado soon equalled her instructress; and she sought to teach her the value of useful books; and while one read aloud to the other of deeds historic and names re-nowned, Frado experienced a *new impulse*. She felt herself capable of elevation; she felt that this book information sup-plied an *undefined dissatisfaction* she had long felt, but could not express. Every leisure moment was carefully applied to self-improvement, ... [emphasis added]

In these final scenes of instruction, Harriet Wilson's text reflects upon its own creation, just as surely as Frado's awakened speaking voice signifies her consciousness of herself as a subject. With the act of speaking alone, Frado assumes a large measure of control over the choices she can possibly make each day. The "free and independent thoughts" she first feels upon speaking are repeated with variation in phrases such as "a new impulse," and "an undefined dissatisfaction," emotions she experiences while learning to read. "This book information," as the narrator tells us, enables Frado to *name things* by reading books. That such an apparently avid reader transformed the salient and tragic details of her life into the stuff of the novel— and was so daring in rendering the structures of fiction—is only one of the wonders of *Our Nig*.

What, finally, is the import of *Our Nig*? Its presence attests to a direct relation between the will and being of a sort rarely so explicit. Harriet E. Wilson's project, as bold and as unsure as it promised to be, failed to allow her to regain possession of her son. In this sense, Mrs. Wilson's project was a failure. Nevertheless, her legacy is an attestation of the will to power as the will to write. The transformation of the black-as-object into the black-as-subject: this is what Mrs. Harriet E. Wilson manifests for the first time in the writings of Afro-American women.

Henry Louis Gates, Jr.
November 26, 1982

A Note on the Text

Harriet E. Wilson published *Our Nig* herself. George C. Rand and Avery printed the 1859 edition for the author. Rand, Avery, located in 1859 at 117 Franklin Street in Boston, was a printer of some distinction; it advertised its services extensively in local business directories and newspapers, frequently in full-size advertisements. Rand, Avery, however, was not a commercial publisher, in a strict sense; we can only speculate on the terms of the agreement that Wilson struck with her printers. Nevertheless, it is this 1859 first edition that appears to have been the *only* edition of *Our Nig*, and that we have used to print this second edition.

Lyle Wright's three-volume bibliography of *American Fiction, 1774–1900* lists seven copies of *Our Nig* held in the following libraries: American Antiquarian Society, Henry E. Huntington Library and Art Gallery, Newberry Library, New York Historical Society Library, New York Public Library, University of Chicago Library, and the Yale University Library. There is a copy at the Schomburg Collection of Negro History and Literature, and another at the Moorland-Spingarn Collection at Howard University, as listed in their dictionary catalogues. Geraldine O. Matthews, in *Black American Writers, 1773–1949*, lists copies at Atlanta University and Fisk University. There are no doubt other copies, held at institutions and in private collections. The editor of this edition includes two copies among the titles in his private library; it is one of these that has been used for the printing of this edition, which is signed "Miss Mary A. Whitcomb, Hampton, N.H., February 1, 1861," and is listed as "No. 100."

This second, annotated edition of *Our Nig* reprints the 1859 edition exactly. Because there appears to be extant no holograph manuscript, no corrected proofs, no subsequent editions, no external evidence of authorial revisions, no other contemporary editions, and only one impression of the text, there would seem to be no textual questions or quandaries necessary for the editor to address.

We have adopted the clear-copy method of annotation, so that Mrs. Wilson's carefully designed text, and her intentional strategies of presentation, are neither interrupted by scholarly commentary, nor revised or altered in any manner by the interests of a readership one full century removed from the novel's initial manner of publication. All notes and comments we list in a section entitled Notes to the Text, which immediately follows the novel's Appendix, as Mrs. Wilson labeled it and which is composed of three letters included obstensibly to attest to the truth of the events depicted in the novel, to confirm both the character and the authorship of the text, and to urge black and white readers to buy the book so that its author might be able to support herself and her son.

These notes to the text consist of several sorts. Mrs. Wilson introduces each of the twelve chapters of *Our Nig*, and its title page, with an epigraph. We have identified eight of these, and list their identities by page number. We have, in addition, compared the biographical statements made by the three writers found in the Appendix to elements in the novel's plot. We have, furthermore, included in the notes evidence gathered from public documents pertaining to Harriet, Thomas, and George Mason Wilson, and juxtaposed this with both events of the plot as well as the letters of the Appendix. To facilitate comparisons among these three, rather different, sorts of "evidence," we have compiled a "Chronology of Harriet E. Adams Wilson," in a convenient outline form. This Chronology follows the Notes to the Text.

What we know to be the case about the life of Harriet E. Wilson, although sufficient to establish her existence and her authorship, remains frustratingly sparse. The three biographical letters appended to the novel concern themselves essentially with the decade of Mrs. Wilson's life between 1850 and 1860; accordingly, our capacity to verify, or to qualify, the statements made in these painfully brief biographical statements is more extensive than it is for any other period in the author's life. Nevertheless, even in this decade, as is true of the preceding and subsequent decades of Harriet E. Wilson's life, virtually all of the parts of her story remain to be reassembled. We publish this edition, with its extensive notes, so that other scholars may, with some profit, pursue in ever finer detail the curiously compelling story of the life and times of Harriet E. Wilson. The editor welcomes supplements and emendations to the data collected in this, the second edition of *Our Nig*. For, ultimately, it is to restore an author's presence to the American, the Afro-American, and the Feminist canons that we initially undertook this research, and accordingly share in these pages the tentative and still incomplete results of our search for Harriet E. Wilson.

Following is a Facsimile of the 1859 Edition of *Our Nig*

OUR NIG;

OR,

Sketches from the Life of a Free Black,

IN A TWO-STORY WHITE HOUSE, NORTH.

SHOWING THAT SLAVERY'S SHADOWS FALL EVEN THERE.

BY "OUR NIG."

"I know
That care has iron crowns for many brows;
That Calvaries are everywhere, whereon
Virtue is crucified, and nails and spears
Draw guiltless blood; that sorrow sits and drinks
At sweetest hearts, till all their life is dry;
That gentle spirits on the rack of pain
Grow faint or fierce, and pray and curse by turns;
That hell's temptations, clad in heavenly guise
And armed with might, lie evermore in wait
Along life's path, giving assault to all." — HOLLAND.

BOSTON:
PRINTED BY GEO. C. RAND & AVERY.
1859.

PREFACE.

In offering to the public the following pages, the writer confesses her inability to minister to the refined and cultivated, the pleasure supplied by abler pens. It is not for such these crude narrations appear. Deserted by kindred, disabled by failing health, I am forced to some experiment which shall aid me in maintaining myself and child without extinguishing this feeble life. I would not from these motives even palliate slavery at the South, by disclosures of its appurtenances North. My mistress was wholly imbued with *southern* principles. I do not pretend to divulge every transaction in my own life, which the unprejudiced would declare unfavorable in comparison with treatment of legal bondmen; I have purposely omitted what would most provoke shame in our good anti-slavery friends at home.

My humble position and frank confession of errors will, I hope, shield me from severe criticism. Indeed, defects are so apparent it requires no skilful hand to expose them.

I sincerely appeal to my colored brethren universally for patronage, hoping they will not condemn this attempt of their sister to be erudite, but rally around me a faithful band of supporters and defenders.

H. E. W.

OUR NIG.

CHAPTER I.

MAG SMITH, MY MOTHER.

Oh, Grief beyond all other griefs, when fate
First leaves the young heart lone and desolate
In the wide world, without that only tie
For which it loved to live or feared to die;
Lorn as the hung-up lute, that ne'er hath spoken
Since the sad day its master-chord was broken!

MOORE.

LONELY MAG SMITH! See her as she walks with downcast eyes and heavy heart. It was not always thus. She *had* a loving, trusting heart. Early deprived of parental guardianship, far removed from relatives, she was left to guide her tiny boat over life's surges alone and inexperienced. As she merged into womanhood, unprotected, uncherished, uncared for, there fell on her ear the music of love, awakening an intensity of emotion long dormant. It whispered of an elevation before unaspired to; of ease and plenty

1*

her simple heart had never dreamed of as hers.
She knew the voice of her charmer, so ravishing,
sounded far above her. It seemed like an angel's, alluring her upward and onward. She
thought she could ascend to him and become an
equal. She surrendered to him a priceless gem,
which he proudly garnered as a trophy, with
those of other victims, and left her to her fate.
The world seemed full of hateful deceivers and
crushing arrogance. Conscious that the great
bond of union to her former companions was severed, that the disdain of others would be insupportable, she determined to leave the few friends
she possessed, and seek an asylum among strangers.
Her offspring came unwelcomed, and before its
nativity numbered weeks, it passed from earth,
ascending to a purer and better life.

"God be thanked," ejaculated Mag, as she saw
its breathing cease; "no one can taunt *her* with
my ruin."

Blessed release! may we all respond. How
many pure, innocent children not only inherit a
wicked heart of their own, claiming life-long
scrutiny and restraint, but are heirs also of parental disgrace and calumny, from which only

long years of patient endurance in paths of recti-
tude can disencumber them.

Mag's new home was soon contaminated by
the publicity of her fall; she had a feeling of
degradation oppressing her; but she resolved to
be circumspect, and try to regain in a measure
what she had lost. Then some foul tongue would
jest of her shame, and averted looks and cold
greetings disheartened her. She saw she could
not bury in forgetfulness her misdeed, so she
resolved to leave her home and seek another in
the place she at first fled from.

Alas, how fearful are we to be first in extending a helping hand to those who stagger in the
mires of infamy; to speak the first words of hope
and warning to those emerging into the sunlight
of morality! Who can tell what numbers, ad-
vancing just far enough to hear a cold welcome
and join in the reserved converse of professed
reformers, disappointed, disheartened, have cho-
sen to dwell in unclean places, rather than encounter these "holier-than-thou" of the great
brotherhood of man!

Such was Mag's experience; and disdaining to
ask favor or friendship from a sneering world,

she resolved to shut herself up in a hovel she
had often passed in better days, and which she
knew to be untenanted. She vowed to ask no
favors of familiar faces; to die neglected and forgotten before she would be dependent on any.
Removed from the village, she was seldom seen
except as upon your introduction, gentle reader,
with downcast visage, returning her work to her
employer, and thus providing herself with the
means of subsistence. In two years many hands
craved the same avocation; foreigners who
cheapened toil and clamored for a livelihood,
competed with her, and she could not thus sustain herself. She was now above no drudgery.
Occasionally old acquaintances called to be favored with help of some kind, which she was glad
to bestow for the sake of the money it would
bring her; but the association with them was
such a painful reminder of by-gones, she returned to her hut morose and revengeful, re-
fusing all offers of a better home than she possessed. Thus she lived for years, hugging her
wrongs, but making no effort to escape. She
had never known plenty, scarcely competency;
but the present was beyond comparison with

those innocent years when the coronet of virtue was hers.

Every year her melancholy increased, her means diminished. At last no one seemed to notice her, save a kind-hearted African, who often called to inquire after her health and to see if she needed any fuel, he having the responsibility of furnishing that article, and she in return mending or making garments.

"How much you earn dis week, Mag?" asked he one Saturday evening.

"Little enough, Jim. Two or three days without any dinner. I washed for the Reeds, and did a small job for Mrs. Bellmont; that's all. I shall starve soon, unless I can get more to do. Folks seem as afraid to come here as if they expected to get some awful disease. I do n't believe there is a person in the world but would be glad to have me dead and out of the way."

"No, no, Mag! do n't talk so. You shan't starve so long as I have barrels to hoop. Peter Greene boards me cheap. I'll help you, if nobody else will."

A tear stood in Mag's faded eye. "I'm glad," she said, with a softer tone than before, "if there is *one* who is n't glad to see me suffer. I b'lieve all Singleton wants to see me punished, and feel as if they could tell when I 've been punished long enough. It 's a long day ahead they 'll set it, I reckon."

After the usual supply of fuel was prepared, Jim returned home. Full of pity for Mag, he set about devising measures for her relief. "By golly!" said he to himself one day—for he had become so absorbed in Mag's interest that he had fallen into a habit of musing aloud—"By golly! I wish she 'd *marry* me."

"Who?" shouted Pete Greene, suddenly starting from an unobserved corner of the rude shop.

"Where you come from, you sly nigger!" exclaimed Jim.

"Come, tell me, who is 't?" said Pete; "Mag Smith, you want to marry?"

"Git out, Pete! and when you come in dis shop again, let a nigger know it. Do n't steal in like a thief."

Pity and love know little severance. One attends the other. Jim acknowledged the presence of the former, and his efforts in Mag's behalf told also of a finer principle.

This sudden expedient which he had unintentionally disclosed, roused his thinking and inventive powers to study upon the best method of introducing the subject to Mag.

He belted his barrels, with many a scheme revolving in his mind, none of which quite satisfied him, or seemed, on the whole, expedient. He thought of the pleasing contrast between her fair face and his own dark skin; the smooth, straight hair, which he had once, in expression of pity, kindly stroked on her now wrinkled but once fair brow. There was a tempest gathering in his heart, and at last, to ease his pent-up passion, he exclaimed aloud, "By golly!" Recollecting his former exposure, he glanced around to see if Pete was in hearing again. Satisfied on this point, he continued: "She'd be as much of a prize to me as she'd fall short of coming up to the mark with white folks. I do n't care for past things. I 've done things 'fore now I's 'shamed of. She's good enough for me, any how."

One more glance about the premises to be sure Pete was away.

The next Saturday night brought Jim to the hovel again. The cold was fast coming to tarry its apportioned time.   Mag was nearly despairing of meeting its rigor.

" How's the wood, Mag?" asked Jim.

" All gone; and no more to cut, any how," was the reply.

" Too bad!" Jim said.   His truthful reply would have been, I'm glad.

" Anything to eat in the house ? " continued he.

" No," replied Mag.

" Too bad!" again, orally, with the same *inward* gratulation as before.

" Well, Mag," said Jim, after a short pause, " you's down low enough.   I do n't see but I've got to take care of ye.   'Sposin' we marry! "

Mag raised her eyes, full of amazement, and uttered a sonorous " What?"

Jim felt abashed for a moment.   He knew well what were her objections.

" You's had trial of white folks, any how.   They run off and left ye, and now none of 'em come near ye to see if you's dead or alive.   I's black outside, I know, but I's got a white heart inside.   Which you rather have, a black heart in a white skin, or a white heart in a black one ? "

"Oh, dear!" sighed Mag; "Nobody on earth cares for *me* — "

"I do," interrupted Jim.

"I can do but two things," said she, "beg my living, or get it from you."

"Take me, Mag. I can give you a better home than this, and not let you suffer so."

He prevailed; they married. You can philosophize, gentle reader, upon the impropriety of such unions, and preach dozens of sermons on the evils of amalgamation. Want is a more powerful philosopher and preacher. Poor Mag. She has sundered another bond which held her to her fellows. She has descended another step down the ladder of infamy.

2

CHAPTER II.

MY FATHER'S DEATH.

Misery ! we have known each other,
Like a sister and a brother,
Living in the same lone home
Many years — we must live some
Hours or ages yet to come.
                            SHELLEY.

JIM, proud of his treasure, — a white wife, —
tried hard to fulfil his promises; and furnished
her with a more comfortable dwelling, diet, and
apparel. It was comparatively a comfortable
winter she passed after her marriage. When
Jim could work, all went on well. Industrious,
and fond of Mag, he was determined she should
not regret her union to him. Time levied an
additional charge upon him, in the form of two
pretty mulattos, whose infantile pranks amply
repaid the additional toil. A few years, and a
severe cough and pain in his side compelled him
to be an idler for weeks together, and Mag had

thus a reminder of by-gones. She cared for him only as a means to subserve her own comfort; yet she nursed him faithfully and true to marriage vows till death released her. He became the victim of consumption. He loved Mag to the last. So long as life continued, he stifled his sensibility to pain, and toiled for her sustenance long after he was able to do so.

A few expressive wishes for her welfare; a hope of better days for her; an anxiety lest they should not all go to the " good place;" brief advice about their children; a hope expressed that Mag would not be neglected as she used to be; the manifestation of Christian patience; these were *all* the legacy of miserable Mag. A feeling of cold desolation came over her, as she turned from the grave of one who had been truly faithful to her.

She was now expelled from companionship with white people; this last step — her union with a black — was the climax of repulsion.

Seth Shipley, a partner in Jim's business, wished her to remain in her present home; but she declined, and returned to her hovel again, with obstacles threefold more iusurmountable

than before. Seth accompanied her, giving her
a weekly allowance which furnished most of the
food necessary for the four inmates. After a
time, work failed; their means were reduced.

How Mag toiled and suffered, yielding to fits
of desperation, bursts of anger, and uttering
curses too fearful to repeat. When both were
supplied with work, they prospered; if idle, they
were hungry together. In this way their interests became united; they planned for the future
together. Mag had lived an outcast for years.
She had ceased to feel the gushings of peni-
tence; she had crushed the sharp agonies of an
awakened conscience. She had no longings for
a purer heart, a better life. Far easier to
descend lower. She entered the darkness of
perpetual infamy. She asked not the rite of
civilization or Christianity. Her will made her
the wife of Seth. Soon followed scenes familiar
and trying.

"It's no use," said Seth one day; "we must
give the children away, and try to get work in
some other place."

"Who'll take the black devils?" snarled Mag.

" They 're none of mine," said Seth ; " what you growling about ? "

" Nobody will want any thing of mine, or yours either," she replied.

" We 'll make 'em, p'r'aps," he said. " There 's Frado 's six years old, and pretty, if she is yours, and white folks 'll say so. She 'd be a prize somewhere," he continued, tipping his chair back against the wall, and placing his feet upon the rounds, as if he had much more to say when in the right position.

Frado, as they called one of Mag's children, was a beautiful mulatto, with long, curly black hair, and handsome, roguish eyes, sparkling with an exuberance of spirit almost beyond restraint.

Hearing her name mentioned, she looked up from her play, to see what Seth had to say of her.

" Would n't the Bellmonts take her ? " asked Seth.

" Bellmonts ? " shouted Mag. " His wife is a right she-devil ! and if —"

" Had n't they better be all together ? " inter-

2*

rupted Seth, reminding her of a like epithet used in reference to her little ones.

Without seeming to notice him, she continued, " She can't keep a girl in the house over a week ; and Mr. Bellmont wants to hire a boy to work for him, but he can't find one that will live in the house with her ; she 's so ugly, they can't."

" Well, we 've got to make a move soon," answered Seth ; " if you go with me, we shall go right off. Had you rather spare the other one ? " asked Seth, after a short pause.

" One 's as bad as t' other," replied Mag. " Frado is such a wild, frolicky thing, and means to do jest as she 's a mind to ; she wo n't go if she do n't want to. I do n't want to tell her she is to be given away."

" I will," said Seth. " Come here, Frado ? "

The child seemed to have some dim fore-shadowing of evil, and declined.

" Come here," he continued ; " I want to tell you something."

She came reluctantly. He took her hand and said : " We 're going to move, by-'m-bye ; will you go ? "

"No!" 'screamed she; and giving a sudden jerk which destroyed Seth's equilibrium, left him sprawling on the floor, while she escaped through the open door.

"She's a hard one," said Seth, brushing his patched coat sleeve. "I'd risk her at Bellmont's."

They discussed the expediency of a speedy departure. Seth would first seek employment, and then return for Mag. They would take with them what they could carry, and leave the rest with Pete Greene, and come for them when they were wanted. They were long in arranging affairs satisfactorily, and were not a little startled at the close of their conference to find Frado missing. They thought approaching night would bring her. Twilight passed into darkness, and she did not come. They thought she had understood their plans, and had, perhaps, permanently withdrawn. They could not rest without making some effort to ascertain her retreat. Seth went in pursuit, and returned without her. They rallied others when they discovered that another little colored girl was missing, a favorite playmate of Frado's. All effort proved unavailing. Mag felt sure her fears were realized, and that she might never see her again. Before her anxieties became realities, both were safely returned, and from them and their attendant they learned that they went to walk, and not minding the direction soon found themselves lost. They had climbed fences and walls, passed through thickets and marshes, and when night approached selected a thick cluster of shrubbery as a covert for the night. They were discovered by the person who now restored them, chatting of their prospects, Frado attempting to banish the childish fears of her companion. As they were some miles from home, they were kindly cared for until morning. Mag was relieved to know her child was not driven to desperation by their intentions to relieve themselves of her, and she was inclined to think severe restraint would be healthful.

The removal was all arranged; the few days necessary for such migrations passed quickly, and one bright summer morning they bade farewell to their Singleton hovel, and with budgets and bundles commenced their weary march. As they neared the village, they heard the merry shouts of children gathered around the schoolroom, awaiting the coming of their teacher.

"Halloo!" screamed one, "Black, white and yeller!" "Black, white and yeller," echoed a dozen voices.

It did not grate so harshly on poor Mag as once it would. She did not even turn her head to look at them. She had passed into an insensibility no childish taunt could penetrate, else she would have reproached herself as she passed familiar scenes, for extending the separation once so easily annihilated by steadfast integrity. Two miles beyond lived the Bellmonts, in a large, old fashioned, two-story white house, environed by fruitful acres, and embellished by shrubbery and shade trees. Years ago a youthful couple consecrated it as home; and after many little feet had worn paths to favorite fruit trees, and over its green hills, and mingled at last with brother man in the race which belongs neither to the swift or strong, the sire became grey-haired and decrepid, and went to his last repose. His aged consort soon followed him. The old homestead thus passed into the hands of a son, to whose wife Mag had applied the

epithet " she-devil," as may be remembered.
John, the son, had not in his family arrangements departed from the example of the father.
The pastimes of his boyhood were ever freshly
revived by witnessing the games of his own sons
as they rallied about the same goal his youthful
feet had often won; as well as by the amuse-
ments of his daughters in their imitations of
maternal duties.

At the time we introduce them, however,
John is wearing the badge of age. Most of his
children were from home; some seeking employment; some were already settled in homes
of their own. A maiden sister shared with him
the estate on which he resided, and occupied a
portion of the house.

Within sight of the house, Seth seated himself
with his bundles and the child he had been leading, while Mag walked onward to the house
leading Frado. A knock at the door brought
Mrs. Bellmont, and Mag asked if she would be
willing to let that child stop there while she
went to the Reed's house to wash, and when she
came back she would call and get her. It
seemed a novel request, but she consented.

Why the impetuous child entered the house, we cannot tell; the door closed, and Mag hastily departed. Frado waited for the close of day, which was to bring back her mother. Alas! it never came. It was the last time she ever saw or heard of her mother.

CHAPTER III.

A NEW HOME FOR ME.

Oh! did we but know of the shadows so nigh,
   The world would indeed be a prison of gloom;
All light would be quenched in youth's eloquent eye,
   And the prayer-lisping infant would ask for the tomb.

For if Hope be a star that may lead us astray,
   And " deceiveth the heart," as the aged ones preach;
Yet 'twas Mercy that gave it, to beacon our way,
   Though its halo illumes where it never can reach.

ELIZA COOK.

As the day closed and Mag did not appear,
surmises were expressed by the family that she
never intended to return. Mr. Bellmont was a
kind, humane man, who would not grudge hospi-
tality to the poorest wanderer, nor fail to sympathize with any sufferer, however humble.
The child's desertion by her mother appealed to
his symathy, and he felt inclined to succor her.
To do this in opposition to Mrs. Bellmont's
wishes, would be like encountering a whirlwind

charged with fire, daggers and spikes. She was
not as susceptible of fine emotions as her spouse.
Mag's opinion of her was not without foundation. She was self-willed, haughty, undisciplined,
arbitrary and severe. In common parlance, she
was a *scold*, a thorough one. Mr. B. remained
silent during the consultation which follows,
engaged in by mother, Mary and John, or Jack,
as he was familiarly called.

"Send her to the County House," said Mary,
in reply to the query what should be done with
her, in a tone which indicated self-importance in
the speaker. She was indeed the idol of her
mother, and more nearly resembled her in disposition and manners than the others.

Jane, an invalid daughter, the eldest of those
at home, was reclining on a sofa apparently un-
interested.

"Keep her," said Jack. "She's real handsome and bright, and not very black, either."

"Yes," rejoined Mary; "that's just like you,
Jack. She'll be of no use at all these three
years, right under foot all the time."

"Poh! Miss Mary; if she should stay, it
would n't be two days before you would be tell-

ing the girls about *our* nig, *our* nig!" retorted Jack.

" I do n't want a nigger 'round *me*, do you, mother?" asked Mary.

" I do n't mind the nigger in the child. I should like a dozen better than one," replied her mother. " If I could make her do my work in a few years, I would keep her. I have so much trouble with girls I hire, I am almost persuaded if I have one to train up in my way from a child, I shall be able to keep them awhile. I am tired of changing every few months."

" Where could she sleep?" asked Mary. " I do n't want her near me."

" In the L chamber," answered the mother.

" How 'll she get there?" asked Jack. " She'll be afraid to go through that dark passage, and she can't climb the ladder safely."

" She 'll have to go there; it 's good enough for a nigger," was the reply.

Jack was sent on horseback to ascertain if Mag was at her home. He returned with the testimony of Pete Greene that they were fairly departed, and that the child was intentionally thrust upon their family.

The imposition was not at all relished by Mrs. B., or the pert, haughty Mary, who had just glided into her teens.

"Show the child to bed, Jack," said his mother. "You seem most pleased with the little nigger, so you may introduce her to her room."

He went to the kitchen, and, taking Frado gently by the hand, told her he would put her in bed now; perhaps her mother would come the next night after her.

It was not yet quite dark, so they ascended the stairs without any light, passing through nicely furnished rooms, which were a source of great amazement to the child. He opened the door which connected with her room by a dark, unfinished passage-way. "Don't bump your head," said Jack, and stepped before to open the door leading into her apartment,— an unfinished chamber over the kitchen, the roof slanting nearly to the floor, so that the bed could stand only in the middle of the room. A small half window furnished light and air. Jack returned to the sitting room with the remark that the child would soon outgrow those quarters.

"When she *does,* she'll outgrow the house," remarked the mother.

"What can she do to help you?" asked Mary. "She came just in the right time, did n't she? Just the very day after Bridget left," continued she.

"I'll see what she can do in the morning," was the answer.

While this conversation was passing below, Frado lay, revolving in her little mind whether she would remain or not until her mother's return. She was of wilful, determined nature, a stranger to fear, and would not hesitate to wander away should she decide to. She remembered the conversation of her mother with Seth, the words " given away " which she heard used in reference to herself; and though she did not know their full import, she thought she should, by remaining, be in some relation to white people she was never favored with before. So she resolved to tarry, with the hope that mother would come and get her some time. The hot sun had penetrated her room, and it was long before a cooling breeze reduced the temperature so that she could sleep.

Frado was called early in the morning by her new mistress. Her first work was to feed the hens. She was shown how it was *always* to be done, and in no other way; any departure from this rule to be punished by a whipping. She was then accompanied by Jack to drive the cows to pasture, so she might learn the way. Upon her return she was allowed to eat her breakfast, consisting of a bowl of skimmed milk, with brown bread crusts, which she was told to eat, standing, by the kitchen table, and must not be over ten minutes about it. Meanwhile the family were taking their morning meal in the dining-room. This over, she was placed on a cricket to wash the common dishes; she was to be in waiting always to bring wood and chips, to run hither and thither from room to room.

A large amount of dish-washing for small hands followed dinner. Then the same after tea and going after the cows finished her first day's work. It was a new discipline to the child. She found some attractions about the place, and she retired to rest at night more willing to remain. The same routine followed day after day, with slight variation; adding a little more work, and

3*

spicing the toil with "words that burn," and frequent blows on her head. These were great
annoyances to Frado, and had she known where
her mother was, she would have gone at once to
her. She was often greatly wearied, and silently
wept over her sad fate. At first she wept aloud,
which Mrs. Bellmont noticed by applying a raw-
hide, always at hand in the kitchen. It was a
symptom of discontent and complaining which
must be "nipped in the bud," she said.

Thus passed a year. No intelligence of Mag.
It was now certain Frado was to become a permanent member of the family. Her labors were
multiplied; she was quite indispensable, although
but seven years old. She had never learned to
read, never heard of a school until her residence
in the family.

Mrs. Bellmont was in doubt about the utility
of attempting to educate people of color, who
were incapable of elevation. This subject occa-
sioned a lengthy discussion in the family. Mr.
Bellmont, Jane and Jack arguing for Frado's
education; Mary and her mother objecting. At
last Mr. Bellmont declared decisively that she
should go to school. He was a man who seldom

decided controversies at home. The word once spoken admitted of no appeal; so, notwithstanding Mary's objection that she would have to attend the same school she did, the word became law.

It was to be a new scene to Frado, and Jack had many queries and conjectures to answer. He was himself too far advanced to attend the summer school, which Frado regretted, having had too many opportunities of witnessing Miss Mary's temper to feel safe in her company alone.

The opening day of school came. Frado sauntered on far in the rear of Mary, who was ashamed to be seen "walking with a nigger." As soon as she appeared, with scanty clothing and bared feet, the children assembled, noisily published her approach: "See that nigger," shouted one. "Look! look!" cried another. "I won't play with her," said one little girl. "Nor I neither," replied another.

Mary evidently relished these sharp attacks, and saw a fair prospect of lowering Nig where, according to her views, she belonged. Poor Frado, chagrined and grieved, felt that her anticipations of pleasure at such a place were far

from being realized. She was just deciding
to return home, and never come there again,
when the teacher appeared, and observing the
downcast looks of the child, took her by the
hand, and led her into the school-room. All followed, and, after the bustle of securing seats
was over, Miss Marsh inquired if the children
knew " any cause for the sorrow of that little
girl ? " pointing to Frado. It was soon all told.
She then reminded them of their duties to the
poor and friendless; their cowardice in attack-
ing a young innocent child; referred them to
one who looks not on outward appearances, but
on the heart. "She looks like a good girl; I
think *I* shall love her, so lay aside all prejudice,
and vie with each other in shewing kindness
and good-will to one who seems different from
you," were the closing remarks of the kind lady.
Those kind words! The most agreeable sound
which ever meets the ear of sorrowing, griev-
ing childhood.

Example rendered her words efficacious. Day
by day there was a manifest change of de-
portment towards "Nig." Her speeches often
drew merriment from the children; no one

could do more to enliven their favorite pastimes
than Frado. Mary could not endure to see her
thus noticed, yet knew not how to prevent it.
She could not influence her schoolmates as she
wished. She had not gained their affections
by winning ways and yielding points of controversy. On the contrary, she was self-willed,
domineering; every day reported "mad" by
some of her companions. She availed herself
of the only alternative, abuse and taunts, as
they returned from school. This was not satis-
factory; she wanted to use physical force "to
subdue her," to "keep her down."

There was, on their way home, a field intersected by a stream over which a single plank
was placed for a crossing. It occurred to Mary that it would be a punishment to Nig to
compel her to cross over; so she dragged her
to the edge, and told her authoritatively to go
over. Nig hesitated, resisted. Mary placed
herself behind the child, and, in the struggle
to force her over, lost her footing and plunged
into the stream. Some of the larger scholars
being in sight, ran, and thus prevented Mary
from drowning and Frado from falling. Nig

scampered home fast as possible, and Mary went to the nearest house, dripping, to procure a change of garments. She came loitering home, half crying, exclaiming, "Nig pushed me into the stream!" She then related the particulars. Nig was called from the kitchen. Mary stood with anger flashing in her eyes. Mr. Bellmont sat quietly reading his paper. He had witnessed too many of Miss Mary's outbreaks to be startled. Mrs. Bellmont interrogated Nig.

"I didn't do it! I didn't do it!" answered Nig, passionately, and then related the occurrence truthfully.

The discrepancy greatly enraged Mrs. Bellmont. With loud accusations and angry gestures she approached the child. Turning to her husband, she asked,

"Will you sit still, there, and hear that black nigger call Mary a liar?"

"How do we know but she has told the truth? I shall not punish her," he replied, and left the house, as he usually did when a tempest threatened to envelop him. No sooner was he out of sight than Mrs. B. and Mary commenced beating her inhumanly;

then propping her mouth open with a piece
of wood, shut her up in a dark room, without any supper. For employment, while the
tempest raged within, Mr. Bellmont went for
the cows, a task belonging to Frado, and thus
unintentionally prolonged her pain. At dark
Jack came in, and seeing Mary, accosted her
with, "So you thought you'd vent your spite
on Nig, did you? Why can't you let her
alone? It was good enough for you to get
a ducking, only you did not stay in half long
enough."

"Stop!" said his mother. "You shall never
talk so before me. You would have that little
nigger trample on Mary, would you? She
came home with a lie; it made Mary's story
false."

"What was Mary's story?" asked Jack.

It was related.

"Now," said Jack, sallying into a chair, "the
school-children happened to see it all, and they
tell the same story Nig does. Which is most
likely to be true, what a dozen agree they
saw, or the contrary?"

"It is very strange you will believe what

others say against your sister," retorted his mother, with flashing eye. "I think it is time your father subdued you."

"Father is a sensible man," argued Jack. "He would not wrong a dog. Where *is* Frado?" he continued.

"Mother gave her a good whipping and shut her up," replied Mary.

Just then Mr. Bellmont entered, and asked if Frado was "shut up yet."

The knowledge of her innocence, the perfidy of his sister, worked fearfully on Jack. He bounded from his chair, searched every room till he found the child; her mouth wedged apart, her face swollen, and full of pain.

How Jack pitied her! He relieved her jaws, brought her some supper, took her to her room, comforted her as well as he knew how, sat by her till she fell asleep, and then left for the sitting room. As he passed his mother, he remarked, "If that was the way Frado was to be treated, he hoped she would never wake again!" He then imparted her situation to his father, who seemed untouched, till a glance at Jack exposed a tearful eye. Jack went early to her next morning.

She awoke sad, but refreshed.   After breakfast
Jack took her with him to the field, and kept
her through the day.   But it could not be so
generally.   She must return to school, to her
household duties.   He resolved to do what he
could to protect her from Mary and his mother.
He bought her a dog, which became a great
favorite with both.   The invalid, Jane, would
gladly befriend her ;   but she had not the
strength to brave the iron will of her mother.
Kind words and affectionate glances were the
only expressions of sympathy she could safely
indulge in.   The men employed on the farm
were always glad to hear her prattle ; she was
a great favorite with them.   Mrs. Bellmont allowed them the privilege of talking with her in
the kitchen.   She did not fear but she should
have ample opportunity of subduing her when
they were away.   Three months of schooling,
summer and winter, she enjoyed for three years.
Her winter over-dress was a cast-off overcoat,
once worn by Jack, and a sun-bonnet.   It was a
source of great merriment to the scholars, but
Nig's retorts were so mirthful, and their satisfac-
tion so evident in attributing the selection to

4

" Old Granny Bellmont," that it was not painful to Nig or pleasurable to Mary. Her jollity was not to be quenched by whipping or scolding. In Mrs. Bellmont's presence she was under restraint; but in the kitchen, and among her schoolmates, the pent up fires burst forth. She was ever at some sly prank when unseen by her teacher, in school hours; not unfrequently some outburst of merriment, of which she was the original, was charged upon some innocent mate, and punishment inflicted which she merited. They enjoyed her antics so fully that any of them would suffer wrongfully to keep open the avenues of mirth. She would venture far beyond propriety, thus shielded and countenanced.

The teacher's desk was supplied with drawers, in which were stored his books and other *et ceteras* of the profession. The children observed Nig very busy there one morning before school, as they flitted in occasionally from their play outside. The master came; called the children to order; opened a drawer to take the book the occasion required; when out poured a volume of smoke. " Fire ! fire !" screamed he, at the top of his voice. By this time he had become sufficiently acquainted with the peculiar odor, to know he was imposed upon. The scholars shouted with laughter to see the terror of the dupe, who, feeling abashed at the needless fright, made no very strict investigation, and Nig once more escaped punishment. She had provided herself with cigars, and puffing, puffing away at the crack of the drawer, had filled it with smoke, and then closed it tightly to deceive the teacher, and amuse the scholars. The interim of terms was filled up with a variety of duties new and peculiar. At home, no matter how powerful the heat when sent to rake hay or guard the grazing herd, she was never permitted to shield her skin from the sun. She was not many shades darker than Mary now; what a calamity it would be ever to hear the contrast spoken of. Mrs. Bellmont was determined the sun should have full power to darken the shade which nature had first bestowed upon her as best befitting.

CHAPTER IV.

A FRIEND FOR NIG.

" Hours of my youth ! when nurtured in my breast,
To love a stranger, friendship made me blest ; —
Friendship, the dear peculiar bond of youth,
When every artless bosom throbs with truth ;
Untaught by worldly wisdom how to feign ;
And check each impulse with prudential reign ;
When all we feel our honest souls disclose —
In love to friends, in open hate to foes ;
No varnished tales the lips of youth repeat,
No dear-bought knowledge purchased by deceit."

BYRON.

WITH what differing emotions have the denizens of earth awaited the approach of to-day. Some sufferer has counted the vibrations of the pendulum impatient for its dawn, who, now that it has arrived, is anxious for its close. The votary of pleasure, conscious of yesterday's void, wishes for power to arrest time's haste till a few more hours of mirth shall be enjoyed. The unfortunate are yet gazing in vain for golden-edged clouds they fancied would appear in their horizon. The good man feels that he has accom-

plished too little for the Master, and sighs that
another day must so soon close. Innocent childhood, weary of its stay, longs for another morrow; busy manhood cries, hold! hold! and pur-
sues it to another's dawn. All are dissatisfied.
All crave some good not yet possessed, which
time is expected to bring with all its morrows.

Was it strange that, to a disconsolate child,
three years should seem a long, long time?
During school time she had rest from Mrs. Bellmont's tyranny. She was now nine years old;
time, her mistress said, such privileges should
cease.

She could now read and spell, and knew the
elementary steps in grammar, arithmetic, and
writing. Her education completed, as *she* said, Mrs.
Bellmont felt that her time and person belonged
solely to her. She was under her in every sense
of the word. What an opportunity to indulge
her vixen nature! No matter what occurred to
ruffle her, or from what source provocation came,
real or fancied, a few blows on Nig seemed to
relieve her of a portion of ill-will.

These were days when Fido was the entire
confidant of Frado. She told him her griefs as

4*

though he were human; and he sat so still, and
listened so attentively, she really believed he
knew her sorrows.   All the leisure moments she
could gain were used in teaching him some feat
of dog-agility, so that Jack pronounced him
very knowing, and was truly gratified to know
he had furnished her with a gift answering his
intentions.

Fido was the constant attendant of Frado,
when sent from the house on errands, going and
returning with the cows, out in the fields, to the
village. If ever she forgot her hardships it was
in his company.

Spring was now retiring.   James, one of the
absent sons, was expected home on a visit.   He
had never seen the last acquisition to the family.
Jack had written faithfully of all the merits of
his colored *protegé*, and hinted plainly that
mother did not always treat her just right.
Many were the preparations to make the visit
pleasant, and as the day approached when he
was to arrive, great exertions were made to
cook the favorite viands, to prepare the choicest
table-fare.

The morning of the arrival day was a busy

one. Frado knew not who would be of so much importance; her feet were speeding hither and thither so unsparingly. Mrs. Bellmont seemed a trifle fatigued, and her shoes which had, early in the morning, a methodic squeak, altered to an irregular, peevish snap.

"Get some little wood to make the fire burn," said Mrs. Bellmont, in a sharp tone. Frado obeyed, bringing the smallest she could find.

Mrs. Bellmont approached her, and, giving her a box on her ear, reiterated the command.

The first the child brought was the smallest to be found; of course, the second must be a trifle larger. She well knew it was, as she threw it into a box on the hearth. To Mrs. Bellmont it was a greater affront, as well as larger wood, so she "taught her" with the raw-hide, and sent her the third time for "little wood."

Nig, weeping, knew not what to do. She had carried the smallest; none left would suit her mistress; of course further punishment awaited her; so she gathered up whatever came first, and threw it down on the hearth. As she expected, Mrs. Bellmont, enraged, approached her, and kicked her so forcibly as to throw her upon

the floor.   Before she could rise, another foiled
the attempt, and then followed kick after kick in
quick succession and power, till she reached the
door.   Mr. Bellmont and Anut Abby, hearing the
noise, rushed in, just in time to see the last of
the performance.   Nig jumped up, and rushed
from the house, out of sight.

Aunt Abby returned to her apartment, followed by John, who was muttering to himself.

"What were you saying?" asked Aunt Abby.

"I said I hoped the child never would come
into the house again."

"What would become of her?   You cannot
mean *that*," continued his sister.

"I do mean it.   The child does as much work
as a woman ought to; and just see how she is
kicked about!"

"Why do you have it so, John?" asked his
sister.

"How am I to help it?   Women rule the
earth, and all in it."

"I think I should rule my own house, John,"—

"And live in hell meantime," added Mr.
Bellmont.

John now sauntered out to the barn to await the quieting of the storm.

Aunt Abby had a glimpse of Nig as she passed out of the yard; but to arrest her, or shew her that *she* would shelter her, in Mrs. Bellmont's presence, would only bring reserved wrath on her defenceless head. Her sister-in-law had great prejudices against her. One cause of the alienation was that she did not give her right in the homestead to John, and leave it forever; another was that she was a professor of religion, (so was Mrs. Bellmont;) but Nab, as she called her, did not live according to her profession; another, that she *would* sometimes give Nig cake and pie, which she was never allowed to have at home. Mary had often noticed and spoken of her inconsistencies.

The dinner hour passed. Frado had not appeared. Mrs. B. made no inquiry or search. Aunt Abby looked long, and found her concealed in an outbuilding. "Come into the house with me," implored Aunt Abby.

"I ain't going in any more," sobbed the child.

"What will you do?" asked Aunt Abby.

" I 've got to stay out here and die. I ha' n't got no mother, no home. I wish I was dead."

" Poor thing," muttered Aunt Abby; and slyly providing her with some dinner, left her to her grief.

Jane went to confer with her Aunt about the affair; and learned from her the retreat. She would gladly have concealed her in her own chamber, and ministered to her wants; but she was dependent on Mary and her mother for care, and any displeasure caused by attention to Nig, was seriously felt.

Toward night the coach brought James. A time of general greeting, inquiries for absent members of the family, a visit to Aunt Abby's room, undoing a few delicacies for Jane, brought them to the tea hour.

" Where 's Frado?" asked Mr. Bellmont, observing she was not in her usual place, behind her mistress' chair.

" I don't know, and I don't care. If she makes her appearance again, I 'll take the skin from her body," replied his wife.

James, a fine looking young man, with a pleasant countenance, placid, and yet decidedly serious, yet not stern, looked up confounded. He was no stranger to his mother's nature; but years of absence had erased the occurrences once so familiar, and he asked, "Is this that pretty little Nig, Jack writes to me about, that you are so severe upon, mother?"

"I'll not leave much of her beauty to be seen, if she comes in sight; and now, John," said Mrs, B., turning to her husband, "you need not think you are going to learn her to treat me in this way; just see how saucy she was this morning. She shall learn her place."

Mr. Bellmont raised his calm, determined eye full upon her, and said, in a decisive manner: "You shall not strike, or scald, or skin her, as you call it, if she comes back again. Remember!" and he brought his hand down upon the table. "I have searched an hour for her now, and she is not to be found on the premises. Do *you* know where she is? Is she *your* prisoner?"

"No! I have just told you I did not know where she was. Nab has her hid somewhere, I suppose. Oh, dear! I did not think it would come to this; that my own husband would treat me so." Then came fast flowing tears, which no

one but Mary seemed to notice. Jane crept
into Aunt Abby's room; Mr. Bellmont and
James went out of doors, and Mary remained to
condole with her parent.

"Do you know where Frado is?" asked Jane
of her aunt.

"No," she replied. "I have hunted everywhere. She has left her first hiding-place. I
cannot think what has become of her. There
comes Jack and Fido; perhaps he knows;" and
she walked to a window near, where James and
his father were conversing together.

The two brothers exchanged a hearty greeting, and then Mr. Bellmont told Jack to eat his
supper; afterward he wished to send him away.
He immediately went in. Accustomed to all
the phases of indoor storms, from a whine to
thunder and lightning, he saw at a glance marks
of disturbance. He had been absent through
the day, with the hired men.

"What's the fuss?" asked he, rushing into
Aunt Abby's.

"Eat your supper," said Jane; "go home,
Jack."

Back again through the dining-room, and out to his father.

"What's the fuss?" again inquired he of his father.

"Eat your supper, Jack, and see if you can find Frado. She's not been seen since morning, and then she was kicked out of the house."

"I shan't eat my supper till I find her," said Jack, indignantly. " Come, James, and see the little creature mother treats so."

They started, calling, searching, coaxing, all their way along. No Frado. They returned to the house to consult. James and Jack declared they would not sleep till she was found.

Mrs. Bellmont attempted to dissuade them from the search. "It was a shame a little *nigger* should make so much trouble."

Just then Fido came running up, and Jack exclaimed, "Fido knows where she is, I'll bet."

"So I believe," said his father; "but we shall not be wiser unless we can outwit him. He will not do what his mistress forbids him."

"I know how to fix him," said Jack. Taking a plate from the table, which was still waiting, he called, " Fido! Fido! Frado wants some sup-

5

per. Come!" Jack started, the dog followed,
and soon capered on before, far, far into the
fields, over walls and through fences, into a
piece of swampy land. Jack followed close, and
soon appeared to James, who was quite in the
rear, coaxing and forcing Frado along with him.

A frail child, driven from shelter by the cruelty of his mother, was an object of interest to
James. They persuaded her to go home with
them, warmed her by the kitchen fire, gave her
a good supper, and took her with them into the
sitting-room.

" Take that nigger out of my sight," was Mrs.
Bellmont's command, before they could be
seated.

James led her into Aunt Abby's, where he
knew they were welcome. They chatted awhile
until Frado seemed cheerful; then James led
her to her room, and waited until she retired.

" Are you glad I've come home?" asked
James.

" Yes; if you won't let me be whipped tomorrow."

" You won't be whipped. You must try to
be a good girl," counselled James.

"If I do, I get whipped;" sobbed the child. "They won't believe what I say. Oh, I wish I had my mother back; then I should not be kicked and whipped so. Who made me so?"

"God;" answered James.

"Did God make you?"

"Yes."

"Who made Aunt Abby?"

"God."

"Who made your mother?"

"God."

"Did the same God that made her make me?"

"Yes."

"Well, then, I don't like him."

"Why not?"

"Because he made her white, and me black. Why didn't he make us *both* white?"

"I don't know; try to go to sleep, and you will feel better in the morning," was all the reply he could make to her knotty queries. It was a long time before she fell asleep; and a number of days before James felt in a mood to visit and entertain old associates and friends.

CHAPTER V.

DEPARTURES.

Life is a strange avenue of various trees and flowers;
Lightsome at commencement, but darkening to its end in a distant,
    massy portal.
It beginneth as a little path, edged with the violet and primrose,
A little path of lawny grass and soft to tiny feet.
Soon, spring thistles in the way.

TUPPER.

JAMES' visit concluded. Frado had become
greatly attached to him, and with sorrow she
listened and joined in the farewells which pre-
ceded his exit. The remembrance of his kindness cheered her through many a weary month,
and an occasional word to her in letters to Jack,
were like " cold waters to a thirsty soul." Intelligence came that James would soon marry;
Frado hoped he would, and remove her from
such severe treatment as she was subject to.
There had been additional burdens laid on her
since his return. She must now *milk* the cows,
she had then only to drive. Flocks of sheep
had been added to the farm, which daily claimed

a portion of her time. In the absence of the
men, she must harness the horse for Mary and
her mother to ride, go to mill, in short, do the
work of a boy, could one be procured to endure
the tirades of Mrs. Bellmont. She was first up
in the morning, doing what she could towards
breakfast. Occasionally, she would utter some
funny thing for Jack's benefit, while she was
waiting on the table, provoking a sharp look
from his mother, or expulsion from the room.

On one such occasion, they found her on the
roof of the barn. Some repairs having been
necessary, a staging had been erected, and was
not wholly removed. Availing herself of lad-
ders, she was mounted in high glee on the top-
most board. Mr. Bellmont called sternly for her
to come down; poor Jane nearly fainted from
fear. Mrs. B. and Mary did not care if she
" broke her neck," while Jack and the men
laughed at her fearlessness. Strange, one spark
of playfulness could remain amid such constant
toil; but her natural temperament was in a
high degree mirthful, and the encouragement
she received from Jack and the hired men, constantly nurtured the inclination. When she had

5*

none of the family around to be merry with, she would amuse herself with the animals. Among the sheep was a willful leader, who always persisted in being first served, and many times in his fury he had thrown down Nig, till, provoked, she resolved to punish him. The pasture in which the sheep grazed was bounded on three sides by a wide stream, which flowed on one side at the base of precipitous banks. The first spare moments at her command, she ran to the pasture with a dish in her hand, and mounting the highest point of land nearest the stream, called the flock to their mock repast. Mr Bellmont, with his laborers, were in sight, though unseen by Frado. They paused to see what she was about to do. Should she by any mishap lose her footing, she must roll into the stream, and, without aid, must drown. They thought of shouting; but they feared an unexpected salute might startle her, and thus ensure what they were anxious to prevent. They watched in breathless silence. The willful sheep came furiously leaping and bounding far in advance of the flock. Just as he leaped for the dish, she suddenly jumped one side, when down he rolled

into the river, and swimming across, remained
alone till night. The men lay down, convulsed
with laughter at the trick, and guessed at once
its object. Mr. Bellmont talked seriously to the
child for exposing herself to such danger; but
she hopped about on her toes, and with laugha-
ble grimaces replied, she knew she was quick
enough to " give him a slide."

But to return. James married a Baltimorean
lady of wealthy parentage, an indispensable
requisite, his mother had always taught him.
He did not marry her wealth, though; he loved
her, sincerely. She was not unlike his sister
Jane, who had a social, gentle, loving nature,
rather *too* yielding, her brother thought. His
Susan had a firmness which Jane needed to
complete her character, but which her ill health
may in a measure have failed to produce. Although an invalid, she was not excluded from
society. Was it strange *she* should seem a desirable companion, a treasure as a wife?

Two young men seemed desirous of possessing her. One was a neighbor, Henry Reed, a
tall, spare young man, with sandy hair, and blue,
sinister eyes. He seemed to appreciate her

wants, and watch with interest her improvement
or decay.   His kindness she received, and by it
was almost won.   Her mother wished her to encourage his attentions.   She had counted the
acres which were to be transmitted to an only
son; she knew there was silver in the purse;
she would not have Jane too sentimental.

The eagerness with which he amassed wealth,
was repulsive to Jane; he did not spare his person or beasts in its pursuit.   She felt that to
such a man she should be considered an incum-
brance; she doubted if he would desire her, if
he did not know she would bring a handsome
patrimony.   Her mother, full in favor with the
parents of Henry, commanded her to accept
him.   She engaged herself, yielding to her
mother's wishes, because she had not strength to
oppose them; and sometimes, when witness of
her mother's and Mary's tyranny, she felt any
change would be preferable, even such a one as
this.   She knew her husband should be the man
of her own selecting, one she was conscious of
preferring before all others.   She could not say
this of Henry.

In this dilemma, a visitor came to Aunt

Abby's ; one of her boy-favorites, George Means,
from an adjoining State. Sensible, plain looking,
agreeable, talented, he could not long be a
stranger to any one who wished to know him.
Jane was accustomed to sit much with Aunt
Abby always; her presence now seemed necessary to assist in entertaining this youthful friend.
Jane was more pleased with him each day, and
silently wished Henry possessed more refinement,
and the polished manners of George. She felt
dissatisfied with her relation to him. His calls
while George was there, brought their opposing
qualities vividly before her, and she found it
disagreeable to force herself into those attentions belonging to him. She received him apparently only as a neighbor.

George returned home, and Jane endeavored
to stifle the risings of dissatisfaction, and had
nearly succeeded, when a letter came which
needed but one glance to assure her of its birthplace; and she retired for its perusal. Well
was it for her that her mother's suspicion was
not aroused, or her curiosity startled to inquire
who it came from. After reading it, she glided
into Aunt Abby's, and placed it in her hands,
who was no stranger to Jane's trials.

George could not rest after his return, he
wrote, until he had communicated to Jane the
emotions her presence awakened, and his desire
to love and possess her as his own. He begged
to know if his affections were reciprocated, or
could be; if she would permit him to write to
her; if she was free from all obligation to
another.

"What would mother say?" queried Jane, as
she received the letter from her aunt.

"Not much to comfort you."

"Now, aunt, George is just such a man as I
could really love, I think, from all I have seen
of him; you know I never could say that of
Henry" —

"Then do n't marry him," interrupted Aunt
Abby.

"Mother will make me."

"Your father wo n't."

"Well, aunt, what can I do? Would you
answer the letter, or not?"

"Yes, answer it. Tell him your situation."

"I shall not tell him all my feelings."

Jane answered that she had enjoyed his company much; she had seen nothing offensive in

his manner or appearance; that she was under no obligations which forbade her receiving letters from him as a friend and acquaintance. George was puzzled by the reply. He wrote to Aunt Abby, and from her learned all. He could not see Jane thus sacrificed, without making an effort to rescue her. Another visit followed. George heard Jane say she preferred *him*. He then conferred with Henry at his home. It was not a pleasant subject to talk upon. To be thus supplanted, was not to be thought of. He would sacrifice everything but his inheritance to secure his betrothed.

" And so you are the cause of her late coldness towards me. Leave! I will talk no more about it; the business is settled between us; there it will remain," said Henry.

" Have you no wish to know the real state of Jane's affections towards you?" asked George.

" No! Go, I say! go!" and Henry opened the door for him to pass out.

He retired to Aunt Abby's. Henry soon followed, and presented his cause to Mrs. Bellmont.

Provoked, surprised, indignant, she summoned Jane to her presence, and after a lengthy tirade

upon Nab, and her satanic influence, told her
she could not break the bonds which held her
to Henry; she should not.   George Means was
rightly named ; he was, truly, mean enough ;
she knew his family of old ; his father had four
wives, and five times as many children.

"Go to your room, Miss Jane," she continued.
"Do n't let me know of your being in Nab's for
one while."

The storm was now visible to all beholders.
Mr. Bellmont sought Jane. She told him her objections to Henry; showed him George's letter;
told her answer, the occasion of his visit. He
bade her not make herself sick; he would see
that she was not compelled to violate her free
choice in so important a transaction. He then
sought the two young men; told them he could
not as a father see his child compelled to an un-
congenial union; a free, voluntary choice was of
such importance to one of her health. She must
be left free to her own choice.

Jane sent Henry a letter of dismission; he her
one of a legal bearing, in which he balanced his
disappointment by a few hundreds.

To brave her mother's fury, nearly overcame

her, but the consolations of a kind father and
aunt cheered her on.   After a suitable interval
she was married to George, and removed to his
home in Vermont.   Thus another light disappeared from Nig's horizon.   Another was soon to
follow.   Jack was anxious to try his skill in providing for his own support; so a situation as
clerk in a store was procured in a Western city,
and six months after Jane's departure, was Nig
abandoned to the tender mercies of Mary and
her mother.   As if to remove the last vestige of
earthly joy, Mrs. Bellmont sold the companion and
pet of Frado, the dog Fido.

6

CHAPTER VI.

VARIETIES.

" Hard are life's early steps; and but that youth is buoyant, con-
fident, and strong in hope, men would behold its threshold and
despair."

THE sorrow of Frado was very great for her
pet, and Mr. Bellmont by great exertion obtained
it again, much to the relief of the child.   To be
thus deprived of all her sources of pleasure was a
sure way to exalt their worth, and Fido became,
in her estimation, a more valuable presence than
the human beings who surrounded her.

James had now been married a number of
years, and frequent requests for a visit from the
family were at last accepted, and Mrs. Bellmont
made great preparations for a fall sojourn in
Baltimore.   Mary was installed housekeper — in
name merely, for Nig was the only moving power
in the house.   Although suffering from their joint
severity, she felt safer than to be thrown wholly

upon an ardent, passionate, unrestrained young lady, whom she always hated and felt it hard to be obliged to obey. The trial she must meet. Were Jack or Jane at home she would have some refuge; one only remained; good Aunt Abby was still in the house.

She saw the fast receding coach which conveyed her master and mistress with regret, and begged for one favor only, that James would send for her when they returned, a hope she had confidently cherished all these five years.

She was now able to do all the washing, ironing, baking, and the common *et cetera* of household duties, though but fourteen. Mary left all for her to do, though she affected great responsibility. She would show herself in the kitchen long enough to relieve herself of some command, better withheld; or insist upon some compliance to her wishes in some department which she was very imperfectly acquainted with, very much less than the person she was addressing; and so impetuous till her orders were obeyed, that to escape the turmoil, Nig would often go contrary to her own knowledge to gain a respite.

Nig was taken sick! What could be done

The *work*, certainly, but not by Miss Mary. So Nig would work while she could remain erect, then sink down upon the floor, or a chair, till she could rally for a fresh effort. Mary would look in upon her, chide her for her laziness, threaten to tell mother when she came home, and so forth.

"Nig!" screamed Mary, one of her sickest days, "come here, and sweep these threads from the carpet." She attempted to drag her weary limbs along, using the broom as support. Impatient of delay, she called again, but with a different request. "Bring me some wood, you lazy jade, quick." Nig rested the broom against the wall, and started on the fresh behest.

Too long gone. Flushed with anger, she rose and greeted her with, "What are you gone so long, for? Bring it in quick, I say."

"I am coming as quick as I can," she replied, entering the door.

"Saucy, impudent nigger, you! is this the way you answer me?" and taking a large carving knife from the table, she hurled it, in her rage, at the defenceless girl.

Dodging quickly, it fastened in the ceiling a

few inches from where she stood. There rushed on Mary's mental vision a picture of bloodshed, in which she was the perpetrator, and the sad consequences of what was so nearly an actual occurrence.

"Tell anybody of this, if you dare. If you tell Aunt Abby, I'll certainly kill you," said she, terrified. She returned to her room, brushed her threads herself; was for a day or two more guarded, and so escaped deserved and merited penalty.

Oh, how long the weeks seemed which held Nig in subjection to Mary; but they passed like all earth's sorrows and joys. Mr. and Mrs. B. returned delighted with their visit, and laden with rich presents for Mary. No word of hope for Nig. James was quite unwell, and would come home the next spring for a visit.

This, thought Nig, will be my time of release. I shall go back with him.

From early dawn until after all were retired, was she toiling, overworked, disheartened, longing for relief.

Exposure from heat to cold, or the reverse, often destroyed her health for short intervals.

6*

She wore no shoes until after frost, and snow even, appeared; and bared her feet again before the last vestige of winter disappeared. These sudden changes she was so illy guarded against, nearly conquered her physical system. Any word of complaint was severely repulsed or cruelly punished.

She was told she had much more than she deserved. So that manual labor was not in reality her only burden; but such an incessant torrent of scolding and boxing and threatening, was enough to deter one of maturer years from remaining within sound of the strife.

It is impossible to give an impression of the manifest enjoyment of Mrs. B. in these kitchen scenes. It was her favorite exercise to enter the appartment noisily, vociferate orders, give a few sudden blows to quicken Nig's pace, then return to the sitting room with *such* a satisfied expression, congratulating herself upon her thorough house-keeping qualities.

She usually rose in the morning at the ringing of the bell for breakfast; if she were heard stirring before that time, Nig knew well there was an extra amount of scolding to be borne.

No one now stood between herself and Frado, but Aunt Abby. And if *she* dared to interfere in the least, she was ordered back to her " own quarters." Nig would creep slyly into her room, learn what she could of her regarding the absent, and thus gain some light in the thick gloom of care and toil and sorrow in which she was immersed.

The first of spring a letter came from James, announcing declining health. He must try northern air as a restorative; so Frado joyfully prepared for this agreeable increase of the family, this addition to her cares.

He arrived feeble, lame, from his disease, so changed Frado wept at his appearance, fearing he would be removed from her forever. He kindly greeted her, took her to the parlor to see his wife and child, and said many things to kindle smiles on her sad face.

Frado felt so happy in his presence, so safe from maltreatment! He was to her a shelter. He observed, silently, the ways of the house a few days; Nig still took her meals in the same manner as formerly, having the same allowance

of food.   He, one day, bade her not remove the
food, but sit down to the table and eat.

"She *will*, mother," said he, calmly, but imperatively; I'm determined; she works hard; I've
watched her.   Now, while I stay, she is going to
sit down *here*, and eat such food as we eat."

A few sparks from the mother's black eyes
were the only reply; she feared to oppose where
she knew she could not prevail.   So Nig's standing attitude, and selected diet vanished.

Her clothing was yet poor and scanty; she was
not blessed with a Sunday attire; for she was
never permitted to attend church with her mistress.   "Religion was not meant for niggers," *she*
said; when the husband and brothers were
absent, she would drive Mrs. B. and Mary there,
then return, and go for them at the close of the
service, but never remain.   Aunt Abby would
take her to evening meetings, held in the neigh-
borhood, which Mrs. B. never attended; and im-
part to her lessons of truth and grace as they
walked to the place of prayer.

Many of less piety would scorn to present so
doleful a figure; Mrs. B. had shaved her glossy
ringlets; and, in her coarse cloth gown and an-

cient bonnet, she was anything but an enticing object. But Aunt Abby looked within. She saw a soul to save, an immortality of happiness to secure.

These evenings were eagerly anticipated by Nig; it was such a pleasant release from labor.

Such perfect contrast in the melody and prayers of these good people to the harsh tones which fell on her ears during the day.

Soon she had all their sacred songs at command, and enlivened her toil by accompanying it with this melody.

James encouraged his aunt in her efforts. He had found the *Saviour*, he wished to have Frado's desolate heart gladdened, quieted, sustained, by *His* presence. He felt sure there were elements in her heart which, transformed and purified by the gospel, would make her worthy the esteem and friendship of the world. A kind, affectionate heart, native wit, and common sense, and the pertness she sometimes exhibited, he felt if restrained properly, might become useful in originating a self-reliance which would be of service to her in after years.

Yet it was not possible to compass all this, while she remained where she was. He wished to be cautious about pressing too closely her claims on his mother, as it would increase the burdened one he so anxiously wished to relieve. He cheered her on with the hope of returning with his family, when he recovered sufficiently.

Nig seemed awakened to new hopes and aspirations, and realized a longing for the future, hitherto unknown.

To complete Nig's enjoyment, Jack arrived unexpectedly. His greeting was as hearty to herself as to any of the family.

"Where are your curls, Fra?" asked Jack, after the usual salutation.

"Your mother cut them off."

"Thought you were getting handsome, did she? Same old story, is it; knocks and bumps? Better times coming; never fear, Nig."

How different this appellative sounded from him; he said it in such a tone, with such a rogueish look!

She laughed, and replied that he had better take her West for a housekeeper.

Jack was pleased with James's innovations of

table discipline, and would often tarry in the dining-room, to see Nig in her new place at the family table. As he was thus sitting one day, after the family had finished dinner, Frado seated herself in her mistress' chair, and was just reaching for a clean dessert plate which was on the table, when her mistress entered.

"Put that plate down; you shall not have a clean one; eat from mine," continued she. Nig hesitated. To eat after James, his wife or Jack, would have been pleasant; but to be commanded to do what was disagreeable by her mistress, *because* it was disagreeable, was trying. Quickly looking about, she took the plate, called Fido to wash it, which he did to the best of his ability; then, wiping her knife and fork on the cloth, she proceeded to eat her dinner.

Nig never looked toward her mistress during the process. She had Jack near; she did not fear her now.

Insulted, full of rage, Mrs. Bellmont rushed to her husband, and commanded him to notice this insult; to whip that child; if he would not do it, James ought.

James came to hear the kitchen version of the

affair. Jack was boiling over with laughter. He related all the circumstances to James, and pulling a bright, silver half-dollar from his pocket, he threw it at Nig, saying, "There, take that; 't was worth paying for."

James sought his mother; told her he "would not excuse or palliate Nig's impudence; but she should not be whipped or be punished at all. You have not treated her, mother, so as to gain her love; she is only exhibiting your remissness in this matter."

She only smothered her resentment until a convenient opportunity offered. The first time she was left alone with Nig, she gave her a thorough beating, to bring up arrearages; and threatened, if she ever exposed her to James, she would "cut her tongue out."

James found her, upon his return, sobbing; but fearful of revenge, she dared not answer his queries. He guessed their cause, and longed for returning health to take her under his protection.

CHAPTER VII.

SPIRITUAL CONDITION OF NIG.

"What are our joys but dreams? and what our hopes
   But goodly shadows in the summer cloud?"

                                        H. K. W.

JAMES did not improve as was hoped. Month
after month passed away, and brought no prospect of returning health. He could not walk
far from the house for want of strength; but he
loved to sit with Aunt Abby in her quiet room,
talking of unseen glories, and heart-experiences,
while planning for the spiritual benefit of those
around them. In these confidential interviews,
Frado was never omitted. They would discuss
the prevalent opinion of the public, that people
of color are really inferior; incapable of cultivation and refinement. They would glance at the
qualities of Nig, which promised so much if
rightly directed. "I wish you would take her,
James, when you are well, home with *you*," said
Aunt Abby, in one of these seasons.

7

"Just what I am longing to do, Aunt Abby. Susan is just of my mind, and we intend to take her; I have been wishing to do so for years."

"She seems much affected by what she hears at the evening meetings, and asks me many questions on serious things; seems to love to read the Bible; I feel hopes of her."

"I hope she *is* thoughtful; no one has a kinder heart, one capable of loving more devotedly. But to think how prejudiced the world are towards her people; that she must be reared in such ignorance as to drown all the finer feelings. When I think of what she might be, of what she will be, I feel like grasping time till opinions change, and thousands like her rise into a noble freedom. I have seen Frado's grief, because she is black, amount to agony. It makes me sick to recall these scenes. Mother pretends to think she don't know enough to sorrow for anything; but if she could see her as I have, when she supposed herself entirely alone, except her little dog Fido, lamenting her loneliness and complexion, I think, if she is not past feeling, she would retract. In the summer I was walking near the barn, and as I stood I heard sobs. 'Oh! oh!' I heard,

' why was I made ? why can't I die ? Oh, what have I to live for ? No one cares for me only to get my work. And I feel sick; who cares for that ? Work as long as I can stand, and then fall down and lay there till I can get up. No mother, father, brother or sister to care for me, and then it is, You lazy nigger, lazy nigger — all because I am black ! Oh, if I could die !'

"I stepped into the barn, where I could see her. She was crouched down by the hay with her faithful friend Fido, and as she ceased speaking, buried her face in her hands, and cried bitterly; then, patting Fido, she kissed him, saying, ' You love me, Fido, don't you ? but we must go work in the field.' She started on her mission; I called her to me, and told her she need not go, the hay was doing well.

"She has such confidence in me that she will do just as I tell her; so we found a seat under a shady tree, and there I took the opportunity to combat the notions she seemed to entertain respecting the loneliness of her condition and want of sympathizing friends. I assured her that mother's views were by no means general; that in our part of the country there were thousands upon thousands who favored the elevation of her race, disapproving of oppression in all its forms; that she was not unpitied, friendless, and utterly despised; that she might hope for better things in the future. Having spoken these words of comfort, I rose with the resolution that if I recovered my health I would take her home with me, whether mother was willing or not."

"I don't know what your mother would do without her; still, I wish she was away."

Susan now came for her long absent husband, and they returned home to their room.

The month of November was one of great anxiety on James's account. He was rapidly wasting away.

A celebrated physician was called, and performed a surgical operation, as a last means. Should this fail, there was no hope. Of course he was confined wholly to his room, mostly to his bed. With all his bodily suffering, all his anxiety for his family, whom he might not live to protect, he did not forget Frado. He shielded her from many beatings, and every day imparted religious instructions. No one, but his wife, could move him so easily as Frado; so that in addition to her daily toil she was often deprived of her rest at night.

Yet she insisted on being called; she wished to show her love for one who had been such a friend to her. Her anxiety and grief increased as the probabilities of his recovery became doubtful.

Mrs. Bellmont found her weeping on his account, shut her up, and whipped her with the raw-hide, adding an injunction never to be seen snivelling again because she had a little work to do. She was very careful never to shed tears on his account, in her presence, afterwards.

7*

CHAPTER VIII.

VISITOR AND DEPARTURE.

— " Other cares engross me, and my tired soul with emulative haste,
    Looks to its God."

THE brother associated with James in business, in Baltimore, was sent for to confer with one who might never be able to see him there.

James began to speak of life as closing; of heaven, as of a place in immediate prospect; of aspirations, which waited for fruition in glory. His brother, Lewis by name, was an especial favorite of sister Mary; more like her, in disposition and preferences than James or Jack.

He arrived as soon as possible after the request, and saw with regret the sure indications of fatality in his sick brother, and listened to his admonitions — admonitions to a Christian life — with tears, and uttered some promises of attention to the subject so dear to the heart of James.

How gladly he would have extended healing

aid. But, alas! it was not in his power; so, after listening to his wishes and arrangements for his family and business, he decided to return home.

Anxious for company home, he persuaded his father and mother to permit Mary to attend him. She was not at all needed in the sick room; she did not choose to be useful in the kitchen, and then she was fully determined to go.

So all the trunks were assembled and crammed with the best selections from the wardrobe of herself and mother, where the last-mentioned articles could be appropriated.

"Nig was never so helpful before," Mary remarked, and wondered what had induced such a change in place of former sullenness.

Nig was looking further than the present, and congratulating herself upon some days of peace, for Mary never lost opportunity of informing her mother of Nig's delinquincies, were she otherwise ignorant.

Was it strange if she were officious, with such relief in prospect?

The parting from the sick brother was tearful and sad. James prayed in their presence for their renewal in holiness; and urged their immediate attention to eternal realities, and gained a promise that Susan and Charlie should share their kindest regards.

No sooner were they on their way, than Nig slyly crept round to Aunt Abby's room, and tiptoeing and twisting herself into all shapes, she exclaimed, —

"She's gone, Aunt Abby, she's gone, fairly gone;" and jumped up and down, till Aunt Abby feared she would attract the notice of her mistress by such demonstrations.

"Well, she's gone, gone, Aunt Abby. I hope she'll never come back again."

"No! no! Frado, that's wrong! you would be wishing her dead; that won't do."

"Well, I'll bet she'll never come back again; somehow, I feel as though she would n't."

"She is James's sister," remonstrated Aunt Abby.

"So is our cross sheep just as much, that I ducked in the river; I'd like to try my hand at curing *her* too."

"But you forget what our good minister told us last week, about doing good to those that hate us."

"Did n't I do good, Aunt Abby, when I washed and ironed and packed her old duds to get rid of her, and helped her pack her trunks, and run here and there for her?"

"Well, well, Frado; you must go finish your work, or your mistress will be after you, and remind you severely of Miss Mary, and some others beside."

Nig went as she was told, and her clear voice was heard as she went, singing in joyous notes the relief she felt at the removal of one of her tormentors.

Day by day the quiet of the sick man's room was increased. He was helpless and nervous; and often wished change of position, thereby hoping to gain momentary relief. The calls upon Frado were consequently more frequent, her nights less tranquil. Her health was impaired by lifting the sick man, and by drudgery in the kitchen. Her ill health she endeavored to conceal from James, fearing he might have less repose if there should be a change of attendants; and Mrs. Bellmont, she well knew, would have no sympathy for her. She was at last so much reduced as to be unable to stand

erect for any great length of time. She would
sit at the table to wash her dishes; if she heard
the well-known step of her mistress, she would
rise till she returned to her room, and then sink
down for further rest. Of course she was longer
than usual in completing the services assigned
her. This was a subject of complaint to Mrs.
Bellmont; and Frado endeavored to throw off
all appearance of sickness in her presence.

But it was increasing upon her, and she could
no longer hide her indisposition. Her mistress
entered one day, and finding her seated, commanded her to go to work. "I am sick," replied
Frado, rising and walking slowly to her unfinished task, "and cannot stand long, I feel so
bad."

Angry that she should venture a reply to her
command, she suddenly inflicted a blow which
lay the tottering girl prostrate on the floor. Ex-
cited by so much indulgence of a dangerous passion, she seemed left to unrestrained malice; and
snatching a towel, stuffed the mouth of the sufferer, and beat her cruelly.

Frado hoped she would end her misery by
whipping her to death. She bore it with the

hope of a martyr, that her misery would soon close. Though her mouth was muffled, and the sounds much stifled, there was a sensible commotion, which James' quick ear detected.

"Call Frado to come here," he said faintly, "I have not seen her to-day."

Susan retired with the request to the kitchen, where it was evident some brutal scene had just been enacted.

Mrs. Bellmont replied that she had " some work to do just now ; when that was done, she might come."

Susan's appearance confirmed her husband's fears, and he requested his father, who sat by the bedside, to go for her. This was a messenger, as James well knew, who could not be denied; and the girl entered the room, sobbing and faint with anguish.

James called her to him, and inquired the cause of her sorrow. She was afraid to expose the cruel author of her misery, lest she should provoke new attacks. But after much entreaty, she told him all, much which had escaped his watchful ear. Poor James shut his eyes in silence, as if pained to forgetfulness by the re-

cital. Then turning to Susan, he asked her to
take Charlie, and walk out; " she needed the
fresh air," he said. " And say to mother I wish
Frado to sit by me till you return. I think you
are fading, from staying so long in this sick
room." Mr. B. also left, and Frado was thus left
alone with her friend. Aunt Abby came in to
make her daily visit, and seeing the sick countenance of the attendant, took her home with
her to administer some cordial. She soon returned, however, and James kept her with him
the rest of the day; and a comfortable night's
repose following, she was enabled to continue, as
usual, her labors. James insisted on her attend-
ing religious meetings in the vicinity with Aunt
Abby.

Frado, under the instructions of Aunt Abby
and the minister, became a believer in a future
existence — one of happiness or misery. Her
doubt was, *is* there a heaven for the black? She
knew there was one for James, and Aunt Abby,
and all good white people; but was there any
for blacks? She had listened attentively to all
the minister said, and all Aunt Abby had told
her; but then it was all for white people.

As James approached that blessed world, she felt a strong desire to follow, and be with one who was such a dear, kind friend to her.

While she was exercised with these desires and aspirations, she attended an evening meeting with Aunt Abby, and the good man urged all, young or old, to accept the offers of mercy, to receive a compassionate Jesus as their Saviour. " Come to Christ," he urged, " all, young or old, white or black, bond or free, come all to Christ for pardon ; repent, believe."

This was the message she longed to hear; it seemed to be spoken for her. But he had told them to repent; "what was that?" she asked. She knew she was unfit for any heaven, made for whites or blacks. She would gladly repent, or do anything which would admit her to share the abode of James.

Her anxiety increased; her countenance bore marks of solicitude unseen before; and though she said nothing of her inward contest, they all observed a change.

James and Aunt Abby hoped it was the springing of good seed sown by the Spirit of God. Her tearful attention at the last meeting

encouraged his aunt to hope that her mind was
awakened, her conscience aroused. Aunt Abby
noticed that she was particularly engaged in
reading the Bible; and this strengthened her
conviction that a heavenly Messenger was striving with her. The neighbors dropped in to inquire after the sick, and also if Frado was "serious?" They noticed she seemed very thoughtful and tearful at the meetings. Mrs. Reed was
very inquisitive; but Mrs. Bellmont saw no appearance of change for the better. She did not
feel responsible for her spiritual culture, and
hardly believed she had a soul.

Nig was in truth suffering much; her feelings
were very intense on any subject, when once
aroused. She read her Bible carefully, and as
often as an opportunity presented, which was
when entirely secluded in her own apartment,
or by Aunt Abby's side, who kindly directed her
to Christ, and instructed her in the way of salva-
tion.

Mrs. Bellmont found her one day quietly
reading her Bible. Amazed and half crediting
the reports of officious neighbors, she felt it was
time to interfere. Here she was, reading and

shedding tears over the Bible. She ordered her
to put up the book, and go to work, and not be
snivelling about the house, or stop to read
again.

But there was one little spot seldom penetrated by her mistress' watchful eye : this was her
room, uninviting and comfortless; but to herself a safe retreat. Here she would listen to the
pleadings of a Saviour, and try to penetrate the
veil of doubt and sin which clouded her soul,
and long to cast off the fetters of sin, and rise
to the communion of saints.

Mrs. Bellmont, as we before said, did not trouble herself about the future destiny of her servant. If she did what she desired for *her* benefit, it was all the responsibility she acknowledged.
But she seemed to have great aversion to the
notice Nig would attract should she become
pious. How could she meet this case? She resolved to make her complaint to John. Strange,
when she was always foiled in this direction, she
should resort to him. It was time something
was done; she had begun to read the Bible
openly.

The night of this discovery, as they were

retiring, Mrs. Bellmont introduced the conversation, by saying:

"I want your attention to what I am going
to say. I have let Nig go out to evening meetings a few times, and, if you will believe it, I
found her reading the Bible to-day, just as
though she expected to turn pious nigger, and
preach to white folks. So now you see what
good comes of sending her to school. If she
should get converted she would have to go to
meeting: at least, as long as James lives. I wish
he had not such queer notions about her. It
seems to trouble him to know he must die and
leave her. He says if he should get well he
would take her home with him, or educate her
here. Oh, how awful! What can the child
mean? So careful, too, of her! He says we
shall ruin her health making her work so hard,
and sleep in such a place. O, John! do you
think he is in his right mind?"

"Yes, yes; she is slender."

"Yes, *yes!*" she repeated sarcastically, "you
know these niggers are just like black snakes;
you *can't* kill them. If she wasn't tough she

would have been killed long ago. There was never one of my girls could do half the work."

"Did they ever try?" interposed her husband. "I think she can do more than all of them together."

"What a man!" said she, peevishly. "But I want to know what is going to be done with her about getting pious?"

"Let her do just as she has a mind to. If it is a comfort to her, let her enjoy the privilege of being good. I see no objection."

"I should think *you* were crazy, sure. Do n't you know that every night she will want to go toting off to meeting? and Sundays, too? and you know we have a great deal of company Sundays, and she can't be spared."

"I thought you Christians held to going to church," remarked Mr. B.

"Yes, but who ever thought of having a nigger go, except to drive others there? Why, according to you and James, we should very soon have her in the parlor, as smart as our own girls. It's of no use talking to you or James. If you should go on as you would like, it would not be six months before she would be leaving me; and that won't do. Just think how much profit she was to us last summer. We had no work hired out; she did the work of two girls — "

"And got the whippings for two with it!" remarked Mr. Bellmont.

"I'll beat the money out of her, if I can't get her worth any other way," retorted Mrs. B. sharply. While this scene was passing, Frado was trying to utter the prayer of the publican, " God be merciful to me a sinner."

CHAPTER IX.

DEATH.

We have now
But a small portion of what men call time,
To hold communion.

SPRING opened, and James, instead of rallying,
as was hoped, grew worse daily. Aunt Abby
and Frado were the constant allies of Susan.
Mrs. Bellmont dared not lift him. She was not
"strong enough," she said.

It was very offensive to Mrs. B. to have Nab
about James so much. She had thrown out
many a hint to detain her from so often visiting
the sick-room; but Aunt Abby was too well
accustomed to her ways to mind them. After
various unsuccessful efforts, she resorted to the
following expedient. As she heard her cross
the entry below, to ascend the stairs, she slipped
out and held the latch of the door which led
into the upper entry.

"James does not want to see you, or any one
else," she said.

Aunt Abby hesitated, and returned slowly to her own room; wondering if it were really James' wish not to see her. She did not venture again that day, but still felt disturbed and anxious about him. She inquired of Frado, and learned that he was no worse. She asked her if James did not wish her to come and see him; what could it mean?

Quite late next morning, Susan came to see what had become of her aunt.

"Your mother said James did not wish to see me, and I was afraid I tired him."

Why, aunt, that is a mistake, I *know*. W at could mother mean?" asked Susan.

The next time she went to the sitting-room she asked her mother, —

"Why does not Aunt Abby visit James as she has done? Where is she?"

"At home. I hope that she will stay there," was the answer.

"I should think she would come in and see James," continued Susan.

"I told her he did want to see her, and to stay out. You need make no stir about it; remember:" she added, with one of her fiery glances.

Susan kept silence. It was a day or two before James spoke of her absence. The family were at dinner, and Frado was watching beside him. He inquired the cause of her absence, and *she* told him all. After the family returned he sent his wife for her. When she entered, he took her hand, and said, " Come to me often, Aunt. Come any time, — I am always glad to see you. I have but a little longer to be with you, — come often, Aunt. Now please help lift me up, and see if I can rest a little."

Frado was called in, and Susan and Mrs. B. all attempted; Mrs. B. was too weak; she did not feel able to lift so much. So the three succeeded in relieving the sufferer.

Frado returned to her work. Mrs. B. followed. Seizing Frado, she said she would " cure her of tale-bearing," and, placing the wedge of wood between her teeth, she beat her cruelly with the raw-hide. Aunt Abby heard the blows, and came to see if she could hinder them.

Surprised at her sudden appearance, Mrs. B. suddenly stopped, but forbade her removing the wood till she gave her permission, and commanded Nab to go home.

She was thus tortured when Mr. Bellmont came in, and, making inquiries which she did not, because she could not, answer, approached her; and seeing her situation, quickly removed the instrument of torture, and sought his wife. Their conversation we will omit; suffice it to say, a storm raged which required many days to exhaust its strength.

Frado was becoming seriously ill. She had no relish for food, and was constantly over-worked, and then she had such solicitude about the future. She wished to pray for pardon. She did try to pray. Her mistress had told her it would "do no good for her to attempt prayer; prayer was for whites, not for blacks. If she minded her mistress, and did what she commanded, it was all that was required of her."

This did not satisfy her, or appease her long-ings. She knew her instructions did not har-monize with those of the man of God or Aunt Abby's. She resolved to persevere. She said nothing on the subject, unless asked. It was evident to all her mind was deeply exercised. James longed to speak with her alone on the subject. An opportunity presented soon, while the family were at tea It was usual to summon Aunt Abby to keep company with her, as his death was expected hourly.

As she took her accustomed seat, he asked, " Are you afraid to stay with me alone, Frado ? "

" No," she replied, and stepped to the window to conceal her emotion.

" Come here, and sit by me ; I wish to talk with you."

She approached him, and, taking her hand, he remarked :

" How poor you are, Frado ! I want to tell you that I fear I shall never be able to talk with you again. It is the last time, perhaps, I shall *ever* talk with you. You are old enough to remember my dying words and profit by them. I have been sick a long time ; I shall die pretty soon. My Heavenly Father is calling me home. Had it been his will to let me live I should take you to live with me ; but, as it is, I shall go and leave you. But, Frado, if you will be a good girl, and love and serve God, it will be but a short time before we are in a *heavenly* home together. There will never be any sickness or sorrow there."

Frado, overcome with grief, sobbed, and buried her face in his pillow. She expected he would die; but to hear him speak of his departure himself was unexpected.

"Bid me good bye, Frado."

She kissed him, and sank on her knees by his bedside; his hand rested on her head; his eyes were closed; his lips moved in prayer for this disconsolate child.

His wife entered, and interpreting the scene, gave him some restoratives, and withdrew for a short time.

It was a great effort for Frado to cease sobbing; but she dared not be seen below in tears; so she choked her grief, and descended to her usual toil. Susan perceived a change in her husband. She felt that death was near.

He tenderly looked on her, and said, "Susan, my wife, our farewells are all spoken. I feel prepared to go. I shall meet you in heaven. Death is indeed creeping fast upon me. Let me see them all once more. Teach Charlie the way to heaven; lead him up as you come."

The family all assembled. He could not talk as he wished to them. He seemed to

sink into unconsciousness. They watched him
for hours. He had labored hard for breath
some time, when he seemed to awake suddenly, and exclaimed, "Hark! do you hear
it?"

"Hear what, my son?" asked the father.

"Their call. Look, look, at the shining
ones! Oh, let me go and be at rest!"

As if waiting for this petition, the Angel of
Death severed the golden thread, and he was
in heaven. At midnight the messenger came.

They called Frado to see his last struggle.
Sinking on her knees at the foot of his bed,
she buried her face in the clothes, and wept
like one inconsolable. They led her from the
room. She seemed to be too much absorbed
to know it was necessary for her to leave.
Next day she would steal into the chamber
as often as she could, to weep over his remains,
and ponder his last words to her. She moved
about the house like an automaton. Every
duty performed—but an abstraction from all,
which shewed her thoughts were busied elsewhere. Susan wished her to attend his burial
as one of the family. Lewis and Mary and

9

Jack it was not thought best to send for, as the season would not allow them time for the journey. Susan provided her with a dress for the occasion, which was her first intimation that she would be allowed to mingle her grief with others.

The day of the burial she was attired in her mourning dress; but Susan, in her grief, had forgotten a bonnet.

She hastily ransacked the closets, and found one of Mary's, trimmed with bright pink ribbon.

It was too late to change the ribbon, and she was unwilling to leave Frado at home; she knew it would be the wish of James she should go with her. So tying it on, she said, "Never mind, Frado, you shall see where our dear James is buried." As she passed out, she heard the whispers of the by-standers, "Look there! see there! how that looks, — a black dress and a pink ribbon!"

Another time, such remarks would have wounded Frado. She had now a sorrow with which such were small in comparison.

As she saw his body lowered in the grave she wished to share it; but she was not fit to die. She could not go where he was if she did. She did not love God; she did not serve him or know how to.

She retired at night to mourn over her unfitness for heaven, and gaze out upon the stars, which, she felt, studded the entrance of heaven, above which James reposed in the bosom of Jesus, to which her desires were hastening. She wished she could see God, and ask him for eternal life. Aunt Abby had taught her that He was ever looking upon her. Oh, if she could see him, or hear him speak words of forgiveness. Her anxiety increased; her health seemed impaired, and she felt constrained to go to aunt Abby and tell her all about her conflicts.

She received her like a returning wanderer; seriously urged her to accept of Christ; explained the way; read to her from the Bible, and remarked upon such passages as applied to her state. She warned her against stifling that voice which was calling her to heaven; echoed the farewell words of James, and told her to come to her with her difficulties, and

not to delay a duty so important as attention
to the truths of religion, and her soul's interests.

Mrs. Bellmont would occasionally give instruction, though far different. She would tell
her she could not go where James was; she
need not try. If she should get to heaven at
all, she would never be as high up as he.

He was the attraction. Should she "want
to go there if she could not see him?"

Mrs. B. seldom mentioned her bereavement,
unless in such allusion to Frado. She donned
her weeds from custom; kept close her crape
veil for so many Sabbaths, and abated nothing
of her characteristic harshness.

The clergyman called to minister consolation
to the afflicted widow and mother. Aunt Abby
seeing him approach the dwelling, knew at once
the object of his visit, and followed him to the
parlor, unasked by Mrs. B! What a daring
affront! The good man dispensed the consolations, of which he was steward, to the apparently grief-smitten mother, who talked like one
schooled in a heavenly atmosphere. Such resig-
nation expressed, as might have graced the trial
of the holiest. Susan, like a mute sufferer,

bared her soul to his sympathy and godly counsel, but only replied to his questions in short syllables. When he offered prayer, Frado stole to the door that she might hear of the heavenly bliss of one who was her friend on earth. The prayer caused profuse weeping, as any tender reminder of the heaven-born was sure to. When the good man's voice ceased, she returned to her toil, carefully removing all trace of sorrow. Her mistress soon followed, irritated by Nab's impudence in presenting herself unasked in the parlor, and upraided her with indolence, and bade her apply herself more diligently. Stung by unmerited rebuke, weak from sorrow and anxiety, the tears rolled down her dark face, soon followed by sobs, and then losing all control of herself, she wept aloud. This was an act of disobedience. Her mistress grasping her raw-hide, caused a longer flow of tears, and wounded a spirit that was craving healing mercies.

CHAPTER X.

PERPLEXITIES. — ANOTHER DEATH.

Neath the billows of the ocean,
Hidden treasures wait the hand,
That again to light shall raise them
With the diver's magic wand.

G. W. Cook.

The family, gathered by James' decease, returned to their homes. Susan and Charles returned to Baltimore. Letters were received from the absent, expressing their sympathy and grief. The father bowed like a " bruised reed," under the loss of his beloved son. He felt desirous to die the death of the righteous ; also, conscious that he was unprepared, he resolved to start on the narrow way, and some time solicit entrance through the gate which leads to the celestial city. He acknowledged his too ready acquiescence with Mrs. B., in permitting Frado to be deprived of her only religious privileges for weeks together. He accordingly asked his sister to take her to meeting once more, which she was ready at once to do.

The first opportunity they once more attended meeting together. The minister conversed faithfully with every person present. He was surprised to find the little colored girl so solicitous, and kindly directed her to the flowing fountain where she might wash and be clean. He inquired of the origin of her anxiety, of her progress up to this time, and endeavored to make Christ, instead of James, the attraction of Heaven. He invited her to come to his house, to speak freely her mind to him, to pray much, to read her Bible often.

The neighbors, who were at meeting,—among them Mrs. Reed, — discussed the opinions Mrs. Bellmont would express on the subject. Mrs. Reed called and informed Mrs. B. that her colored girl " related her experience the other night at the meeting."

" What experience?" asked she, quickly, as if she expected to hear the number of times she had whipped Frado, and the number of lashes set forth in plain Arabic numbers.

"Why, you know she is serious, don't you? She told the minister about it."

Mrs. B. made no reply, but changed the subject adroitly. Next morning she told Frado she "should not go out of the house for one while, except on errands; and if she did not stop trying to be religious, she would whip her to death."

Frado pondered; her mistress was a professor of religion; was *she* going to heaven? then she did not wish to go. If she should be near James, even, she could not be happy with those fiery eyes watching her ascending path. She resolved to give over all thought of the future world, and strove daily to put her anxiety far from her.

Mr. Bellmont found himself unable to do what James or Jack could accomplish for her. He talked with her seriously, told her he had seen her many times punished undeservedly; he did not wish to have her saucy or disrespectful, but when she was *sure* she did not deserve a whipping, to avoid it if she could. "You are looking sick," he added, "you cannot endure beating as you once could."

It was not long before an opportunity offered of profiting by his advice. She was sent for wood, and not returning as soon as Mrs. B. calculated, she followed her, and, snatching from the pile a stick, raised it over her.

"Stop!" shouted Frado, "strike me, and I'll never work a mite more for you;" and throwing down what she had gathered, stood like one who feels the stirring of free and independent thoughts.

By this unexpected demonstration, her mistress, in amazement, dropped her weapon, desisting from her purpose of chastisement. Frado walked towards the house, her mistress following with the wood she herself was sent after. She did not know, before, that she had a power to ward off assaults. Her triumph in seeing her enter the door with *her* burden, repaid her for much of her former suffering.

It was characteristic of Mrs. B. never to rise in her majesty, unless she was sure she should be victorious.

This affair never met with an "after clap," like many others.

Thus passed a year. The usual amount of

scolding, but fewer whippings. Mrs. B. longed
once more for Mary's return, who had been
absent over a year; and she wrote imperatively
for her to come quickly to her. A letter came
in reply, announcing that she would comply as
soon as she was sufficiently recovered from an
illness which detained her.

No serious apprehensions were cherished by
either parent, who constantly looked for notice
of her arrival, by mail. Another letter brought
tidings that Mary was seriously ill; her mother's
presence was solicited.

She started without delay. Before she reached
her destination, a letter came to the parents
announcing her death.

No sooner was the astounding news received,
than Frado rushed into Aunt Abby's, exclaiming: —

"She's dead, Aunt Abby!"

"Who?" she asked, terrified by the unpre-
faced announcement.

"Mary; they 've just had a letter."

As Mrs. B. was away, the brother and sister
could freely sympathize, and she sought him in
this fresh sorrow, to communicate such solace as

she could, and to learn particulars of Mary's untimely death, and assist him in his journey thither.

It seemed a thanksgiving to Frado. Every hour or two she would pop in into Aunt Abby's room with some strange query:

"She got into the *river* again, Aunt Abby, did n't she; the Jordan is a big one to tumble into, any how. S'posen she goes to hell, she 'll be as black as I am. Would n't mistress be mad to see her a nigger!" and others of a similar stamp, not at all acceptable to the pious, sympathetic dame; but she could not evade them.

The family returned from their sorrowful journey, leaving the dead behind. Nig looked for a change in her tyrant; what could subdue her, if the loss of her idol could not?

Never was Mrs. B. known to shed tears so profusely, as when she reiterated to one and another the sad particulars of her darling's sickness and death. There was, indeed, a season of quiet grief; it was the lull of the fiery elements. A few weeks revived the former tempests, and so at variance did they seem with chastisement sanctified, that Frado felt them to be unbear-

able. She determined to flee. But where?
Who would take her? Mrs. B. had always repre-
sented her ugly. Perhaps every one thought
her so. Then no one would take her. She was
black, no one would love her. She might have
to return, and then she would be more in her
mistress' power than ever.

She remembered her victory at the wood-pile.
She decided to remain to do as well as she could;
to assert her rights when they were trampled
on; to return once more to her meeting in
the evening, which had been prohibited. She
had learned how to conquer; she would not
abuse the power while Mr. Bellmont was at
home.

But had she not better run away? Where?
She had never been from the place far enough
to decide what course to take. She resolved to
speak to Aunt Abby. *She* mapped the dangers
of her course, her liability to fail in finding so
good friends as John and herself. Frado's mind
was busy for days and nights. She contem-
plated administering poison to her mistress, to
rid herself and the house of so detestable a
plague.

But she was restrained by an overruling Providence ; and finally decided to stay contentedly through her period of service, which would expire when she was eighteen years of age.

In a few months Jane returned home with her family, to relieve her parents, upon whom years and affliction had left the marks of age. The years intervening since she had left her home, had, in some degree, softened the opposition to her unsanctioned marriage with George. The more Mrs. B. had about her, the more energetic seemed her directing capabilities, and her fault-finding propensities. Her own, she had full power over ; and Jane after vain endeavors, became disgusted, weary, and perplexed, and decided that, though her mother might suffer, she could not endure her home. They followed Jack to the West. Thus vanished all hopes of sympathy or relief from this source to Frado. There seemed no one capable of enduring the oppressions of the house but her. She turned to the darkness of the future with the determination previously formed, to remain until she should be eighteen. Jane begged her to follow her so

10

soon as she should be released; but so wearied out was she by her mistress, she felt disposed to flee from any and every one having her similitude of name or feature.

CHAPTER XI.

MARRIAGE AGAIN.

Crucified the hopes that cheered me,
All that to the earth endeared me ;
Love of wealth and fame and power,
Love, — all have been crucified.

C. E.

DARKNESS before day.   Jane left, but Jack was
now to come again.   After Mary's death he visited home, leaving a wife behind.   An orphan
whose home was with a relative, gentle, loving,
the true mate of kind, generous Jack.   His
mother was a stranger to her, of course, and
had perfect right to interrogate :

" Is she good looking, Jack ? " asked his
mother.

" Looks well to me," was the laconic reply.

" Was her *father* rich ? "

" Not worth a copper, as I know of; I never
asked him," answered Jack.

" Hadn't she any property ?   What did you
marry her for," asked his mother.

"Oh, she's *worth a million* dollars, mother, though not a cent of it is in money."

"Jack! what do you want to bring such a poor being into the family, for? You'd better stay here, at home, and let your wife go. Why could n't you try to do better, and not disgrace your parents?"

"Don't judge, till you see her," was Jack's reply, and immediately changed the subject. It was no recommendation to his mother, and she did not feel prepared to welcome her cordially now he was to come with his wife. He was indignant at his mother's advice to desert her. It rankled bitterly in his soul, the bare suggestion. He had more to bring. He now came with a child also. He decided to leave the West, but not his family.

Upon their arrival, Mrs. B. extended a cold welcome to her new daughter, eyeing her dress with closest scrutiny. Poverty was to her a disgrace, and she could not associate with any thus dishonored. This coldness was felt by Jack's worthy wife, who only strove the harder to recommend herself by her obliging, winning ways.

Mrs. B. could never let Jack be with her alone without complaining of this or that deficiency in his wife.

He cared not so long as the complaints were piercing his own ears. He would not have Jenny disquieted. He passed his time in seeking employment.

A letter came from his brother Lewis, then at the South, soliciting his services. Leaving his wife, he repaired thither.

Mrs. B. felt that great restraint was removed, that Jenny was more in her own power. She wished to make her feel her inferiority; to relieve Jack of his burden if he would not do it himself. She watched her incessantly, to catch at some act of Jenny's which might be construed into conjugal unfaithfulness.

Near by were a family of cousins, one a young man of Jack's age, who, from love to his cousin, proffered all needful courtesy to his stranger relative. Soon news reached Jack that Jenny was deserting her covenant vows, and had formed an illegal intimacy with his cousin. Meantime Jenny was told by her mother-in-law that Jack did not marry her untrammelled.

10*

He had another love whom he would be glad, even now, if he could, to marry. It was very doubtful if he ever came for her.

Jenny would feel pained by her unwelcome gossip, and, glancing at her child, she decided, however true it might be, she had a pledge which would enchain him yet. Ere long, the mother's inveterate hate crept out into some neighbor's enclosure, and, caught up hastily, they passed the secret round till it became none, and Lewis was sent for, the brother by whom Jack was employed. The neighbors saw her fade in health and spirits; they found letters never reached their destination when sent by either. Lewis arrived with the joyful news that he had come to take Jenny home with him.

What a relief to her to be freed from the gnawing taunts of her adversary.

Jenny retired to prepare for the journey, and Mrs. B. and Henry had a long interview. Next morning he informed Jenny that new clothes would be necessary, in order to make her presentable to Baltimore society, and he should return without her, and she must stay till she was suitably attired.

Disheartened, she rushed to her room, and, after relief from weeping, wrote to Jack to come ; to have pity on her, and take her to him. No answer came. Mrs. Smith, a neighbor, watchful and friendly, suggested that she write away from home, and employ some one to carry it to the office who would elude Mrs. B., who, they very well knew, had intercepted Jenny's letter, and influenced Lewis to leave her behind. She accepted the offer, and Frado succeeded in managing the affair so that Jack soon came to the rescue, angry, wounded, and forever after alienated from his early home and his mother. Many times would Frado steal up into Jenny's room, when she knew she was tortured by her mistress' malignity, and tell some of her own encounters with her, and tell her she might "be sure it would n't kill her, for she should have died long before at the same treatment."

Susan and her child succeeded Jenny as visitors. Frado had merged into womanhood, and, retaining what she had learned, in spite of the few privileges enjoyed formerly, was striving to enrich her mind. Her school-books were her constant companions, and every leisure moment was applied to them. Susan was delighted to witness her progress, and some little book from her was a reward sufficient for any task imposed, however difficult. She had her book always fastened open near her, where she could glance from toil to soul refreshment. The approaching spring would close the term of years which Mrs. B. claimed as the period of her servitude. Often as she passed the way-marks of former years did she pause to ponder on her situation, and wonder if she *could* succeed in providing for her own wants. Her health was delicate, yet she resolved to try.

Soon she counted the time by days which should release her. Mrs. B. felt that she could not well spare one who could so well adapt herself to all departments—man, boy, housekeeper, domestic, etc. She begged Mrs. Smith to talk with her, to show her how ungrateful it would appear to leave a home of such comfort—how wicked it was to be ungrateful! But Frado replied that she had had enough of such comforts; she wanted some new ones; and as it was so wicked to be ungrateful, she would go from temptation; Aunt Abby said "we must n't put ourselves in the way of temptation."

Poor little Fido! She shed more tears over him than over all beside.

The morning for departure dawned. Frado engaged to work for a family a mile distant. Mrs. Bellmont dismissed her with the assurance that she would soon wish herself back again, and a present of a silver half dollar.

Her wardrobe consisted of one decent dress, without any superfluous accompaniments. A Bible from Susan she felt was her greatest treasure.

Now was she alone in the world. The past year had been one of suffering resulting from a fall, which had left her lame.

The first summer passed pleasantly, and the wages earned were expended in garments neces- sary for health and cleanliness. Though feeble, she was well satisfied with her progress. Shut up in her room, after her toil was finished, she studied what poor samples of apparel she had, and, for the first time, prepared her own gar- ments.

Mrs. Moore, who employed her, was a kind friend to her, and attempted to heal her wounded spirit by sympathy and advice, burying the past in the prospects of the future. But her failing health was a cloud no kindly human hand could dissipate. A little light work was all she could accomplish. A clergyman, whose family was small, sought her, and she was removed there. Her engagement with Mrs. Moore finished in the fall. Frado was anxious to keep up her reputation for efficiency, and often pressed far beyond prudence. In the winter she entirely gave up work, and confessed herself thoroughly sick. Mrs. Hale, soon overcome by additional cares, was taken sick also, and now it became necessary to adopt some measures for Frado's comfort, as well as to relieve Mrs. Hale. Such dark forebodings as visited her as she lay, solitary and sad, no moans or sighs could relieve.

The family physician pronounced her case one of doubtful issue. Frado hoped it was final. She could not feel relentings that her former home was abandoned, and yet, should she be in need of succor could she obtain it from one who would now so grudgingly bestow it? The family were applied to, and it was decided to take her there. She was removed to a room

built out from the main building, used formerly
as a workshop, where cold and rain found unob-
structed access, and here she fought with bitter
reminiscences and future prospects till she became reckless of her faith and hopes and person,
and half wished to end what nature seemed so
tardily to take.

Aunt Abby made her frequent visits, and at
last had her removed to her own apartment,
where she might supply her wants, and minister
to her once more in heavenly things.

Then came the family consultation.

" What is to be done with her," asked Mrs. B.,
" after she is moved there with Nab ? "

" Send for the Dr., your brother," Mr. B. replied.

" When ? "

" To-night."

" To-night ! and for her !   Wait till morning,"
she continued.

" She has waited too long now ; I think something should be done soon."

" I doubt if she is much sick," sharply interrupted Mrs. B.

" Well, we'll see what our brother thinks."

His coming was longed for by Frado, who had
known him well during her long sojourn in the
family; and his praise of her nice butter and
cheese, from which his table was supplied, she
knew he felt as well as spoke.

"You're sick, very sick," he said, quickly,
after a moment's pause. "Take good care of
her, Abby, or she'll never get well. All broken
down."

"Yes, it was at Mrs. Moore's," said Mrs. B.,
"all this was done. She did but little the latter
part of the time she was here."

"It was commenced longer ago than last summer. Take good care of her; she may never
get well," remarked the Dr.

"We sha'n't pay you for doctoring her; you
may look to the town for that, sir," said Mrs. B.,
and abruptly left the room.

"Oh dear! oh dear!" exclaimed Frado, and
buried her face in the pillow.

A few kind words of consolation, and she was
once more alone in the darkness which envel-
oped her previous days. Yet she felt sure they
owed her a shelter and attention, when disabled,
and she resolved to feel patient, and remain till

she could help herself. Mrs. B. would not attend her, nor permit her domestic to stay with
her at all. Aunt Abby was her sole comforter.
Aunt Abby's nursing had the desired effect, and
she slowly improved. As soon as she was able
to be moved, the kind Mrs. Moore took her to
her home again, and completed what Aunt Abby
had so well commenced. Not that she was well,
or ever would be; but she had recovered so far
as rendered it hopeful she might provide for her
own wants. The clergyman at whose house she
was taken sick, was now seeking some one to
watch his sick children, and as soon as he heard
of her recovery, again asked for her services.

What seemed so light and easy to others, was
too much for Frado; and it became necessary
to ask once more where the sick should find an
asylum.

All felt that the place where her declining
health began, should be the place of relief; so
they applied once more for a shelter.

"No," exclaimed the indignant Mrs. B.; "she
she shall never come under this roof again;
never! never!" she repeated, as if each repeti-
tion were a bolt to prevent admission.

11

One only resource; the public must pay the expense. So she was removed to the home of two maidens, (old,) who had principle enough to be willing to earn the money a charitable public disburses.

Three years of weary sickness wasted her, without extinguishing a life apparently so feeble. Two years had these maidens watched and cared for her, and they began to weary, and finally to request the authorities to remove her.

Mrs. Hoggs was a lover of gold and silver, and she asked the favor of filling her coffers by caring for the sick. The removal caused severe sickness.

By being bolstered in the bed, after a time she could use her hands, and often would ask for sewing to beguile the tedium. She had become very expert with her needle the first year of her release from Mrs. B., and she had forgotten none of her skill. Mrs. H. praised her, and as she improved in health, was anxious to employ her. She told her she could in this way replace her clothes, and as her board would be paid for, she would thus gain something.

Many times her hands wrought when her

body was in pain ; but the hope that she might yet help herself, impelled her on.

Thus she reckoned her store of means by a few dollars, and was hoping soon to come in possession, when she was startled by the announcement that Mrs. Hoggs had reported her to the physician and town officers as an impostor. That she was, in truth, able to get up and go to work.

This brought on a severe sickness of two weeks, when Mrs. Moore again sought her, and took her to her home. She had formerly had wealth at her command, but misfortune had deprived her of it, and unlocked her heart to sympathies and favors she had never known while it lasted. Her husband, defrauded of his last means by a branch of the Bellmont family, had supported them by manual labor, gone to the West, and left his wife and four young children. But she felt humanity required her to give a shelter to one she knew to be worthy of a hospitable reception. Mrs. Moore's physician was called, and pronounced her a very sick girl, and encouraged Mrs. M. to keep her and care for her, and he would see that the authorities were informed of Frado's helplessness, and pledged assistance.

Here she remained till sufficiently restored to sew again. Then came the old resolution to take care of herself, to cast off the unpleasant charities of the public.

She learned that in some towns in Massachusetts, girls make straw bonnets — that it was easy and profitable. But how should *she*, black, feeble and poor, find any one to teach her. But God prepares the way, when human agencies see no path. Here was found a plain, poor, simple woman, who could see merit beneath a dark skin ; and when the invalid mulatto told her sorrows, she opened her door and her heart, and took the stranger in. Expert with the needle, Frado soon equalled her instructress; and she sought also to teach her the value of useful books ; and while one read aloud to the other of deeds historic and names renowned, Frado experienced a new impulse. She felt herself capable of elevation ; she felt that this book information supplied an undefined dissatisfaction she had long felt, but could not express. Every leisure moment was carefully applied to self-improvement, and a devout and Christian exterior invited confidence from the villagers. Thus she passed months of quiet, growing in the confidence of her neighbors and new found friends.

11*

CHAPTER XII.

THE WINDING UP OF THE MATTER.

Nothing new under the sun.
SOLOMON.

A FEW years ago, within the compass of my narrative, there appeared often in some of our New England villages, professed fugitives from slavery, who recounted their personal experience in homely phrase, and awakened the indignation of non-slaveholders against brother Pro. Such a one appeared in the new home of Frado; and as people of color were rare there, was it strange she should attract her dark brother; that he should inquire her out; succeed in seeing her; feel a strange sensation in his heart towards her; that he should toy with her shining curls, feel proud to provoke her to smile and expose the ivory concealed by thin, ruby lips; that her sparkling eyes should fascinate; that he should propose; that they should marry? A short acquaintance was indeed an objection, but she saw

him often, and thought she knew him. He
never spoke of his enslavement to her when
alone, but she felt that, like her own oppression,
it was painful to disturb oftener than was
needful.

He was a fine, straight negro, whose back
showed no marks of the lash, erect as if it never
crouched beneath a burden. There was a silent
sympathy which Frado felt attracted her, and
she opened her heart to the presence of love —
that arbitrary and inexorable tyrant.

She removed to Singleton, her former residence, and there was married. Here were Frado's first feelings of trust and repose on human
arm. She realized, for the first time, the relief
of looking to another for comfortable support.
Occasionally he would leave her to " lecture."

Those tours were prolonged often to weeks.
Of course he had little spare money. Frado was
again feeling her self-dependence, and was at
last compelled to resort alone to that. Samuel
was kind to her when at home, but made no pro-
vision for his absence, which was at last unprece-
dented.

He left her to her fate — embarked at sea,

with the disclosure that he had never seen the
South, and that his illiterate harangues were
humbugs for hungry abolitionists. Once more
alone! Yet not alone. A still newer companionship would soon force itself upon her. No
one wanted her with such prospects. Herself
was burden enough ; who would have an · additional one ?

The horrors of her condition nearly prostrated
her, and she was again thrown upon the public
for sustenance. Then followed the birth of her
child. The long absent Samuel unexpectedly
returned, and rescued her from charity. Recov-
ering from her expected illness, she once more
commenced toil for herself and child, in a room
obtained of a poor woman, but with better fortune. One so well known would not be wholly
neglected. Kind friends watched her when Samuel was from home, prevented her from suffering,
and when the cold weather pinched the warmly
clad, a kind friend took them in, and thus pre-
served them. At last Samuel's business became
very engrossing, and after long desertion, news
reached his family that he had become a victim
of yellow fever, in New Orleans.

So much toil as was necessary to sustain Frado, was more than she could endure. As soon
as her babe could be nourished without his
mother, she left him in charge of a Mrs. Capon,
and procured an agency, hoping to recruit her
health, and gain an easier livelihood for herself
and child. This afforded her better maintenance than she had yet found. She passed into
the various towns of the State she lived in, then
into Massachusetts. Strange were some of her
adventures. Watched by kidnappers, maltreated
by professed abolitionists, who did n't want
slaves at the South, nor niggers in their own
houses, North. Faugh! to lodge one; to eat
with one; to admit one through the front door;
to sit next one; awful!

Traps slyly laid by the vicious to ensnare her,
she resolutely avoided. In one of her tours,
Providence favored her with a friend who, pity-
ing her cheerless lot, kindly provided her with a
valuable recipe, from which she might herself
manufacture a useful article for her maintenance.
This proved a more agreeable, and an easier way
of sustenance.

And thus, to the present time, may you see

her busily employed in preparing her merchandise; then sallying forth to encounter many frowns, but some kind friends and purchasers. Nothing turns her from her steadfast purpose of elevating herself. Reposing on God, she has thus far journeyed securely. Still an invalid, she asks your symyathy, gentle reader. Refuse not, because some part of her history is unknown, save by the Omniscient God. Enough has been unrolled to demand your sympathy and aid.

Do you ask the destiny of those connected with her *early* history? A few years only have elapsed since Mr. and Mrs. B. passed into another world. As age increased, Mrs. B. became more irritable, so that no one, even her own children, could remain with her; and she was accompanied by her husband to the home of Lewis, where, after an agony in death unspeakable, she passed away. Only a few months since, Aunt Abby entered heaven. Jack and his wife rest in heaven, disturbed by no intruders; and Susan and her child are yet with the living. Jane has silver locks in place of auburn tresses, but she has the early love of Henry still, and has never regretted her exchange of lovers. Frado has passed from their memories, as Joseph from the butler's, but she will never cease to track them till beyond mortal vision.

APPENDIX.

"TRUTH is stranger than fiction;" and whoever reads the narrative of Alfrado, will find the assertion verified.

About eight years ago I became acquainted with the author of this book, and I feel it a privilege to speak a few words in her behalf. Through the instrumentality of an itinerant colored lecturer, she was brought to W——, Mass. This is an ancient town, where the mothers and daughters seek, not "wool and flax," but *straw*, — working willingly with their hands! Here she was introduced to the family of Mrs. Walker, who kindly consented to receive her as an inmate of her household, and immediately succeeded in procuring work for her as a "straw sewer." Being very ingenious, she soon acquired the art of making hats; but on account of former hard treatment, her constitution was greatly impaired, and she was subject to seasons of sickness. On this account Mrs. W. gave her a room joining her own chamber, where she could hear her faintest call. Never shall I forget the expression of her "black, but comely" face, as she came to me one day, exclaiming, "O, aunt J——, I have at last found a *home*, — and not only a home, but a *mother*. My cup runneth over. What shall I render to the Lord for all his benefits?"

Months passed on, and she was *happy* — truly happy. Her health began to improve under the genial sunshine in which she lived, and she even looked forward with *hope* — joyful hope to the future. But, alas, "it is not in man that walketh to direct his steps." One beautiful morning in the early spring of 1842, as she was taking her usual walk, she chanced to meet her old friend, the " lecturer," who brought her to W——, and with him was a fugitive slave. Young, well-formed and very handsome, he said he had been a *house-* servant, which seemed to account in some measure for his gentlemanly manners and pleasing address. The meeting was entirely accidental; but it was a sad occurrence for poor Alfrado, as her own sequel tells. Suffice it to say, an acquaintance and attachment was formed, which, in due time, resulted in marriage. In a few days she left W——, and *all* her home comforts, and took up her abode in New Hampshire. For a while everything went on well, and she dreamed not of danger; but in an evil hour he left his young and trusting wife, and embarked for sea. She knew nothing of all this, and waited for his return. But she waited in vain. Days passed, weeks passed, and he came not; then her heart failed her. She felt herself deserted at a time, when, of all others, she most needed the care and soothing attentions of a devoted husband. For a time she tried to sustain *herself*, but this was impossible. She had friends, but they were mostly of that class who are poor in the things of earth, but " rich in faith." The charity on which she depended failed at last, and there was nothing to save her from the " County House;" *go she must.* But her feelings on her way thither, and after her arrival, can be given better in her own language; and I trust it will be no breach of confidence if I here insert part of a letter she wrote her mother Walker, concerning the matter.

* * * " The evening before I left for my dreaded journey to the 'house' which was to be my abode, I packed my trunk, carefully placing in it every little memento of affection received from *you* and my friends in W——, among which was the portable inkstand, pens and paper. My beautiful

little Bible was laid aside, as a place nearer my heart was reserved for that. I need not tell you I slept not a moment that night. My home, my peaceful, quiet home with you, was before me. I could see my dear little room, with its pleasant eastern window opening to the morning; but more than all, I beheld *you*, my mother, gliding softly in and kneeling by my bed to read, as no one but you *can* read, 'The Lord is my shepherd, — I shall not want' But I cannot go on, for tears blind me. For a description of the morning, and of the scant breakfast, I must wait until another time.

"We started. The man who came for me was kind as he could be, — helped me carefully into the wagon, (for I had no strength,) and drove on. For miles I spoke not a word. Then the silence would be broken by the driver uttering some sort of word the horse seemed to understand ; for he invariably quickened his pace. And so, just before nightfall, we halted at the institution, prepared for the *homeless*. With cold civility the matron received me, and bade one of the inmates shew me my room. She did so ; and I followed up two flights of stairs. I crept as I was able ; and when she said, 'Go in there,' I obeyed, asking for my trunk, which was soon placed by me. My room was furnished some like the 'prophet's chamber,' except there was no ' candlestick ; ' so when I could creep down I begged for a light, and it was granted. Then I flung myself on the bed and cried, until I could cry no longer. I rose up and tried to pray ; the Saviour seemed near. I opened my precious little Bible, and the first verse that caught my eye was — 'I am poor and needy, yet the Lord thinketh upon me.' O, my mother, could I tell you the comfort this was to me. I sat down, calm, almost happy, took my pen and wrote on the inspiration of the moment —

"O, holy Father, by thy power,
   Thus far in life I'm brought;
And now in this dark, trying hour,
   O God, forsake me not.

" Dids't thou not nourish and sustain
    My infancy and youth ?
Have I not testimonials plain,
    Of thy unchanging truth ?

" Though I 've no home to call my own,
    My heart shall not repine ;
The saint may live on earth unknown,
    And yet in glory shine.

" When my Redeemer dwelt below,
    He chose a lowly lot ;
He came unto his own, but lo !
    His own received him not.

" Oft was the mountain his abode,
    The cold, cold earth his bed ;
The midnight moon shone softly down
    On his unsheltered head.

" But *my* head *was sheltered,* and I tried to feel thankful."
    *   *   *   *   *   *   *

Two or three letters were received after this by her friends in
W——, and then all was silent.   No one of us knew whether
she still lived or had gone to her home on high.   But it seems
she remained in this house until after the birth of her babe ;
then her faithless husband returned, and took her to some town
in New Hampshire, where, for a time, he supported her and his
little son decently well.   But again he left her as before — suddenly and unexpectedly, and she saw him no more.   Her efforts
were again successful in a measure in securing a meagre maintenance for a time ; but her struggles with poverty and sickness
were severe.   At length, a door of hope was opened.   A kind
gentleman and lady took her little boy into their own family,
and provided everything necessary for his good ; and all this without the hope of remuneration.   But let them know, they shall

be " recompensed at the resurrection of the just." God is not
unmindful of this work, — this labor of love. As for the
afflicted mother, she too has been remembered. The heart of a
stranger was moved with compassion, and bestowed a recipe
upon her for restoring gray hair to its former color. She availed
herself of this great help, and has been quite successful; but
her health is again falling, and she has felt herself obliged to
resort to another method of procuring her bread — that of writing an Autobiography.

I trust she will find a ready sale for her interesting work;
and let all the friends who purchase a volume, remember they
are doing good to one of the most worthy, and I had almost
said most unfortunate, of the human family. I will only add
in conclusion, a few lines, calculated to comfort and strengthen
this sorrowful, homeless one. " I will help thee, saith the
Lord."

> " I will help thee," promise kind,
>   Made by our High Priest above;
> Soothing to the troubled mind,
>   Full of tenderness and love.

> " I will help thee " when the storm
>   Gathers dark on every side;
> Safely from impending harm,
>   In my sheltering bosom hide.

> " I will help thee," weary saint,
>   Cast thy burdens *all on me;*
> Oh, how cans't thou tire or faint,
>   While my arm encircles thee.

> I have pitied every tear,
>   Heard and *counted* every sigh;
> Ever lend a gracious ear
>   To thy supplicating cry.

What though thy wounded bosom bleed,
  Pierced by affliction's dart ;
Do I not all thy sorrows heed,
  And bear thee on my heart ?

Soon will the lowly grave become
  Thy quiet resting place ;
Thy spirit find a peaceful home
  In mansions *near my face.*

There are thy robes and glittering crown,
  Outshining yonder sun ;
Soon shalt thou lay the body down,
  And put those glories on.

Long has thy golden lyre been strung,
  Which angels cannot move ;
No song to this is ever sung,
  But bleeding, dying Love.

ALLIDA.

TO THE FRIENDS OF OUR DARK-COMPLEXIONED BRETHREN AND SISTERS, THIS NOTE IS INTENDED.

Having known the writer of this book for a number of years, and knowing the many privations and mortifications she has had to pass through, I the more willingly add my testimony to the truth of her assertions. She is one of that class, who by some are considered not only as little lower than the angels, but far beneath them ; but I have long since learned that we are not to look at the color of the hair, the eyes, or the skin, for the man or woman ; their life is the criterion we are to judge by. The writer of this book has seemed to be a child of misfortune.

Early in life she was deprived of her parents, and all those endearing associations to which childhood clings. Indeed, she may be said not to have had that happy period; for, being taken from home so young, and placed where she had nothing to love or cling to, I often wonder she had not grown up a *monster;* and those very people calling themselves Christians, (the good Lord deliver me from such,) and they likewise ruined her health by hard work, both in the field and house. She was indeed a slave, in every sense of the word; and a lonely one, too.

But she has found some friends in this degraded world, that were willing to do by others as they would have others do by them; that were willing she should live, and have an existence on the earth with them. She has never enjoyed any degree of comfortable health since she was eighteen years of age, and a great deal of the time has been confined to her room and bed. She is now trying to write a book; and I hope the public will look favorably on it, and patronize the same, for she is a worthy woman.

Her own health being poor, and having a child to care for, (for, by the way, she has been married,) and she wishes to educate him; in her sickness he has been taken from her, and sent to the county farm, because she could not pay his board every week; but as soon as she was able, she took him from that *place*, and now he has a home where he is contented and happy, and where he is considered as good as those he is with. He is an intelligent, smart boy, and no doubt will make a smart man, if he is rightly managed. He is beloved by his playmates, and by all the friends of the family; for the family do not recognize those as friends who do not include him in their family, or as one of them, and his mother as a daughter — for they treat her as such; and she certainly deserves all the affection and kindness that is bestowed upon her, and they are always happy to have her visit them whenever she will. They are not wealthy, but the latch-string is always out when suffering humanity needs a shelter; the last loaf they are willing to divide with those more needy than themselves, remembering these words, Do good as we have opportunity ; and we can always find opportunity, if we have the disposition.

And now I would say, I hope those who call themselves friends of our dark-skinned brethren, will lend a helping hand, and assist our sister, not in giving, but in buying a book ; the expense is trifling, and the reward of doing good is great. Our duty is to our fellow-beings, and when we let an opportunity pass, we know not what we lose. Therefore we should do with all our might what our hands find to do ; and remember the words of Him who went about doing good, that inasmuch as ye have done a good deed to one of the least of these my brethren, ye have done it to me ; and even a cup of water is not forgotten. Therefore, let us work while the day lasts, and we shall in no wise lose our reward.

                                              MARGARETTA THORN.

_____

MILFORD, JULY 20th, 1859.

Feeling a deep interest in the welfare of the writer of this book, and hoping that its circulation will be extensive, I wish to say a few words in her behalf. I have been acquainted with her for several years, and have always found her worthy the esteem of all friends of humanity ; one whose soul is alive to the work to which she puts her hand. . Although her complexion is a little darker than my own, I esteem it a privilege to associate with her, and assist her whenever an opportunity presents itself. It is with this motive that I write these few lines, knowing this book must be interesting to all who have any knowledge of the writer's character, or wish to have. I hope no one will refuse to aid her in her work, as she is worthy the sympathy of all Christians, and those who have a spark of humanity in their breasts.

Thinking it unnecessary for me to write a long epistle, I will close by bidding her God speed.   C. D. S.

The End of the Facsimile Edition

AFTERWORD

New Information on Harriet Wilson and the Bellmont Family

by Barbara A. White

The recent rediscovery of Harriet E. Adams Wilson's *Our Nig*, a narrative first published in 1859, was an important event in the history of African American letters and American literature as a whole. As Alice Walker has confessed, "I sat up most of the night reading and pondering the enormous significance of Harriet Wilson's novel *Our Nig*. It is as if we'd just discovered Phillis Wheatley—or Langston Hughes."[1] The discovery radically alters the standard chronology, dislodging an 1892 work previously considered the first novel by an African American woman and establishing Harriet Wilson as the first black person known to have published a novel in the United States.[2] Moreover, *Our Nig* expands the literary terrain in other ways with its unconventional treatment of racism in the North. The heroine is a Northern servant, not a Southern slave; at the tender age of six Frado finds herself indentured to the Bellmont family, becoming "our nig" to Mrs. Bellmont, a "she-devil" who overworks and beats her (17).

But if the text provides, as Walker asserts, a "vastness of heretofore unexamined experience, a whole new layer of time and existence in American life and literature," we know very little about the author. It was only in 1982 that Professor Henry Louis Gates, Jr., set out to trace the "Mrs. H. E. Wilson" mentioned in the copyright of *Our Nig* and to demonstrate that she was a black woman. Gates's spectacular success in tracking down Harriet E. Adams Wilson of New Hampshire restored the narrative to American literature, but at the same time he had to conclude, "What we know to be the case about the life of Harriet E. Wilson, although sufficient to establish her existence and her authorship, remains frustratingly sparse" (lix).

In this essay I undertake to increase our knowledge of Wilson's life on the basis of documents I have discovered. I have also found the true identity of the "Bellmont" family; the family has interesting features, some of which should have a bearing on interpretations of *Our Nig*. In the next section of the paper I will discuss the rediscovery of the narrative and the findings of Professor Gates, and in the third section I will provide new information about Harriet Wilson and her son. The fourth section describes the "Bellmont" family and begins to connect some of the prominent facts in their history to *Our Nig;* the fifth section treats the most important aspect of the family in regard to Wilson's narrative—their abolitionist connections. Except for this one detail, the lives of the real-life family correspond very closely to the lives of the Bellmonts; in my conclusion I will take up the often asked and still difficult question of whether *Our Nig* is primarily autobiography or fiction.

Our Nig opens with the marriage of Frado's parents—Mag, a "fallen" white woman, and Jim, a "kind-hearted African" (9).

After Jim dies of consumption, the poverty-stricken Mag abandons Frado at the Bellmonts' farm. Only six years old, Frado is overtasked and mistreated by the evil Mrs. Bellmont. Although Frado is befriended by other members of the family—Mr. Bellmont, his sister Abby, and the sons James and Jack—the cruelties of Mrs. Bellmont and her vicious daughter Mary ruin Frado's health so that she has trouble supporting herself once she escapes the indenture at age eighteen. The last chapter shows Frado marrying a professed fugitive slave who turns out to be a fake and leaves her with a son to feed. Thus the writing of *Our Nig*: Wilson tells us in her preface that having been "deserted by kindred, disabled by failing health, I am forced to some experiment which shall aid me in maintaining myself and child without extinguishing this feeble life."

The writing experiment had succeeded for many a white woman, beginning in the 1820s with New Hampshire widow Sarah Josepha Hale, who became a famous editor and sent her son to Harvard. It cannot have worked at all for Wilson because, even though we know she managed to publish *Our Nig* at her own expense, the book was not reviewed or even mentioned in the periodicals of the day (xxx). *Our Nig* was never completely lost, for it is sometimes referred to in literary histories and bibliographies, but the title alone put people off—one writer even decided to change it, renaming the book *Our Meg*.[3] The title may also have contributed to the rumor that the author was white. Rare book dealers debated the question for years until the enterprising Henry Louis Gates, Jr., resolved to prove that Harriet Wilson was truly a black woman. Gates and his colleagues turned to Milford,

New Hampshire, a town mentioned in one of the testimonials appended to the narrative, and found the evidence they sought.[4]

The proof of Wilson's race, sadly and ironically, turned out to be the death certificate of her son. George Mason Wilson died of fever in February 1860, only six months after the publication of the book intended to raise money for his support. The death record lists his parents as Thomas and Harriet E. Wilson and his "color" as "Black." In the obituary notice in the *Farmer's Cabinet*, Milford's local paper, George Mason is referred to as the "only son of H. E. Wilson," the name given on the copyright notice in *Our Nig*.[5] Having established that *Our Nig* was written by Harriet E. Wilson, a black woman, Gates went on to find two other documents. First, Milford marriage records show that a Harriet Adams of Milford married Thomas Wilson of Virginia on 6 October 1851 in Milford (about nine months before George Mason was born). Second, the 1850 federal census for Milford lists Harriet Adams, a twenty-two-year-old black woman born in New Hampshire, as residing with the family of Samuel Boyles, a white carpenter. The Boyles family, Gates speculates, may have been the Bellmonts, and Mary Louisa Boyles, Samuel's wife, the original of the she-devil Mrs. Bellmont.[6] At the least it would seem that H. E. Wilson was originally Harriet Adams, who was born in New Hampshire in 1827 or 1828.

Our Nig ends, however, with Frado leaving New Hampshire, and we know the narrative was printed in Boston and entered into copyright in Massachusetts. In investigating the Massachusetts connection, Gates found in Boston city directories a "Harriet Wilson, widow," living at 4 Webster Avenue from

1856 to 1863. This Harriet Wilson has the same address as an African American widow listed in the 1860 federal census; the widow's birthplace is given as Fredericksburg, Virginia, and her age as 52. Can we assume that this older "Harriet Wilson, widow," is the same woman who wrote *Our Nig*? Gates suggests that we might, and either the 1850 Milford or the 1860 Boston census is wrong or unclear (as early censuses so frequently were) about her age. Or, alternatively, there might have been two widowed Harriet Wilsons living in Boston, one on Webster Avenue and the other our author, who either died sometime between February 1860 when her son died and the summer of 1860 when the census was taken or has not yet been located in the unindexed census records. The contradictions are reflected in the second edition of *Our Nig* (1983): while Gates favors 1828 as Wilson's probable birthdate, the Library of Congress catalogers chose to credit the 1860 Boston census instead, assigning Wilson the dates 1808–ca. 1870.

The dearth of information about Wilson's life has made interpretation of *Our Nig* even more difficult than it might otherwise have proved. The narrative is often puzzling. Why, for instance, is there so much emphasis on Frado's near conversion to Christianity and Frado's newfound independence (105) when the subjects are never resolved? Is the narrative a straightforward account of Wilson's life or is it truly fiction? Why, if Wilson wrote the narrative to earn money, did she do everything possible, seemingly, to make it unpopular—from using the epithet "nig" to portraying an interracial marriage involving an "immoral woman" and "bad mother" to introducing a fake fugitive slave when the very idea would guarantee enmity from abolitionists? Indeed, it seems odd to attack one's most likely source of support, as Wilson does when Frado is "maltreated by professed abolitionists, who didn't want slaves at the South, nor niggers in their own houses, North" (129). We might speculate that Wilson was too naive or untalented to disguise autobiographical fact; but in that case how do we account for the art of the ironic use of "our nig" or the brilliant employment of the dog motif whereby Frado's double, Fido, comments on the quality of the white humans?

These are just a few of many questions that have been asked about Wilson and her narrative. My research provides some answers, though before I begin to fill in the gaps I should say that several bits of information I have uncovered raise new difficult questions, and we may expect the search for Harriet Wilson to continue. But it can now be asserted that the Harriet Wilson who lived in Boston from 1856 to 1863 is almost certainly the Harriet Wilson who wrote *Our Nig*. She seems to have been born between 1824 and 1828, whether in New Hampshire or Virginia I do not know, and she was definitely still alive, in fact was back in New Hampshire, in 1863, when she disappears from sight. Wilson spent her childhood serving not the Samuel Boyleses but the Nehemiah Haywards, an established Milford farming family, and she appears in the (1 June) 1840 census for Milford. Although only heads of household were listed by name in 1840, the Nehemiah Hayward family includes for the first time a "free colored person" in addition to the "free white persons"; she is a female and at least 10 years old but under 24 (thus Wilson would be born after 1 June 1816 and before

1 June 1830). The 1840 census does not list any other female "free colored persons" residing in Milford.

Documentary evidence regarding the Haywards shows that many of Wilson's stories in *Our Nig* are literally true. The patriarch (Nehemiah Hayward Jr./Mr. Bellmont) did inherit the family homestead from his parents, who had first established it; his sister (Sally Hayward/Aunt Abby Bellmont) did own a "right in the homestead" (45) and occupy a section of the house; the farm did have orchards and sheep and an energetic river capable of endangering the life of "our nig" as she played the trick on the sheep. Just as in the narrative, the youngest daughter (Rebecca Hayward the younger/Mary Bellmont) died in her teens on a visit to Baltimore; the other daughter (Lucretia Hayward/Jane Bellmont) married a Vermont man and eventually settled in "the West"; the eldest son (George Hayward/James Bellmont) worked in Baltimore and returned home ill with his wife and child to die an early death and be buried in Milford, and so on. This son is even named George M., suggesting that Harriet Wilson named her own son, George Mason, after her favorite in the Hayward family.[7]

The lives of the Haywards correspond so closely to the narrative, in fact, as to remind us that Henry Louis Gates, Jr., not Harriet Wilson, classifies *Our Nig* as fiction; Wilson simply subtitles her work "Sketches from the Life of a Free Black" and refers to her "narrations," while the author of the longest testimonial at the end calls the book "an Autobiography" (137). I will return to the autobiography/fiction issue in my conclusion; suffice it to say at this point that I uncovered information about Wilson and the Haywards by assuming the details of her story to be true. For instance, the comment that

after leaving the Bellmonts Frado was "thrown upon the public for sustenance" (128) led to the discovery of Wilson's
name on Milford reports of expenditures for the town poor. I
found the Haywards by investigating Milford doctors, because
Wilson says the doctor who treats Frado is Mrs. Bellmont's
brother (119); Dr. Jonas Hutchinson had a sister Rebecca
who married a Hayward and moved in her old age to Baltimore, just as Mrs. Bellmont does. But before I discuss the
Haywards in more detail I will review in chronological order
the documents I have discovered that pertain directly to Harriet Wilson and her son.

Two records provide a glimpse of the previously undocu-
mented period of time before Wilson appears on the 1850
federal census. In addition to the 1840 census, where she is a
"free colored person" between 10 and 24, there is the
"Report of the Overseers of the Poor for the Town of Milford,
for the Year ending February 15, 1850."[8] One "Harriet
Adams" appears on the list of "Poor not on the Farm" as costing the town $43.84. Presumably she had managed to avoid
the town pauper farm and lived with a family reimbursed by
the town, either the Boyleses or one of the other families
mentioned in *Our Nig*.[9] The fact that Harriet Adams does not
appear on the overseers' report for the previous year, cover-
ing February 1848 to February 1849, indicates that she sometimes succeeded in supporting herself after leaving the
Haywards (the Haywards went to Baltimore in 1847). Probably the dependency of 1849–50 strengthened her "resolution
to take care of herself, to cast off the unpleasant charities of

the public" (124), and precipitated the move to "W," Massachusetts, where she met her husband.

The reports of the overseers of the poor for 1851–54 are missing, so we do not know what support Wilson received from the town of Milford during the years right after her marriage and the birth of her son. In *Our Nig* she says Frado was "thrown upon the public for sustenance" before her child's birth, and "Allida," the author of the long testimonial, claims that Wilson had to go to the county home to have her baby (according to the boy's death certificate, he was born in Goffstown, the location of the county farm). Then, says Allida, Thomas Wilson returned; but he eventually left his wife for good, and her "struggles with poverty and sickness were severe" (136). In the February 1855 list of "Support of Poor not at the Pauper Farm," Wilson appears as "Harriet E. Wilson" at $45.45, and in the 1856 list the reference is to "Harriet E. Wilson and Child." That this period must have been particularly excruciating for mother and child is attested to by another document from the time. The records of the Hillsborough County Farm show that George Wilson, age three, a "colored" resident of Milford, was admitted for four weeks beginning 19 August 1855. On September 11 he was discharged to Milford to his mother.[10]

Allida recounts the "cold civility" that greeted the pregnant Harriet Wilson in her desperate stay at the county farm (135); the author of *History of the Town of Goffstown* notes the terrible conditions there, including an outbreak of smallpox in 1853, just two years before George Wilson's stay (xxiv). The situation for a "colored" child must have been insupportable, perhaps even worse psychologically than physically. The reminiscences of a Major D. E. Proctor, whose parents ran the Milford poor farm from 1848 to 1854, tell a dismal tale.[11] Proctor recalls Dimon or Diamond Prince, a sixty-year-old "herculean negro" with a crippled hand and hip. Prince sometimes acted "a trifle unruly but his little rebellion was soon quelled by the judicious application of a womans weapon, the broom." He engaged in an "everlasting war" with an old man who "would make faces at the negro just to provoke him to anger." Prince was also harassed by "an insane man by the name of Bradbury," whose claim to fame was having once disrobed at a matron's tea party. Bradbury "tied the old negro up in the stantions with the cows and danced around him swinging his tomahawk just near enough as not to hit him. He also took the negro who was sitting near the kitchen window and threw him out without raising the sash."

Prince's reaction to this treatment is not surprising. Proctor says he "saught to frighten my mother at one time by threatening suicide but my mother asked him to hold on till afternoon till the men folks came home to lay him out. That took the suicide idea out of him." Apparently thoughts of suicide were a common reaction to life at the poor farm, as an "insane" woman named Mollie also "attempted suicide once by jumping into a well but the cold water cooled her ardor and she cried lustily to be saved." Mollie and an "insane" Mrs. Hopkins were both distraught at having been separated from their children, and Proctor's idea of fun was to hide in the woods and call to them, pretending to be a long-lost child. There also lived at the farm a man with delirium tremens, a woman "of simple mind the butt of many good natured jokes," and a Mrs. Foster, who "created a great deal of trouble by telling outside how badly she was abused at the farm."[12] Proctor concludes that the inmates were unlucky in being poor but "fortunate in living in so good a town as Milford as to so kindly care for them in their misfortune."

Although the Milford town farm was not the same as the county farm, the permanent residents were transferred to the Hillsborough County Farm after its purchase in 1849. Dimon Prince definitely lived at the county farm during George Mason Wilson's stay, and one rather hopes he befriended the child.[13] At any rate, it becomes clear why Harriet Wilson would go to any lengths to keep her son off the poor farm, including separating from him and leaving him with a foster family while she sought work in Massachusetts—and later, it should be added, writing *Our Nig*. Knowledge of George Mason Wilson's stay at the county farm and the terrible living conditions at the poor farms should make us very cautious about questioning Wilson's stated motive for authorship, as some recent literary critics have done.[14]

The reports of the Milford overseers of the poor support Wilson's contention that she left her son in New Hampshire and went to Massachusetts; the records indicate that she was gone between February 1856 and the time of the boy's death in 1860. In the 1857, 1858, and 1859 reports Harriet Wilson herself does not appear; there are listings solely for "Harriet E. Wilson's child" and "Wilson Boy." Interestingly, this proves Wilson's friend Allida wrong in one of her statements in the appendix and makes one wonder whether she made other mistakes recounting Wilson's life. Allida claims that a "kind gentleman and lady took her little boy into their own family, and provided everything necessary for his good; and all this without the hope of remuneration" (136), but we know that the town paid approximately $20 a year for the boy's care.

Harriet Wilson's appearances on the overseers' reports form a pattern that points to her as the Harriet Wilson listed in the 1856–63 Boston city directories. For these are the very years the town did not support her, and it seems too much of a coincidence that another Harriet Wilson would reside in Boston during the exact same years that the author of *Our Nig* absented herself from Milford. In the 1863 report Wilson reappears, but she is entered under "Support of County Paupers" instead of "Support of Paupers not on Farm."[15] So she must have been staying at the hated county farm rather than residing with a family as before. Did Harriet Wilson come home to die? Her name does not appear in Milford or Boston records after 1863, and, given her poor health in the past, it seems a strong possibility that she returned to Milford ill and/or in crisis. She tended to retreat to her hometown at critical times of her life, such as to marry and give birth; the latter was an economic practicality because towns would more likely aid long-time residents,[16] but one suspects a more sentimental reason for her return to marry since she did not live in Milford immediately before or after the marriage. At any rate, I have not been able to find a trace of Wilson after 1863, but neither is she listed in the (very incomplete) admission or death records of the Hillsborough County Farm. Maybe she died in 1863 or maybe she recovered and left Milford for another place.

If the author of *Our Nig* lived at 4 Webster Avenue in Boston from 1856 to 1863 and is thus the widowed Harriet Wilson of the 1860 Boston census, the census must err in giving her age as 52 (or perhaps the five was supposed to be a three, which would be consistent with the ages given in the 1840 and 1850 censuses and with the plot of *Our Nig*). The birthplace of Fredericksburg, Virginia, is probably wrong too, as the 1850 census, her marriage record, and the plot of *Our Nig* all indicate she was born in New Hampshire.[17] We may eventually find birth and death records for Harriet Wilson, especially as Milford town papers become more accessible. But it must be remembered that in the early nineteenth-century birth records were sporadically kept, often by the church rather than the town. At a time when some births were recorded years afterwards and some not at all, it would not be surprising if the birth of the socially least valued kind of child, a poor black female, went unrecorded. The most plentiful documents from the time are the property records of white men, and the sparse documentary evidence of Harriet Wilson's existence stands in sharp contrast to the pages and pages of property transactions involving Nehemiah Hayward and his sons.[18] The Hayward family also boasts an extensive genealogy that necessitated research in England and traces the family back to the 1300s.[19]

The Nehemiah Haywards were moderately well off, but not wealthy or formally educated,[20] and the fancy genealogy was prepared by a descendant of the one character in *Our Nig* to end up rich and famous. This is Lewis Bellmont, or Jonas Hayward, the brother associated in a Baltimore business with Frado's beloved James (George Hayward). Wilson presents Lewis in a negative light as "an especial favorite of sister Mary;

more like her, in disposition and preferences than James or Jack" (78). He turned out the better businessman, however; when he arrived in Baltimore, brother George was engaged "in a small way" in a stove business so "little known" that in Jonas's favorite story, told and retold, he could not find his brother until he accidentally stumbled upon him.[21] Jonas quickly became senior partner and transformed the company into what a news article calls "an American industrial giant."[22] He developed a system of hot-water heating for large buildings and employed thousands of men in iron works and heating apparatus plants. Needless to say, Jonas became a leading citizen of Baltimore; in one of the many ironies involving Wilson and *Our Nig*, he acted in the 1860s as "Ward Manager of the Poor" for the eighteenth Baltimore ward.[23] Jonas's descendants rose up rapidly: his son, Thomas Jonas (1847–1909), attended a New England prep school; his grandson, E. Bartlett (b. 1882), studied under private tutors in Europe and then went to Harvard.

The family genealogy set down by one of these descendants shows the early Haywards to have been the proverbial horse thieves, who seem also to have stolen corn and timber. Later they became London merchants and in the 1640s emigrated to Massachusetts, where one finds a long line of Nehemiah Haywards in Beverly, Reading, and the surrounding area. The first Hayward of interest to us, Nehemiah (1738–1825), whom I will call "Nehemiah Sr.," is the "sire" referred to in *Our Nig* who obtained the property and built the "large, old fashioned, two-story white house, environed by fruitful acres" (21). Nehemiah Sr. was born in Hardwick, Massachusetts, but in 1761 went with his brother George to explore New

Jonas Hayward

Brunswick on behalf of the Massachusetts government. He became one of the first settlers of Maugerville, New Brunswick, where he amassed "considerable property" (BG, 47). In 1786 Nehemiah Sr. sold his Maugerville land and bought 118 acres in the "mile slip," an unincorporated (and thus untaxed) bit of land about ten miles long by one mile wide lying between Milford and Wilton, New Hampshire.[24] In 1794 he joined others in petitioning to become part of Milford. Although Nehemiah Sr. was neither one of the biggest landowners in Milford nor a town leader, he made frequent land transactions and participated in local affairs, acting occasionally from 1794 to the early 1800s as "surveyor of highways" and "fence viewer."[25] The census of 1800 lists him as over 45 and having a wife, son, and daughter.

The son, Nehemiah (1779–1849), "Nehemiah Jr.," or John Bellmont in *Our Nig*, inherited the "old homestead," as Wilson describes it (21); his parents, Nehemiah and Mary, gave him half the family farm when he turned 21, and he essentially took over from his father.[26] Wilson notes that "John, the son, had not in his family arrangements departed from the example of the father" (22). Although she goes on to make a sentimental point about boyhood pastimes, the statement is literally true. Nehemiah Jr. continued the pattern his father set in Milford, buying and selling small parcels of land and acting in the same positions, such as surveyor of highways and fence viewer (he was also constable and member of the Committee to Examine Bridges). Nehemiahs Sr. and Jr. either had religious inclinations or wished to appear solid citizens, for in 1805 they bought a church pew together. As Mr. Bellmont in *Our Nig* does not consider himself a believer (89), it may be that the young Nehemiah was trying to impress the woman he would marry the next year, Rebecca S. Hutchinson; they were married in 1806 by Congregational minister and abolitionist Reverend Humphrey Moore. Nehemiah Jr. seems to have departed from his father's example only in marrying a "she-devil" and having a large number of children—nine that we

Milford, 1854, "N. Haywood" residence circled.

know about, seven of whom lived to adulthood (see p. *xxxvii* for Hayward family tree).[27]

In terms of family prominence, at least, Nehemiah Jr. "married up." The Baltimore genealogy claims that Rebecca S. Hutchinson Hayward (1780/81–1850), the evil Mrs. Bellmont in *Our Nig*, was a "direct descendant of Anne Hutchinson, one of the 'Pilgrim Mothers'" (BG, 48). She certainly hailed from one of the most distinguished families in Milford. Her maternal grandfather, William Peabody, was the town's first settler, and her paternal grandfather, Nathan Hutchinson, could match Peabody in being both a town founder and Revolutionary War veteran; he is eulogized throughout *The History of Milford* as "one of the most active and useful citizens" (32). Rebecca's parents were well off, and four of her brothers would own their own farms, the other brother becoming a doctor and her sister marrying a noted physician who was elected state senator.

But if Rebecca was born to social prominence, she also received a less attractive heritage. A startling revelation about her father appears in a chatty history of Milford published in 1963:

> Have you ever been spanked in order to make you remember something? There is an old story about the grandson of one of Milford's earliest settlers who received just such a spanking!
>
> In 1744 Nathan Hutchinson bought a part of the Charlestown School Farm from Benjamin Hopkins. He settled on it in 1748. And it was Nathan Hutchinson's son, Nathan [Rebecca's father], who was said to have taken *his* son Reuben to the large rock which is the southwestern boundary of the Charlestown School Farm. There he gave the boy a serious whipping as a life-long reminder that that particular rock was the southwestern bound of that particular tract of land! Reuben never forgot the lesson, either![28]

In other words, Rebecca's father may have been a child beater. The tone of the passage reminds us that standards for the treatment of children were different 250 years ago (and perhaps 25 years ago) or this story would not have been handed down and repeated with such insouciance. To the modern sensibility it reveals a bit more than the overriding significance of property to men in 1800, for we are told that child abusers have usually been abused themselves when they were children.[29] If Rebecca Hutchinson Hayward received some of her father's "serious whippings," she may have felt all the more entitled to beat her servant. In *Our Nig* Wilson hints that the "she-devil" abused at least one of her children when he was young. When Frado and her beloved James first meet in *Our Nig,* Frado has just been whipped and banished from the house and James is eager to talk with her. Wilson's comment that "a frail child, driven from shelter by the cruelty of his mother, was an object of interest to James" (50) implies that James's identification with Frado might arise from shared experience.

The living patterns of the Hayward family, in addition to the history of violence in Rebecca's background, suggest that Wilson based her characterization of Mrs. Bellmont as a she-devil on reality. Although Wilson was familiar with contemporary novels like Susan Warner's *The Wide, Wide World* (1850), wherein cruel guardians mistreat orphans, she probably did not need fictional models. There is direct evidence, for instance, that Rebecca Hayward had trouble living in the same house with others, just as Mrs. Bellmont does. Mrs. Bellmont cannot keep hired help because no servant "will live in the house with her; she's so ugly, they can't" (18). At the end of *Our Nig* Wilson says Mrs. Bellmont worsened with age so that finally "no one, even her own children, could remain with her" (130). Interestingly, in the 1850 census Rebecca Hayward and her three surviving sons—Jonas, Nehemiah P., and Charles—are all shown residing in Baltimore (Nehemiah Jr. died there early in 1849). Rebecca's address, however, is in a different ward from any of her sons.

Apparently the young Rebecca could not live in the same house as her in-laws. The family was together in Milford at the time of the 1810 census, but in 1818 Nehemiah Jr., Rebecca, and their children moved a short distance away to Wilton (the Hayward farm lay close to the Wilton border).[30] Although land records do not reveal any new financial stresses, Nehemiah Jr. started keeping a store in Wilton Centre, and the 1820 census lists the senior Haywards and their daughter Sally (Aunt Abby) in Milford and Nehemiah and his wife and children in Wilton. As soon as Mary and Nehemiah Sr. were dead, the Nehemiah Jrs. moved back to the family homestead in Milford. In his will Nehemiah Sr. left the farm to his son but specified that his daughter Sally would have during her lifetime "the right of occupying one undivided half of all buildings except the barn," along with the privilege of keeping a cow and a horse in the barn.[31] It would seem that unless there were conflict or some likelihood that Sally might be prevented from living on the homestead, her father need not have provided for her so specifically. Wilson says in *Our Nig* that one reason Mrs. Bellmont hated Aunt Abby was because "she did not give her right in the homestead to John, and leave it forever" (45).

Mrs. Bellmont is also portrayed as greedily pushing her children to marry into affluent families (56, 111), and this characteristic too was probably based on reality. At least Rebecca Hayward's oldest child Elizabeth (Betsey) provided a model for the lucrative matches Mrs. Bellmont tries to set up

District School No. 3, where Wilson would have attended school.
Courtesy of the Milford Historical Society.

for Jane and Jack. Betsey, who is referred to in *Our Nig* only as one of the grown-up children "already settled in homes of their own" (22), married an ambitious man known for his "hardness in driving a bargain."[32] He made the fortune he sought, and the couple's sons were all successful in business, "some unusually successful" (Ramsdell, 483).

There are numerous indications of a strong materialism in the Hayward family, ranging from the decision of the "sire" to buy untaxed land to the overriding emphasis of the Baltimore genealogy a hundred years later on the Haywards' "thrift and economy" and "financial and managerial abilities" (BG, 50, 52). No doubt Rebecca would have been gratified to know that her grandson's "business qualities were similar to those of a great military commander" (BG, 53). While the values of the author may account in part for the genealogy's foregrounding of financial success linked with domination, the same concerns appear in stories that obviously originated with Jonas Hayward and are repeated in several sources. The anecdotes all validate Jonas's status as self-made man. We have already heard the one about his search for his obscure brother; there are also tales of how his brother paid him only fifty cents a day when he joined the business and how throughout his rise Jonas's talisman was "his first dollar, a silver one," which he earned on his father's farm and "has been retained in the family as a useful souvenir, all of his children having cut their teeth upon it."[33]

This coin recalls the silver dollars in *Our Nig*, such as the half dollar Mrs. Bellmont gives Frado as a "present" for twelve years' drudgery (117). The prevalence of "thrift and economy" (or greed and rapaciousness, depending on one's point of view) in the lives of the Haywards should make us take a closer look at economic themes in *Our Nig* and recognize the extent to which economic motives predominate in Wilson's narrative. Even Mrs. Bellmont's cruelty stems from her financial interests; she discourages Frado's religious proclivities, for instance, because she fears they might induce her to leave and "just think how much profit she was to us last summer." Mrs. Bellmont decides to beat Frado because "I'll beat the money out of her, if I can't get her worth any other way" (90). Frado has "worth" to Mrs. Bellmont as a workhorse, but there are other villains in *Our Nig* and almost all human interactions are shown reduced to economic exchanges. Frado learns early that women count not only as workers but as ornaments for men. Her mother gave away her "priceless gem"—virginity—for nothing but was later able to trade her second "treasure"—white skin—to Jim for a living (6, 14). Even a white invalid has more value than a black supergirl. Frado remarks wistfully of Jane Bellmont (Lucretia Hayward), "Although an invalid, she was not excluded from society. Was it strange *she* should seem a desirable companion, a treasure as a wife?" (55). Despite its seemingly happy ending, Jane's courtship story has more to do with bargaining than love; the suitor who fails in "possessing her" ultimately "balanced his disappointment by a few hundreds" (55, 60).

In an environment where everything is for sale, not even Frado can remain untarnished. The first silver half-dollar she receives is for her ornamental value. Although Frado cannot be a "treasure as a wife" to the Bellmont men, throughout the narrative she plays the part of clown for her so-called friends in the household, Jack and Mr. Bellmont. Twice she endangers her life to amuse them (the climb to the roof of the barn and the sheep episode), and the encouragement she receives "constantly nurtured the inclination" (53). The ultimate entertainment for Jack is when Mrs. Bellmont orders Frado to eat from her dirty plate and Frado has the dog lick it first: "Jack was boiling over with laughter. He related all the circumstances to James, and pulling a bright, silver half-dollar from his pocket, he threw it at Nig, saying, 'There, take that; 't was worth paying for'" (72). Although Frado/Wilson seems to relish this silver dollar, it is hard to ignore the dehumanizing parallel between throwing a coin at Frado and tossing a bone to the dog.

The dollar signs that reverberate throughout *Our Nig* and the lives of the Haywards are intriguing, but probably the most important piece of information about the Hayward family, in terms of its implications for interpreting *Our Nig,* is their strong abolitionist connections. Rebecca Hayward, who descended from the eminent Hutchinson family, was related to another branch of the Milford Hutchinsons, the Hutchinson Family Singers. The Hutchinson Family Singers gained international recognition in the late 1840s and 1850s as a group of folksingers who supported progressive causes, most notably abolition but also women's rights and temperance; they were the nineteenth-century equivalent of a Pete Seeger or an Odetta. Brothers Judson, John, and Asa, and sister Abby Hutchinson believed themselves engaged in a "great moral combat" against slavery, as Asa noted in his journal: "Only let knowledge be generally diffused and slavery cannot any way be tolerated. . . . let us, the Hutchinson family, tune our voice for the cause of freedom."[34] The Hutchinson Family Singers knew most of the abolitionist leaders and were considered a huge success in raising consciousness. Frederick Douglass himself wrote John Hutchinson, "I especially have reason to feel a grateful interest in the whole Hutchinson Family—for you have sung the yokes from the necks and the fetters from the limbs of my race."[35]

Milford, New Hampshire, abounded with Hutchinsons, and Rebecca's blood relationship with the Hutchinson Family Singers was not close; so far as I can tell, she and their father were second cousins. However, the relationship was cemented through two marriages. In 1843, the same year as a massive abolitionist rally in Milford, Judson Hutchinson wed Rebecca's niece. The avaricious man whom the Haywards' eldest child Betsey married was the singers' eldest brother David. In a biography of the Hutchinson Family Singers, Betsey's husband is presented as a materialist and skinflint, the only one of the siblings to deny support to a needy sister: "David, the eldest, had always seemed the farthest away from them. The younger boys had resented his Yankee hardness in driving a bargain. He had had a good deep bass voice, but music had been less important to him than was the fortune he was amassing" (Brink, 274).

The character of David Hutchinson reminds us that strong differences can exist between siblings, to say nothing of cousins, and Rebecca Hayward's connection to the Hutchinson Family Singers does not necessarily make her an abolitionist. But there is strong evidence that her son Jonas, the Baltimore entrepreneur, was just that. Both John Hutchinson in his reminiscences and Asa in his journal describe a concert tour to Baltimore in January and February of 1844, at a time when the singers were struggling to establish their national reputation.[36] Not surprisingly, Baltimore gave a chilly response to the singers of "O Liberate the Bondsmen" and "The Slaves' Appeal"; the Hutchinsons complain of small,

The Hutchinson Family Singers, 1846.

"panic stricken" audiences, and they had trouble finding personal accommodations and concert space once people learned who they were. Asa calls himself "an Unwelcomed Stranger" and says bluntly, "I don't like the slave states. Freedom does not reign here." The bright spot of the Baltimore trip was the support of the Haywards, Jonas and Nehemiah P. (not Nehemiah Jr. but his son Nehemiah Peabody, who had joined Jonas in the business after George's death in 1840).

The Hutchinson Family Singers socialized nearly every day

with Jonas and Nehemiah and their wives and for a time even resided with them. Asa notes, "Here I am in the corner of our chamber in the house of our much esteemed townsmen and friends, the Messrs. Hawards, who are a fine specimen of the true Yankee character. Their wives are true-hearted Baltimoreans. ["True-hearted" probably means antislavery.] Jonas' wife is rather more healthy than Nehemiah's, but they are all very kind and therefore we feel very much at home here." The relationship was not merely social, because Jonas acted as an informal manager for the Hutchinsons during their stay. It was he who found lodgings and concert halls, provided an escort to Washington for some concerts, took care of the luggage, and acted as "door agent pro tem." Asa reports that Jonas also sold tickets in advance, once having disposed of a third of the tickets himself. He even dispensed sympathy after unsuccessful concerts and "told of trials he had himself experienced." What these trials were—and whether they stemmed from holding unpopular abolitionist views—is unclear, but Jonas probably would not have gone to all this trouble for the Hutchinsons unless he shared their sentiments.[37] Certainly Asa Hutchinson would have described Jonas less warmly, for a perusal of the journal shows that Asa calls antislavery people "true" and "kind"; proslavery people are quickly dismissed or termed a "disgrace to the country."

Jonas Hayward may thus have been one of the hypocritical (racist) abolitionists Wilson excoriates in *Our Nig*, and it is quite possible that the she-devil herself had abolitionist sympathies. Rebecca could have been influenced not only by her son and Hutchinson cousins but also by her minister, the Reverend Humphrey Moore; he presided at her marriage in

1806, and in *Our Nig* Mrs. Bellmont is still a churchgoer. Milford's most distinguished minister, Moore served as pastor of the Congregational Church from 1802 to 1836. He was such a strong abolitionist that he was elected by antislavery men to the House of Representatives in 1840 and to the New Hampshire State Senate in 1841; in both places he delivered stirring orations against slavery.[38] It is one of the many ironies involving *Our Nig* that Milford, the site of Harriet Wilson's oppression, should have been an abolitionist stronghold and station on the Underground Railroad (Frado's cramped attic chamber would have made a good hiding place). A citizen stated at Milford's centennial celebration in 1894, "If Milford is distinguished for anything, it is for the unselfish and sublime work" of abolitionists.[39]

The likelihood that one or more of the Haywards was an abolitionist provides an answer to the often asked question of why, if Wilson was really writing to earn money for her son, she risked alienating abolitionists. Why suddenly mention in the last chapter being "maltreated by professed abolitionists, who didn't want slaves at the South, nor niggers in their own houses, North" (129) when abolitionists were the most important, if not the only, source of support for African American writers? A reasonable explanation is that a critique of abolitionists' racism was more central to Wilson's story than we have previously supposed. In the narrative the only reason suggested for Frado/Wilson's hostility to abolitionists is not a very compelling one—they simply failed (like Frado herself) to detect that her husband was a fake. Nor is the comment about being maltreated by professed abolitionists developed; it is simply mentioned as one of the several "strange adventures" Frado experienced *after* she left her child in Milford and sought a living elsewhere. It would seem that Wilson may have deliberately pushed the maltreatment by professed abolitionists forward in time in order to disassociate it from the Bellmonts. As she says in the preface, she has not divulged everything about her life, having "purposely omitted what would most provoke shame in our good anti-slavery friends at home." The principal omission may well have been the abolitionist views of the Bellmonts, our bad antislavery friends. If this were the case, it would have intensified the crucial dilemma Wilson faced in publishing her story: how to tell the truth about the racism she experienced in the North without harming the cause of slaves in the South. How could she tell the truth, even slant, about the racism and hypocrisy of abolitionists themselves?

Wilson clearly wanted to tell a more complex story than the political agendas or literary forms of her day could contain. As Barbara Christian has noted, she "questioned the progressive platform of her time—that white northern women were the natural allies of blacks, that the North was not racist, that all Black men were devoted to the women of their race."[40] And, we might add, that all abolitionists were friends of all African Americans. At the same time Wilson found the "progressive platform" of her time too simplistic, she also found the two literary models available to her—the slave narrative and the sentimental novel—inadequate for her purposes. Obviously, she could not plot a clear-cut movement from slavery to freedom, as in the slave narrative. She was supposedly "free" to begin with, and "slavery's shadows" in the North ended up making her economically dependent. Nor could

Wilson create a social world of clear-cut friends and enemies of an orphan on the rise, as in the sentimental novel. At first reading, it may appear that she has divided the Bellmonts very clearly into friends or foes: Mr. Bellmont, James, Jack, Jane, and Aunt Abby are portrayed as empathetic and kind, while Mrs. Bellmont, Mary, and Lewis are mean. But upon closer examination Frado's relationships with the kind Bellmonts dissolve into relations plagued by money and power. The role of Mr. Bellmont provides a good example of the way Wilson complicates her narrative. If the "humane" Mr. Bellmont is Frado's main protector (24), his complicity in Frado's oppression is simultaneously made clear; if Wilson often seems to want to excuse him, the text finally does not.

Although Mr. Bellmont claims that "women rule the earth, and all in it" (44), he in fact makes the big decisions, as when he "declared decisively" that Frado should attend school (30). "The word once spoken admitted of no appeal," and despite Mary's objections "the word became law" (31). The same is the case when he proclaims that Jane can reject Mrs. Bellmont's choice and marry someone else. However much of a "scold" Mrs. Bellmont may be, she accepts her husband's authority as head of the household. When he tells her not to beat Frado, she is reduced to tears and obeys him (47); unfortunately, he usually leaves the house to avoid a confrontation and thus gives Mrs. Bellmont tacit permission to administer a beating (34). Mr. Bellmont's advice to Frado—that "when she was *sure* she did not deserve a whipping, to avoid it if she could"—betrays his belief that sometimes she does deserve to be whipped (104). The mixed character of Mr. Bellmont fits with the complexity of the world portrayed by Wilson, where things are frequently not as they seem. The appearance of a good Northern antislavery society juxtaposed to a bad Southern slave society may be deceiving, just as slavery shadows freedom and just as Frado's father's black outside conceals a white inside (12) and Mrs. Bellmont's light skin covers the inner darkness that can be glimpsed through her "black eyes" (68).

But if Wilson had a complex story, her husband, the fake fugitive slave, did not. In the last chapter of *Our Nig* she says that Samuel recounted his supposed personal experience of slavery "in homely phrase" and that "his illiterate harangues were humbugs for hungry abolitionists" (126, 128). In other words, the content of his narrative was false and the form bad enough to be termed "illiterate." Yet Samuel had no trouble getting an audience from abolitionists, for they were "hungry" for his lies; they preferred his story to hers, even when hers was both highly literate and based on true experience. The tartness of Wilson's appeal to the reader in her last chapter ("Refuse not . . . Enough has been unrolled to demand your sympathy") suggests that she anticipated she would not get much of a hearing and would have to publish the book herself.

As Wilson prepared to publish, she had to face another predicament: although it was necessary to receive the support of at least some "good antislavery friends" to sell her narrative, she could not distribute it very widely without alerting the surviving Haywards, who all had abolitionist connections. Even though most of the family was dead by 1859, Wilson had much to fear from Jonas and Betsey, both of whom still lived, Betsey in the same town as Wilson's son. Both Jonas and Betsey were rich and powerful and had been allied with the she-devil. Jonas may have encouraged abolitionist concerts, but he also took the Hutchinson Family Singers to the grave of his sister Rebecca (Frado's tormentor, Mary Bellmont). Asa writes, "It was a very solemn occasion. Jonas could not refrain from shedding tears, copious tears of grief." (By contrast, Frado had found Mary's death "a thanksgiving," 107). Thus Wilson needed to change the names of the family, even if she intended her narrative as a straight autobiography rather than a work of autobiographical fiction.

There are striking parallels in the circumstances of *Our Nig* and Harriet Jacobs's *Incidents in the Life of a Slave Girl* (1861). Jacobs also had to use different names to protect herself, and until the recent discovery of her letters, which show the book to be an autobiography, *Incidents* was considered a work of fiction heavily edited and possibly even authored by a white woman.[41] Now *Incidents* is classified as autobiography and *Our Nig* as fiction, but the only clear difference in form lies in the point of view, *Incidents* being told in the first person and *Our Nig* in the third. *Our Nig* is told *mostly* in the third person, that is—we need the qualification because Wilson sometimes shifts, as in the early chapter titles "Mag Smith, My Mother," "My Father's Death," and "A New Home for Me." Perhaps these titles are leftovers from an earlier draft Wilson thought too little distanced. At the least, they reveal a strong ambivalence on her part regarding the whole autobiography/fiction issue.

It might seem that my discoveries about the Haywards would allow us to come down firmly on the autobiography side of the frequently asked question of whether *Our Nig* is autobiography or fiction. The similarities between the lives of the Haywards and the lives of the Bellmonts are indeed many, and we now know that because Wilson's enemies were not all dead in 1859 she had to adopt disguises, like changing names and separating the Bellmonts from the abolitionist cause, in order to protect herself. But I think the information I have uncovered could just as well be used to support a description of *Our Nig* as fiction (albeit strongly autobiographical fiction). Even though there are numerous correspondences between the Haywards and the Bellmonts, the correlation is not precise enough to allow us to reconstruct Wilson's life in detail, and I have also found evidence that she deliberately changed some facts.

It first appears that information about the Haywards can be used to determine Wilson's birthdate. If we know the date of Lucretia Hayward's marriage, for instance, can we not count back to Wilson's date of birth? Lucretia married her Vermont lover in September of 1834, just a month after George Hayward's wedding. In *Our Nig* the marriages occur after a spring visit from James (George) when Frado is nine years old. Frado would thus have been born between the summer of 1824 and the spring of 1825. Spring 1825 would be the most likely date because almost all the age markers in *Our Nig* are given in the spring—Frado has just turned six when she goes to the Bellmonts in summer; she is seven when she starts summer school; she is "now nine" when James (George) visits in late spring; and she becomes eighteen and finishes her indenture in spring. But a spring 1825 birthdate for Wilson is problematic for two reasons. First, it contradicts the 1850 census, which gives Wilson's age as twenty-two. Second, in *Our Nig* Mary Bellmont (Rebecca Hayward the younger) has "just glided into her teens" when Frado joins the household (27); Rebecca the younger was born 3 February 1822 and would not enter even her second decade until 1832, a year after Frado would have joined the Bellmonts if she had been born in spring 1825. The puzzle pieces do not fit together if one tries to assume an exact correspondence between Hayward and *Our Nig* chronologies.[42]

But there are strong aesthetic reasons for Wilson's having changed the order of events in *Our Nig*. Let us suppose she was born on 2 June 1827, a date that satisfies most of the requisites: Wilson would thus have been born in the spring, been 22 at the time of the 1 June 1850 census, and have come to the Haywards in the summer of 1833 after she had turned six and Rebecca the younger eleven. In this case she would have met George Hayward during her first year at the Haywards, earlier than in *Our Nig*, and the weddings of Lucretia and George would also have taken place earlier, just after her first year. But it is clearly more effective artistically for Wilson to postpone the weddings, which are uncommon events, and show herself established in a regular routine at the Haywards. Her school experiences need to be described right away because of their importance to her relationships with young Rebecca, Mrs. Hayward, and ultimately George (she must be able to read the Bible when she meets him). Before George and Lucretia can marry, there has to be a context set up for the friendship with George and sufficient leisure for the long courtship story of Lucretia. Wilson did not hesitate to make other alterations in the lives of the Haywards. One change

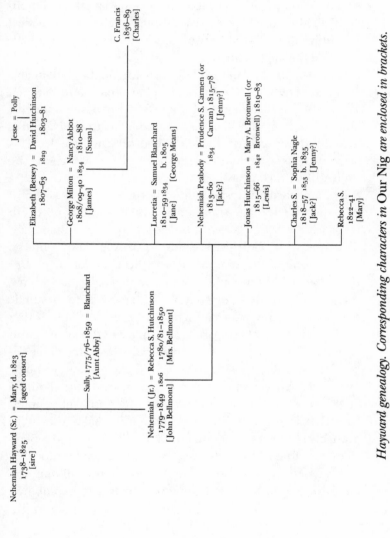

Hayward genealogy. Corresponding characters in **Our Nig** *are enclosed in brackets.*

she may have made out of ignorance—she says the Bellmont "sire" died before his wife (21), though Nehemiah Hayward Sr. outlived Mary—but in two other instances she must have changed the facts deliberately.

Sally Hayward (Aunt Abby) was not really Nehemiah's "maiden sister" because she married at some point between 1825 when her father died and 1837 when she suddenly appears as "Mrs. Sally Blanchard" right beneath the Haywards in Milford tax records. In 1840 "Widow Sally Blanchard" is listed as a taxpayer, and the census of that year suggests she lived with the Haywards; at the time of the 1850 census, a Sally Blanchard was residing in Milford with Betsey Hayward Hutchinson's teenage son and daughter. There is no death record for a Sally Hayward, but in 1859 a Sally Blanchard died in nearby New Ipswich. (Wilson says Aunt Abby "entered heaven" only a few months before the completion of *Our Nig*).[43] Since Wilson would have known that Sally was a widow, she may have made Aunt Abby a "maiden sister" for aesthetic reasons. Certainly it obviates the necessity of going into a long explanation of her past. Wilson makes a slip at one point and introduces some of this material when she describes Jane's husband-to-be as "a visitor [who] came to Aunt Abby's; one of her boy-favorites, George Means, from an adjoining State" (56–57). It is never explained why Aunt Abby should have "boy-favorites" from any state, but in reality they were probably relatives of her late husband. (Sally married a Blanchard and Lucretia wed Samuel Blanchard from Vermont.)

Presumably it was also in the interest of streamlining the narrative that Wilson made another change: she combined two Hayward brothers, Nehemiah P. and Charles, into one character, Jack Bellmont. It appears initially that Jack was based on the youngest Hayward son, Charles, and Nehemiah P. falls into the category of children already away from home when Wilson joined the Haywards. But as I gathered more facts about Nehemiah P. and Charles, it became clear that aspects of both are combined in the character of Jack.[44] It would have been difficult to individualize too many brothers, and Wilson may have further simplified reality by suppressing the presence of a second or even third Hayward son living with the family when she arrived in 1831–33. Nehemiah P. would have been 21 and may already have left home, but Jonas was younger and did not seek his brother in Baltimore until 1837 (BG, 50). These kinds of changes suggest a shaping of the narrative more consistent with autobiographical fiction than "pure" autobiography (if such a thing exists). So there is probably some accuracy in a critic's prediction that "readers of *Our Nig* will be debating for some time the question of whether the work is fiction or autobiography."[45]

Wherever *Our Nig* falls on a fiction/autobiography scale, it can still be considered a link between, as Gates puts it, "the sustained and well-developed tradition of black autobiography and the slow emergence of a distinctive black voice in fiction" (lii). And wherever Wilson's book falls on the scale, she clearly had a strong aesthetic consciousness: we see it at work in her efforts to complicate the narrative and simultaneously provide a clean, dramatic story line; we see it in her struggles to negotiate the Haywards' abolitionist connections. Of course, my discoveries about the Haywards indicate that whatever conscious changes she may have made Wilson adhered closely to her real experience. Much of what she says is literally true, as Wilson herself tells the reader in her preface; she has only "purposely omitted what would most provoke shame in our good anti-slavery friends." In addition, we now know for certain that Wilson's stated motive for writing the narrative, to maintain her child, was no rhetorical device. Her appearance on the lists of the Overseers of the Poor and her boy's month-long stay at the horrid county farm attest to her compelling need. *Our Nig* differs markedly in this respect from *Incidents in the Life of a Slave Girl.* Jacobs told her story to "arouse the women of the North" to political action on behalf of slave women in the South (1), but Wilson could not tie hers to any political agenda of the day, and neither could she demand any action other than buying her book. As she anticipated, her story about a complex North, a "*two-story* [my italics] white house," could be received only by a small group, her "colored brethren" (Preface). And so *Our Nig* disappeared for more than a century.

Yet, if *Our Nig* once fell out of history, it has now fallen back in. The process of restoring the author's identity begun by Henry Louis Gates will surely advance as more researchers pursue her story. In 1983 Gates called the story of the life and times of Harriet E. Wilson . . . "curiously compelling" (lix), and if the latest chapter is any indication, it will continue to be so. Certainly the lives of the real-life Bellmonts are not lacking in drama. The career of Jonas Hayward, in particular, seems the stuff of an overly ironic novel; it is hard to forget his selling tickets to abolitionist concerts while his parents keep a slave at home, or his rising to ward manager of the poor while the family's former "nig" struggles to keep her three-year-old from going "insane" at the county pauper farm. As Wilson's friend Allida proclaims in her testimonial, "'Truth is stranger than fiction;' and whoever reads the narrative of Alfrado, will find the assertion verified" (133).

Notes to Afterword
by Barbara A. White

For valuable assistance in the course of my research, I thank the following: Baltimore County Public Library; City of Baltimore Archives; Maria Fahey; Lucy M. Freibert; Henry Louis Gates, Jr.; Nancy Gray; Hillsborough County Nursing Home; Maryland Historical Society (Francis P. O'Neill); Milford Historical Society; Milford Public Library (Arthur Bryan and Mary Ann Doyle); New Hampshire State Archives (Frank Mevers); and the University of New Hampshire Center for the Humanities (Burt Feintuch), Centra University Research Fund, and Special Collections, Dimond Library.

PAGE

iii   1. Quoted on the cover of H. E. Wilson, *Our Nig; or, Sketches from the Life of a Free Black,* 2nd ed. New York: Vintage, 1983. Further references are from this edition and will be noted in the text.

iii   2. The 1892 work is *Iola Leroy* by Frances E. W. Harper, the most prominent black woman writer in the nineteenth century. The first African American novelist is thought to be William Weals Brown, who published *Clotel* (1853) in England. In his introduction to *Our*

Nig, Henry Louis Gates Jr. calls Harriet Wilson "one of the first two black women to publish a novel in any language" (xiii); also in 1859 the Brazilian Maria F. dos Reis published *Ursula.*

v   3. Presumably after Frado's mother, Mag. See Robert LeRoy Hilldrup, "Cold War against the Yankees in the Antebellum Literature of Southern Women," *North Carolina Historical Review,* vol. 31, July 1954, p. 378. For additional references to *Our Nig,* see Barbara A. White, *American Women's Fiction, 1790–1870: A Reference Guide.* New York: Garland, 1990, p. 246.

vi   4. For an account of the search, see David Ames Curtis and Henry Louis Gates, Jr., "Establishing the Identity of the Author of *Our Nig,*" in *Wild Women in the Whirlwind: Afra-American Culture and the Contemporary Literary Renaissance,* ed. Joanne M. Braxton and Andrée Nicola McLaughlin. New Brunswick: Rutgers Univ. Press, 1990, pp. 48–69. Milford, New Hampshire, is fifty miles from Boston, and its southern border is five miles from the Massachusetts line. At the time *Our Nig* was published, its population was 2,223. For a more thorough description, see George A. Ramsdell, *The History of Milford.* Concord, N.H.: Rumford, 1901, pp. 10–11, 272–77. Further references to this history will be noted in the text.

vi   5. *Farmer's Cabinet,* February 29, 1860. The death record is located at the New Hampshire Bureau of Vital Statistics. Because George Mason Wilson died in 1860, a census year, his death is also recorded in the mortality schedule of the federal census for Milford. This record provides more detail than the death record Gates and Curtis found, establishing that Wilson died of "billious fever" after an illness of 12 days. His

PAGE

"color" is given as "mulatto," the choices being white, black, or mulatto.

vi 6. Henry Louis Gates Jr., "Harriet E. Adams Wilson," in *Afro-American Writers Before the Harlem Renaissance,* ed. Trudier Harris and Thadious M. Davis. Detroit: Gale, 1986, p. 269.

ix 7. For family history, see Afterword Note 19; for description of the farm, see Afterword Note 24. "Inherit the family homestead": *Register of Deeds,* 49/47, Hillsborough County Courthouse, Nashua, N.H. "Right in the homestead": Probate Record 05297, Hillsborough County Courthouse, Nashua, N.H. "Orchards and sheep": "Records [Invoice and Taxes] 1835–56," Milford Public Library.

x 8. This report is located in the Town Clerk's Office in Milford; I thank Nancy Gray for discovering it. According to the WPA Historical Records Survey, the Town Clerk's Office had in 1937 "reports of Treasurer and overseer of poor" from 1839 through 1856. I have seen only 1839 and 1840 (at the Milford Historical Society), 1843, 1845, 1849, 1850, 1855, and 1856. It is not clear whether the others have been temporarily misplaced or permanently lost; the town clerk was uncooperative. For the WPA Historical Records Survey, specifically "Inventory of the Local Archives of New Hampshire/Town of Milford," consult Special Collections, Dimond Library, University of New Hampshire.

x 9. Milford followed national trends in poor relief, moving from the "outdoor" relief of the eighteenth century, in which the poor were auctioned off or bound out, to the "indoor" relief of the nineteenth century, in which they were kept on town and later county poor farms. But there was always overlapping. Around the time Harriet Wilson was born, Milford still made use of the vendue system or "New England method" of disposing of the poor, whereby "the town's poor were sold at auction . . . once a year, usually at the close of the annual town meeting. . . . when the maintenance of the pauper was struck off to the lowest bidder" (Ramsdell, 75). In the 1830s the town established a poor farm, and by the time Wilson needed assistance paupers might either be living on the farm or boarding with a family. As Timothy Dodge notes, "In many instances there was a combination of old and new methods. A town farm might be in operation and at the same time some forms of 'outdoor' relief would also be relied on" (17); see his master's thesis, "Poor Relief in Durham, Lee, and Madbury, 1732–1891," Univ. of New Hampshire, 1982.

One of the "old methods" that probably applied to Harriet Wilson as a child was the binding out of poor children. The terms were usually specified in written contracts setting the period of indenture until adulthood (18 for girls and 21 for boys) and requiring a minimum of education to be provided the child; see Marcus W. Jernegan, *Laboring and Dependent Classes in Colonial America, 1607–1783*. New York: Frederick Ungar, 1965, p. 107. Although Wilson does not mention a formal written contract, and none has been found, she refers to "the term of years which Mrs. B. claimed as the period of her servitude" (116). Also, Frado is allowed three years, and only three years, of education: "Her education completed, as *she* said, Mrs. Bellmont felt that her time and person belonged solely to her" (41). The choice of wording suggests that, no matter how informally, Frado was "bound out" to the Bellmonts.

10. "Paupers Received and Discharged, 1852–1885," Hillsborough County Nursing Home (formerly Hillsborough County Farm), Goffstown, N.H. This is one of the few county farm records listed by the WPA in 1937 to survive the nursing home's move to a new building.

11. Proctor reminisces in two documents, both located at the Milford Historical Society. One is a 1918 letter addressed to George A. Worcester, who was a member of the Town History Committee, and the other document, which contains similar material, in a six-page typed manuscript entitled "Sixty Years Ago."

12. All the paupers at the farm seem to have been badly treated, whether black or white, but one of Proctor's "jokes" attests to the racism there. One day when bread was short, Dimon Prince said "Better kiss the cook," and the cook replied, "I had rather cook another dinner than be kissed by a nigger." Proctor mentions two African Americans at the farm other than Prince, "two boys Henry and James Blanchard mulattoes." During the Civil War, Captain Proctor ran into James, who had "enlisted from Amherst in the 10th N.H. Vols. where he served until his death, in Norfolk, Va. Aug. 19, 1863." It is not certain whether James and Henry Blanchard were ever transferred to the county farm, but their lives may have intersected with Harriet Wilson's in another way. They were sons of Timothy Blanchard, a black man and property owner in Milford, and Dorcas Hood, a white woman. James and Henry were born sometime between 1835 and 1839, when Timothy died (the 1850 census lists

Henry Blanchard, a ten-year-old "mulatto," as residing in the poorhouse). Perhaps they were abandoned by their mother, since one wonders what they were doing at the poor farm when Dorcas remarried (a white property owner, Luther Elliot of Mason). The parallels with *Our Nig* are intriguing. At any rate, the descent of James and Henry happened quickly, as their grandfather was a distinguished Milford citizen; George Blanchard (d. 1824) was a Revolutionary War veteran and "veterinary surgeon" who owed a farm in Milford. His son Timothy (1791–1839) "remained on the homestead for many years." In the 1820 and 1830 censuses Timothy has several "colored" men living with him who are not members of his own family; these residents are prime candidates for Wilson/Frado's father "Jim." (Residing with the Nehemiah Hayward Jrs. in 1820 is a white woman, aged 16–25, whom I cannot identify—a possible candidate for Frado's mother, "Mag.") For information about the Blanchards, see "George Blanchard" family register in Ramsdell, pp. 592–93, and Probate Records 977 and 1872, Hillsborough County Courthouse, Nashua, N.H.

xiii   13. Prince's name also appears in "Paupers Received and Discharged, 1852–1885." The simultaneous existence of a town farm and a county farm for about fifteen years is typical of the overlapping relief systems described in Afterword Note 9; see discussion in Winifred A. Wright, *The Granite Town: Milford, New Hampshire 1902–1978*. Canaan, N.H.: Phoenix, 1979, pp. 339–40.

xiii   14. See the speculations of Blyden Jackson in *A History of Afro-American Literature*. Baton Rouge: Louisiana State Univ. Press, 1989, pp. 351–63; and Claudia Tate, "Allegories of Black Female Desire; or, Rereading

Nineteenth-Century Sentimental Narratives of Black Female Authority," in *Changing Our Own Words: Essays on Criticism, Theory, and Writing by Black Women,* ed. Cheryl A. Wall. New Brunswick: Rutgers Univ. Press, 1989, pp. 111–16. In his introduction to *Our Nig,* Gates accepts Wilson's stated motive for writing.

xiv 15. The smallness of the amount ($12) suggests that she did not reside at the farm for the whole year. Wilson's name appears as "Mrs. Wilson," so it is conceivable, if not very likely, that some other Mrs. Wilson was meant.

xiv 16. From colonial times there were laws to keep out non-resident paupers. New Hampshire citizens could even be fined for bringing an indigent person into the state—*Laws of the State of New Hampshire.* Concord, N.H., 1811, p. 70.

xv 17. It would not be unusual for the census to err. Gates rightly points out that "discrepancies in census data were common even among stable and middle-class white Americans" (xv). He notes that Samuel Boyles, the carpenter with whom Wilson boarded in 1850, is 50 at the time of the 1850 census and 52 in 1860; his birthplace shifts from "Vermont" to "Massachusetts." People often did not know exactly when they had been born, and their recollections could easily be distorted by sickness or trauma. There were also frequent mistakes in birth records. To again use Samuel Boyles as an example, the Boyles family register in Ramsdell's *The History of Milford* has him born in 1806, but his tombstone (West Street cemetery) says he "passed to spirit life" in 1871 at the age of 63. We have three different birthdates for the she-devil herself. According to the Hayward family register in Ramsdell, Rebecca Hutchinson Hayward was born in October of 1780, and according to the Hutchinson family register in November of 1781; the Baltimore genealogy (see Afterword Note 19) gives her birthdate as October 1781.

xv 18. These may be found in the *Register of Deeds,* Hillsborough County Courthouse, Nashua, N.H. It should be remembered that spelling was inconsistent in the nineteenth century and "Hayward" can be given several differing spellings, including Haward, Hawood, Haywood, Heyward, Heywood, and Howard.

xv 19. "Hayward," in *Baltimore: Its History and Its People,* 2 vols. New York: Lewis Historical, 1912, vol. 2, pp. 42–54. I call this work the "Baltimore genealogy" and abbreviate it as BG in further references. There is a more modest "family register" in Ramsdell, p. 735.

xv 20. Jonas provides the information, however, that his parents were "able and willing to assist him" in his ambition to become educated (BG, 49). The Nehemiah Haywards seem solidly middle-class, better off than the "lower middle-class family" Gates views the Bellmonts as being in *Our Nig* (xliii). Their financial position can be assessed through deeds (see Afterword Note 18) and tax records. The latter, thanks to the efforts of Arthur Bryan, may be found at the Milford Public Library. Records mentioning the Haywards include the following: "The South-west Parish Book March 1784"; [Invoice and Taxes 1807–1834]; "Book of Records of Selectmen of the Town of Milford Commencing 1829"; "Records [Invoice and Taxes 1843–1852"; "Invoice and Taxes" [1848–1850]; and "Record of Taxes, 1853–69."

xvi 21. The story is told in the following sources: BG, 50; "Jonas Hutchinson Hayward," in *The Biographical Cyclopedia of Representative Men of Maryland and District of*

Columbia. Baltimore: National Biographical, 1879, pp. 246–47; and William Stump, "Hayward," *Baltimore Sunday Sun Magazine,* June 20, 1954, p. 3. See page *xvii,* for Jonas's portrait in BG.

xvi 22. Stump, 3. Jonas Hayward's accomplishments are also described in "Recollections of George A. Frederick," a speech by an architect on building innovations in Baltimore. The 1912 manuscript may be found at the Maryland Historical Society.

xvi 23. Baltimore, Md., "List of Committees," 1863 (73)-RG.25, S.1, Baltimore City Archives.

xviii 24. The story of the mile slip is told in Christopher D. MacLeod, "The Mile Slip: A New Hampshire Oddity," *New Hampshire Profiles* no. 15, November 1966, pp. 36–39. The Haywards' 118 acres is described in Hillsborough County *Register of Deeds,* 16/423, and Probate Record 05297, Hillsborough County Courthouse, Nashua, N.H. See page *xix,* for the location of the property on the *Map of Milford . . . from Actual Surveys by E. M. Woodford.* Philadelphia: Richard Clark, 1854. Although the white house no longer stands, there are still orchards in the area today (the "fruitful acres" of Wilson's description); according to Ramsdell, Milford farmers produced "large quantities" of apples and a smaller amount of peaches (12). The Souhegan ("crooked") River, which flows nearby, is subject to sudden flooding and energetic enough to have destroyed several bridges; see A. B. Rotch, *Pictures of Old Milford.* Milford, N.H.: Cabinet, 1912, pp. 61–62. The school Wilson attended was probably the District School No. 3 (see page *xxiii*).

xviii 25. See "The South-west Parish Book" (Afterword Note 20) for appointments to town offices and purchase of church pews. The petition to incorporate is discussed

PAGE

in David Goodwin, *Historical Sketch of the Town of Milford, New Hampshire* [1846]. Milford, N.H.: Milford Historical Society, 1987, p. 2.

xviii   26. See *Register of Deeds,* 49/47, Hillsborough County Courthouse, Nashua, N.H. The authors of the Baltimore genealogy must not have seen this deed, for they did not know about Mary and assumed that because Nehemiah Sr. left "no wife" when he died in 1825, he had no wife when he moved to Milford (BG, 48). But Mary died before him, and her name appears on this deed in 1800. See page *xxxvii,* "Hayward genealogy."

xix   27. The two children who did not survive are not mentioned in the Baltimore genealogy or the family registers in Ramsdell. There was a daughter who was born in Wilton February 6, 1820, and died February 9 (Wilton Town Records, Vol. 1, p. 49, New Hampshire State Library). According to "The South-west Parish Book," on August 27, 1814, a child of "N. Haywood" died of dysentery. The Haywards whose graves I have located in Milford are Charles, James, James's wife Nancy, and their son C. Francis (Elm Street Cemetery) and Betsey (North River Cemetery).

xx   28. Alberta T. Hagar and Edith F. Hunter, *Milford: Our Home Town.* Milford, N.H., 1963, p. 24. No source for the anecdote is provided.

xxi   29. See, for instance, Murray A. Straus, Richard J. Gelles, and Suzanne K. Steinmetz, *Behind Closed Doors: Violence in the American Family.* New York: Anchor, 1980, pp. 98–122.

xxii   30. The date can be determined from the Hillsborough County *Register of Deeds,* 116/185 and 117/419, Hillsborough County Courthouse, Nashua, N.H., and [Invoice and Taxes 1807–1834], Milford Public Library.

Afterword

PAGE

The Haywards' residence in Wilton is described briefly in Abiel Abbot Livermore and Sewall Putnam, *History of Wilton*. Lowell, Mass., 1880, pp. 227, 556.

xxii 31. See Probate Record 05297, Hillsborough County Courthouse, Nashua, N.H.

xxiii 32. Carol Brink, *Harps in the Wind: The Story of the Singing Hutchinsons*. New York: Macmillan, 1947, p. 274.

xxiv 33. "Jonas Hutchinson Hayward," p. 246. For various versions of the anecdotes about Jonas, see the three sources listed in Afterword Note 21. Jonas also emphasizes his "military commander" qualities, as when he taught in Milford and felt called upon to "demonstrate in short order who was the master of the school" (BG, 50). Thanks to Maria Fahey for ideas about the silver dollars and economic themes in *Our Nig.*

xxvi 34. Asa B. Hutchinson, "The Journal of Asa" (1844), available at Milford Public Library. In Milford the Hutchinsons were "come-outers," that is, abolitionists who came out of the churches because they felt the churches were not taking a strong enough stand against slavery (see Ramsdell, 106–09). There were various configurations of the Hutchinson Family Singers over the years, as different siblings and their families came and went. Judson, John, Asa, and Abby formed the quartet that originally gained fame; Jesse Jr. composed many of the songs. For an account of the different groupings, see Brink (Afterword Note 32). See page *xxviii,* for a portrait from John Wallace Hutchinson, *Story of the Hutchinsons,* ed. Charles E. Mann, 2 vols. Boston: Lee & Shepard, 1896, vol. 1, p. 142.

xxvii 35. Quoted in Brink, page 286. Douglass wrote an introduction to John Hutchinson's *Story of the Hutchinsons.*

PAGE

xxvii   36.   See *Story of the Hutchinsons,* pp. 102–03. The relevant entries in Asa's journal are January 21–February 21, 1844.

xxix   37.   The Baltimore genealogy says Jonas was "an earnest member of the Whig, and later of the Republican party" (51).

xxx   38.   Moore's papers, including abolitionist sermons and speeches, may be found at the Milford Historical Society. See Ramsdell, pp. 370–75, for a biographical sketch. Humphrey Moore was Rebecca Hayward's cousin by marriage as well as her pastor (he married Hannah Peabody, another granddaughter of the original settler).

xxx   39.   *Celebration of the One Hundredth Anniversary of the Incorporation of Milford, New Hampshire.* Milford, N.H.: Town Committee, 1894, p. 40. See also Cynthia Jones, "Milford House Stationed on Underground Railroad," *Nashua Telegraph,* July 2, 1977, p. 14.

xxxi   40.   Barbara Christian, "'Somebody Forgot to Tell Somebody Something': African-American Women's Historical Novels," in *Wild Women in the Whirlwind,* p. 331.

xxxiv   41.   For an account of the dispute over the authenticity of Jacob's work, see Jean Fagan Yellin "Texts and Contexts of Harriet Jacobs's *Incidents in the Life of a Slave Girl: Written by Herself,*" in *The Slave's Narrative,* ed. Charles T. Davis and Henry Louis Gates Jr. New York: Oxford Univ. Press, 1985, p. 262. For Jacobs's letters, see the Harvard Univ. Press edition of *Incidents* (1987); further references to this edition will be noted in the text.

xxxvi   42.   Other attempts to make a precise match of Hayward dates and the events in *Our Nig* end in similar contradictions. Wilson tells us, for instance, that Frado is 14 when Mr. and Mrs. Bellmont make a fall trip to Baltimore. Since James comes home sick the next spring, and we know that George Hayward returned in May of 1839, Frado must have been 14 in the fall of 1838. If so, she would have been born in 1823 or 1824, yet there are several indications that any date before spring 1824 is too early (for they would make Frado over 18 when Mary dies August 3, 1841, and she hasn't yet completed her indenture; also, if Wilson joined the Haywards at age six she would have appeared on the 1830 census). Spring 1824 is a possible birthdate, but it also runs up against the 1850 census and Mary's entrance into her teens. If we want to take Mary's age into consideration in dating Wilson's birth, she would have to be born in 1826 at the earliest; this would also be the case if we assumed that her father died in the Milford consumption epidemic of 1831. Crediting the census of 1850 leads to an even later birthdate of 1827 or 1828, and Wilson could not have been indentured at age six and spent three years with the family before the weddings of summer 1834.

xxxviii 43. *Our Nig,* p. 130. According to the New Hampshire Bureau of Vital Statistics, Concord, N.H., the Sally Blanchard from New Ipswich died January 18, 1859, of "paralysis." Sally Hayward Blanchard should not be confused with other Sally Blanchards (at least two) with Milford connections. Timothy Blanchard, a black man (see Afterword Note 12), had a daughter Sarah born in 1830. Another "Widow S. Blanchard," once married to Phineas, appears in Milford tax records prior to 1836; she was Sarah, who lived in Milford's fourth district from 1824 to 1835 and then moved to Temple where she died in 1857. There are several Blanchard families whose lives intersect those of Harriet Wilson and the Haywards and who might be more thoroughly investigated. Not only did Sally and Lucretia Hayward both marry Blanchards, but the Haywards' closest neighbors were the Simon Blanchards, and Timothy Blanchard is a possible candidate for Frado's father's associate, "Pete Greene."

xxxix   44.   Charles did not marry until 1853, long after his parents had died, so his wife could not have been the "Jenny" who falls victim to the she-devil's plots. Nor was Charles "forever after alienated from his early home" (115), since he lived on the homestead in the late 1850s. The alienated brother sounds more like Nehemiah P., who seems to have left Milford for Baltimore permanently by 1840. For this same reason, however, he would not have gone West after his youngest sister's death, as Jack does in *Our Nig*, nor would he have had any reason to leave his Baltimorean wife in New Hampshire. Nehemiah P. is an attractive candidate for Jack, if only because he has the same name as his father (as in John-Jack Bellmont). Yet Jack and his wife supposedly "rest[ed] in heaven" (130) by the time Wilson published *Our Nig*, and Nehemiah P. and spouse were still alive (Charles died in 1857. Charles's wife, Sophia, was still alive, however (Probate Record 02794, Hillsborough County Courthouse, Nashua, N.H.).

xxxix   45.   Majorie Pryse, "Introduction" to *Conjuring: Black Women, Fiction and Literary Tradition,* ed. Marjorie Pryse and Hortense J. Spillers. Bloomington: Indiana Univ. Press, 1985, p. 6.

Notes to the Text

title 1. Author is Harriet E. Wilson (b. 1828? d. ?). See Chronology of Harriet E. Adams Wilson hereinafter referred to as Chronology.

title 2. Josiah Gilbert Holland, "Bittersweet: A Poem," in *Bitter-Sweet,* 5th ed. New York: Charles Scribner, 1859, pp. 35–36. R. J. Ellis, who located this 1859 version of the poem, correctly indicates that Wilson's quotation is slightly different than the original, which reads:

> I know
> That care has iron crowns for many brows;
> That Calvaries are everywhere, whereon
> Virtue is crucified, and nails and spears
> Draw guiltless blood; that sorrow sits and drinks
> At sweetest hearts, till all their life is dry;
> That gentle spirits on the rack of pain
> Grow faint or fierce, and pray and curse by turns;
> That Hell's temptations, clad in Heavenly guise
> And armed with might, lie evermore in wait
> Along life's path, giving assault to all—

According to Ellis, the poem continues: "I know the world is full of evil things, / And shudder with the consciousness."

title 3. *Our Nig* was published by Mrs. H. E. Wilson. Copyright date: August 18, 1859; publication date: September 5, 1859.

title 4. The printer, George C. Rand & Avery, was not known as a regular publisher of novels.

Notes to the Text

PAGE

3   5. Mrs. Wilson's "failing health" and impoverished cir-
         cumstances are affirmed by the three letters appended
         to the text (pp. 133–140). In addition, it appears that
         Mrs. Wilson did give birth to her son, George, at the
         Hillsborough County Farm in Goffstown. See "Birth of
         George Mason Wilson" in Chronology.

3   6. Mrs. Wilson's son died of the "fever" within six months
         after she published her novel in order to raise money
         to support him. See "Death of George Mason Wilson"
         in Chronology.

5   7. No information has been found concerning the iden-
         tity, race, age, or place of birth or death of Harriet E.
         (Adams) Wilson's mother, called "Mag" in the novel.

5   8. Thomas Moore, "Lalla Rookh," in *The Poetical Works of
         Thomas Moore, Collected by Himself*. Philadelphia: J. B.
         Lippincott, 1858, p. 257. R. J. Ellis, who located this
         1858 version of the poem, correctly indicates that Wil-
         son's quotation is slightly different than the original,
         which reads:

> Oh, Grief, beyond all other griefs, when fate
> First leaves the young heart alone and desolate
> In the wide world, without that only tie
> For which it lov'd to live or fear'd to die;—
> Lorn as the hung-up lute, that ne'er hath spoken
> Since the sad day its master-chord was broken!

6   9. No information has been found concerning Mrs.
         Wilson's mother's first child, nor the father of this
         child.

9   10. No information has been found concerning Mrs. Wil-
         son's father, called "Jim" in the novel.

13   11.   No record of the marriage of Mrs. Wilson's parents has been found.

14   12.   Percy Bysshe Shelley, "Misery—a Fragment," in *The Poetical Works of Percy Bysshe Shelley, Edited by Mrs. Shelley With a Memoir, vol.* 2. New York: Little, Brown and Co., 1835, p. 399, third stanza. R. J. Ellis, who located this 1835 version of the poem, correctly indicates that Wilson's quotation is slightly different than the original, which reads:

> Misery! we have known each other,
> Like a sister and a brother
> Living in the same lone home,
> Many years—we must live some
> Hours or ages yet to come.

            The next stanza begins: "'Tis an evil lot, and yet / Let us make the best of it."

14   13.   No birth record has been found for Harriet E. (Adams) Wilson, called "Frado" in the novel, nor for the younger brother described here. Mrs. Wilson is listed as "Black," not "Mulatto," on the two records located describing her race (1850 federal census for Milford, New Hampshire, and death record for George Mason Wilson). See Chronology.

15   14.   No death record for Mrs. Wilson's father has been found.

15   15.   No information has been found concerning a "partner" to Mrs. Wilson's father. This partner is called "Seth Shipley" in the novel.

17   16.   Barbara A. White argues convincingly that Harriet Adams spent her early life living with and in service to the Nehemiah Hayward family and not the Samuel

Boyles family as had been previously suggested. See "Early Life of Harriet E. Adams Wilson" in Chronology and Afterword by Barbara A. White.

17   17.   When Frado is six years old the year would be c. 1834, if the 1850 U.S. Federal Census for Harriet Adams in Milford, New Hampshire, is correct and if the novel is true to life at this point.

21   18.   "Bellmonts." See "Early Life of Harriet E. Adams Wilson" in Chronology.

21   19.   "Sire." See "Early Life of Harriet E. Adams Wilson" in Chronology.

22   20.   "John, the son." See "Early Life of Harriet E. Adams Wilson" in Chronology.

22   21.   "Maiden Sister." See "Early Life of Harriet E. Adams Wilson" in Chronology.

22   22.   "She-devil or Mrs. Bellmont." See "Early Life of Harriet E. Adams Wilson" in Chronology.

24   23.   Eliza Cook, "The Future," in *The Poetical Works of Eliza Cook*. London: Frederick Warne and Co.; New York: Scribner, Welford and Co., 1870, p. 187, fourth and fifth stanzas. R. J. Ellis, who located the author of this epigraph, correctly indicates that Wilson's quotation is slightly different than the original, which reads:

> Oh! did we but know of the shadows so nigh,
>> The world would indeed be a prison of gloom;
> All light would be quenched in youth's eloquent eye,
>> And the prayer-lisping infant would ask for the tomb.
> For if Hope be a star that may lead us astray,
>> And "deceiveth the heart," as the aged ones preach;
> Yet 'twas Mercy that gave it, to beacon our way,
>> Though its halo illumes where we never can reach.

25 24. "Mary." See "Early Life of Harriet E. Adams Wilson" in Chronology.

25 25. "Jane." See "Early Life of Harriet E. Adams Wilson" in Chronology.

30 26. The year would be c. 1835 (see Note 17 above).

40 27. George Gordon Noel Byron, 6th Baron Byron, "Child-ish Recollections," from *Hours of Idleness: A Series of Poems, Original and Translated* in *The Poetical Works of Lord Byron: Embracing His Suppressed Poems, and a Sketch of His Life*. London: John Murray, 1845, p. 405, second stanza. R. J. Ellis, who located this 1845 version of the poem, correctly indicates that Wilson's quotation is slightly different than the original, which reads:

> Hours of my youth! when, nurtured in my breast,
> To love a stranger, friendship made me blest;—
> Friendship, the dear peculiar bond of youth,
> When every artless bosom throbs with truth;
> Untaught by worldly wisdom how to feign,
> And check each impulse with prudential reign;
> When all we feel our honest souls disclose—
> In love to friends, in open hate to foes;
> No varnish'd tales the lips of youth repeat,
> No dear-bought knowledge purchased by deceit.

According to Ellis, the poem continues: "Hypocrisy, the gift of lengthen'd years, / Matured by age, the garb of prudence wears."

41 28. The year would be c. 1838 (see Note 17 above).

42 29. "James." See "Early Life of Harriet E. Adams Wilson" in Chronology.

52 30. Martin Farquhar Tupper, "Of Life (Second Series)," in *Tupper's Complete Poetical Works*. Boston: Phillips, Samp-

son, and Company, 1850, p. 192. Fourth stanza, lines
1–5. R. J. Ellis adds that Wilson's quotation includes
slightly different punctuation than the original, which
reads:

> Life is a strange avenue of various trees and flow-
> ers;
> Lightsome at commencement, but darkening to its
> end in a distant, massy portal.
> It beginneth as a little path, edged with the violet
> and primrose,
> A little path of lawny grass, and soft to tiny feet:
> Soon, spring thistles in the way. . . .

The epigraph, Ellis explains, is taken from the final
stanza of "Our Life" and continues:

> Soon, spring thistles in the way, those early griefs of
> school,
> And fruit trees ranged on either hand show holiday
> delights:
> Anon, the rose and the mimosa hint at sensitive
> affection,
> And vipers hide among the grass, and briers are
> woven in the hedges.

62   31. R. J. Ellis attributes the quote to Laetitia Elizabeth
Landon. "Success Alone Seen," in *Life and Literary
Remains of L. E. L.* by Laman Blanchard. London:
Henry Colburn, 1841, p. 261. Ellis, who located the
author of this epigraph, correctly indicates that Wilson's quotation has been reproduced as prose and is
slightly different than the original, which reads:

> Hard are life's early steps; and, but that youth
> Is buoyant, confident, and strong in hope,
> Men would behold its threshold and despair.

63   32. The year would be c. 1842 (see Note 17 above).

73   33. Henry Kirke White, "Time, A Poem," in *The Complete Poetical Works of Henry Kirke White*. Boston: N. H. Whitaker, 1931, p. 136. Third stanza, lines 3 and 4.

75   34. Chapter XI of George A. Ramsdell's *The History of Milford*. Concord, N.H.: The Rumsford Press (Published by The Town), 1901, tells of the "Come-Outer" movements in Milford, New Hampshire, beginning in December 1842. Certain prominent residents of the town (which may be the place where Mrs. Wilson grew up) organized a series of "come-outer" meetings to enlist the support of the town's residents in the anti-slavery cause.

78   35. Henry Kirke White, "Written in the Prospect of Death," in *The Poetical Works of Henry Kirke White*. London: Bell and Daldy, 1830, p. 79. R. J. Ellis, who made this attribution, indicates that Wilson's quotation is slightly different than the original, which reads:

> Now other cares engross me,
> And my tired soul with emulative haste,
> Looks to its God.

Ellis adds that the lines immediately preceding the above quote read: "No more of Hope; the wanton vagrant Hope! / I abjure all."

91   36. Henry Kirke White, "Written in the Prospect of Death," in *The Poetical Works of Henry Kirke White*. London: Bell and Daldy, 1830, p. 79. According to R. J. Ellis, who

Notes to the Text

made this attribution, Wilson's quotation is taken from the same poem she used as the epigraph for Chapter VIII and includes slightly different punctuation than the original, which reads:

—We have now
But a small portion of what men call time
To hold communion;

102 37. R. J. Ellis tentatively attributes this epigraph to George W. Cook, a maritime doctor and author of the 1848 book, *The Mariner's Physician and Surgeon; or a Guide to the Homeopathic Treatment of Those Diseases to Which Seamen Are Liable, Comprising the Treatment of Syphilitic Diseases etc.* New York: J. T. S. Smith.

109 38. The year would be c. 1846 when she reached her majority (see Note 17 above).

111 39. Unable to determine name of the author of this epigraph. The only "C. E." poet found to have been writing at this time was a Charlotte Elliott, a London-based religious poetess. A search of her works available at the Sterling Memorial Library at Yale University yielded no positive results. R. J. Ellis agrees with Henry Louis Gates, Jr., that Charlotte Elliott is the likely author of the epigraph, arguing that the quotation is reminiscent of her other work in both style and content.

116 40. Mrs. Wilson's frequent references to Frado's strong reading habits amidst her social isolation may help to explain Mrs. Wilson's own literary background and abilities.

117 41. The *Boston Directory* lists a "Harriet Wilson, dressmaker." Evidence here and on page 122 indicates that Frado was quite adept at this skill.

Notes to the Text

PAGE

117   42.   No information has been found concerning the character called "Mrs. Moore."

118   43.   No information has been found concerning the character called "Mrs. Hale" in the novel.

122   44.   No information has been found concerning the "two maidens" or the character called "Mrs. Hoggs" in the novel. The Hillsborough County Farm public charity records burned in a fire in the 1880s.

122   45.   "Three years" beyond Mrs. Wilson's age of majority would be c. 1849.

122   46.   See Note 41 above.

124   47.   See "W———, Mass. Period" in Chronology for a discussion of the various possible towns where Mrs. Wilson might have sewn straw bonnets. Allida's letter in the Appendix confirms this aspect of Mrs. Wilson's life, and provides the information that the first letter of the town in Massachusetts was "W" (p. 133).

124   48.   "The plain, poor, simple woman" referred to in the novel was a "Mrs. Walker," according to Allida in her appended letter (p. 133).

126   49.   Solomon, Ecclesiastes, chapter 1, verse 10.

126   50.   Allida confirms in her appended letter (p. 134) that a professed fugitive slave did come to "W———, Mass." and did court Harriet.

127   51.   Harriet Adams, of Milford, married Thomas Wilson, of Virginia, on October 6, 1851, according to the records of the Milford, New Hampshire, Town Clerk. See "Marriage of Thomas Wilson and Harriet Adams" in Chronology. The novel says "she removed to Singleton, her former residence, and there was married." George Mason Wilson's death record confirms that the "birthplace" of Harriet E. Wilson, his mother, was

Milford. Allida merely states that she "took up her abode in New Hampshire." (p. 134).

127   52.   The novel says the character "Samuel"—Frado's husband—"embarked at sea" deserting her. Allida also says (p. 134) that Mrs. Wilson's husband "embarked for sea."

128   53.   While Allida speaks unfavorably of Mrs. Wilson's husband and reports that he was introduced to her by a "colored lecturer," there is no positive indication in her appended letter that Mr. Wilson was an abolitionist lecturer, let alone an abolitionist lecturer *masquerading* as a fugitive slave, but not really so.

128   54.   The birth of George Mason Wilson in Goffstown, site of the Hillsborough County Farm, parallels the novel's account of the birth of Frado's child while "thrown upon the public for sustenance."

128   55.   Allida confirms that Mrs. Wilson's husband returned, and then left for good (p. 136).

128   56.   No records could be obtained for the death of Mrs. Wilson's husband in New Orleans in accordance with the novel at this point.

129   57.   No information has been found concerning the character called "Mrs. Capon." The appended letter from "C.D.S." in "Milford," however, seems to indicate that C.D.S. may be this person (p. 140).

129   58.   There is some possibility that Mrs. Wilson moved to Boston, Massachusetts, as early as 1855, setting up a dress shop there the following year. See "Second Massachusetts Period" in Chronology.

129   59.   Allida describes this "valuable recipe" referred to in the novel as "a recipe ... for restoring gray hair to its former color" (p. 137).

131   60.   "... as Joseph from the butler's ..." R. J. Ellis cites Genesis, chapter 40, verse 22, the passage where

Pharaoh's butler forgets his promise to show kindness to Joseph.

133 61. See "The W———, Massachusetts Period" in the Chronology.

133 62. No information has been found concerning Mrs. Walker of W———, Massachusetts.

133 63. It appears that Allida was called "Aunt J———" by Mrs. Wilson, but no information has been found concerning her identity.

134 64. The date 1842 cannot be correct and probably is a typographical error. See "The W———, Massachusetts, Period" in the Chronology.

134 65. No information has been found concerning the "colored lecturer."

134 66. The alleged fugitive slave is Thomas Wilson of "Virginia," who married Harriet Adams on October 6, 1851, in Milford. See "Marriage of Thomas Wilson and Harriet Adams" in the Chronology.

134 67. The statement of Allida that Mrs. Wilson left W———, Mass., and "took up her abode in New Hampshire" is ambiguous, because it does not confirm or deny that Mrs. Wilson was *born* in New Hampshire. The 1850 federal census records, and George Mason Wilson's death record, as well as other facts, seem to show that Mrs. Wilson was indeed born in New Hampshire and spent her childhood there. See Chronology.

134 68. See Note 52 above, concerning Mrs. Wilson's abandonment by her husband.

134 69. See Chronology and Note 54 above, concerning Mrs. Wilson's time spent in the County Farm.

134 70. Since Allida has a copy of the letter written by Mrs. Wilson to Mrs. Walker, one could assume that Allida is also from W———, Massachusetts.

135   71.   See "Birth of George Mason Wilson" in Chronology for information on the (Goffstown) Hillsborough County (New Hampshire) House, where Mrs. Wilson gave birth to her son. See also Note 54 above.

135–36 72.   Mrs. Wilson's creative abilities in writing poetry are demonstrated here.

136   73.   No information has been found concerning "some town in New Hampshire" where Thomas Wilson took his wife when he returned to her.

136   74.   The "kind gentleman and lady" may be "C.D.S." and his/her spouse. See C.D.S.'s letter on p. 140 of this volume. If Barbara A. White's narrative reconstruction is correct (see Chronology), Allida is incorrect when she states that "a kind gentleman and lady took her little boy into their own family, and provided everything necessary for his good; and all this without the hope of remuneration."

137   75.   See Note 59 above, concerning this "recipe."

137   76.   Allida considers *Our Nig* true-to-life enough to describe it as an "Autobiography."

137–38 77.   It's not clear whether these lines were written by Allida or whether she has quoted them from somewhere else.

138   78.   In addressing this letter in this way, Margaretta Thorn implies that she is white.

138   79.   Margaretta Thorn confirms key aspects of the "Autobiography" including Mrs. Wilson's abandonment by her parents, her state of servitude, her ill health, her child, her time on the "county farm," her poverty, and the placement of her child with foster parents.

139   80.   Margaretta Thorn is ambiguous when she says that Mrs. Wilson "was indeed a slave in every sense of the word." Does she mean "slave" in the *legal* sense? If so, the possible identity of Mrs. Wilson as a fugitive slave from Virginia is strengthened.

139 81. Margaretta Thorn's seeming first-hand knowledge of Mrs. Wilson's son indicates that she was living in Milford, New Hampshire, in 1859. However, a search of tax records, the federal census, and the town history yield no positive confirmation of this hypothesis. It is possible that she lived in a nearby town, or that "Margaretta Thorn," like "Allida" and "C.D.S.," is a pseudonym.

140 82. On her reference to "our dark-skinned brethren," see Note 78 above.

140 83. Presumably the "Milford" address here is Milford, *New Hampshire*. Barbara A. White reminds readers that Milford, New Hampshire, is fifty miles from Boston. At the time *Our Nig* was published, its population was 2,223. George Ramsdell, *The History of Milford*. Concord, N.H.: Rumford, 1901, pp. 10–11, 272–77.

140 84. C.D.S.'s statement that "her complexion is a little darker than my own" is ambiguous. It is not clear if she or he is a light-skinned black, or white. The letters "C.D.S." were a legal abbreviation for "colored indentured servant," and it is just as possible that this legal term is what these letters stand for as it is that they are simply the initials to someone's name. See Note 81 above.

140 85. C.D.S. may be the "kind gentleman" or "lady" referred to by Allida on p. 136. See Note 74 above.

140 86. A search of the tax records, federal census, and Milford town history showed no C.D.S. living in Milford in 1860. The two C.S. names were Catherine Shannahan and Charles Shepard. See also Note 81 above.

Chronology of Harriet E. Adams Wilson*

Compiled By Henry Louis Gates, Jr., David Ames Curtis, and Lisa Rivo

BIRTH OF HARRIET E. ADAMS WILSON

1. Birthplace is "New Hampshire," according to the 1850 Milford, New Hampshire, federal census. Maiden name was "Harriet Adams." She should have been born in 1827 or 1828, as she was "22" years old at the time of the August 24, 1850 census. Her race is listed as "B[lack]."

2. "Birthplace" is Milford, New Hampshire, date unspecified, according to the marriage record of Harriet Adams and Thomas Wilson, 1851, found at the Milford Town Clerk's office.

EARLY LIFE OF HARRIET E. ADAMS WILSON

3. There are no Adams families listed in New Hampshire in Carter G. Woodson's *Free Negro Heads of Families in the United States in 1830,* Washington D.C.: The Association for the Study of Negro Life and History, Inc., 1925. There are, however, almost three dozen Adams families, listed in other states, which fit the description provided in the fictionalized autobiography. There is probably no way to determine if any of these black Adams families are or are not the family of Harriet Adams, since the 1830 federal census, upon which

* See p. lxxxvii

Woodson's book is based, only lists heads of households by name.

4. Only one Adams family in Hillsborough County's 1830 federal census comes close to fitting the description Mrs. Wilson gives of her early family life. The family of Charles Adams, 20–29 years old, of New Ipswich, New Hampshire, included himself, his wife (also aged 20–29), and a daughter, aged 0–4 years old.

   - There is no listing for a Charles Adams in the 1840 federal census for Hillsborough County, New Hampshire, as would be expected, since "Alfrado" was abandoned by her parents.
   - However, no member of this family—which would be interracial if the fictionalized autobiography is true to life at this point—is listed as "colored."
   - The records of the town of New Ipswich, New Hampshire, for the period of 1800 to 1850, are missing.

5. If the fictionalized autobiography is true-to-life concerning Mrs. Wilson's early life—including the event of her natural father's early death—it is possible that there was no Free Black head of household in New Hampshire in 1830 named Adams, and yet still Harriet Adams could have been living with her mother in New Hampshire in 1830 in a family headed by her mother's common-law husband, as the novel suggests.

6. Mrs. Wilson "was taken from home so young," according to Margaretta Thorn.

7. The June 1, 1840, census locates a person closely resembling Harriet Adams' age and race profile at the Hayward family farm in Milford, New Hampshire. Although Nehemiah Hayward is the only person referred to by name, the census lists a female "free colored person" between the age of 10 and 24 along with the Hayward family members and "free white persons" living in the Hayward household. This is the only refer-

ence to a female "free colored person" living in Milford, New Hampshire, in the 1840 census. (BAW)

8. Many of the characters and circumstances of the Hayward family parallel the Bellmont family in *Our Nig,* lending further evidence of Mrs. Wilson's association with the Hayward family. (BAW):

    • Nehemiah Hayward Sr. (1738–1825) was born in Hardwick, Massachusetts, to a family who had emigrated from England to Massachusetts in the 1640s. After amassing considerable property in New Brunswick, he bought 118 acres of land between Milford and Wilton, New Hampshire, in 1786. Like "Sire," Nehemiah Sr. bought land that was unincorporated and thus untaxed. And also like "Sire," he left his holdings to his son along with the stipulation that his daughter had the right to occupy one half of the family farm.

    • Nehemiah Hayward Jr. (1779–1849), like "Mr. John Bellmont," inherited the family farm from his parents who had established it.

    • Rebecca S. Hutchinson (1780/81–1850) married Nehemiah Jr. in 1806. A direct descendent of the Pilgrim Anne Hutchinson and the granddaughter of one of Milford's earliest settlers, she bore nine children, seven of whom lived to adulthood. Like "Mrs. Bellmont," Rebecca Hayward seems to have had a difficult and complex personality.

    • Sally Hayward (1775/76–1859), Nehemiah's sister, like "Aunt Abby Bellmont," owned a "right in the homestead" and occupied a section of the house.

    • The Hayward farm, like the "Bellmont farm," had orchards, sheep flocks, and a vigorous river.

    • The youngest Hayward daughter, Rebecca Hayward (1822–41), like "Mary Bellmont" died in her teens while visiting Baltimore.

- Lucretia Hayward (1810–59), the family's other daughter, like "Jane Bellmont," married (1834) a man from Vermont and eventually settled in the West.
- George Milton Hayward (1808/09–40), Nehemiah's oldest son, like "James Bellmont," worked in Baltimore and returned home with his wife and child after falling ill. He died an early death and was buried in Milford. Barbara A. White argues Mrs. Wilson's son, George Mason, may have been named after Nehemiah Hayward Jr. and Rebecca's son George M.

9. The Haywards had strong abolitionist ties. Rebecca Hayward was related to the Hutchinson Family Singers, folksingers who gained international recognition in the late 1840s and 1850s as supporters of progressive causes, including women's rights, temperance, and abolition. Rebecca's son Jonas, a Baltimore businessman, seems to have been an abolitionist who helped—personally, professionally, and politically—the Hutchinson Family Singers when they visited Baltimore in 1844. The Abolitionist Reverend Humphrey Moore married Nehemiah Jr. and Rebecca and served as the Hayward family pastor until he was elected by antislavery men to the House of Representatives in 1840 and the New Hampshire State Senate in 1841. (BAW)

10. "Mrs. Wilson never enjoyed any degree of comfortable health since she was eighteen years of age," according to Margaretta Thorn.

11. In 1850, Harriet Adams reappears in official documents. In the "Report of the Overseers of the Poor for the Town of Milford, for the Year Ending February 15, 1850," a "Harriet Adams" is listed as "Poor not on the Farm." (BAW) The report itemizes her cost to the town as $43.84. It is clear, then, that Harriet Adams was

unable, in the year 1849–50, to support herself. She would have been placed with a local family who was then reimbursed by the town. (BAW)

12. Harriet Adams does not appear in the "Report of the Overseers of the Poor" from the previous year, 1848–49. The reports from the years 1851–54 have not been located. The 1850 overseers' report is located in the Town Clerk's Office in Milford. (BAW) White has viewed reports from the years 1839, 1840, 1843, 1845, 1849, 1850, 1855, and 1856.

13. According to the 1850 federal census for Milford, New Hampshire, Harriet Adams was a 22-year-old black woman born in New Hampshire, and living with the family of Samuel Boyles:
   • Samuel Boyles is listed as a "50"-year-old carpenter born in Vermont.
   • His wife, Louisa, is said to be "40" years old, and also born in Vermont.
   • Their son Charles was "17" years old and employed as a "clerk." He also was born in Vermont.

14. The 1860 federal census shows that the Boyles' household included three "spinsters" at that time. One could speculate that the Boyleses sometimes took in the aged and the disabled, possibly for remuneration from the county. If this were the case, it is likely that Harriet Adams was living under the Boyles' roof under such circumstances. The Boyles family does not fit the novel's description of any of the families in "Singleton" which took in "Frado."

15. According to William P. Colburn's *Family Registers* printed in George A. Ramsdell's *The History of Milford*, Concord, New Hampshire: The Rumford Press, 1901:
   • Samuel Boyles was born in Beverly, Massachusetts, on January 22, 1806, and died in Milford on March 6,

1871. "He was a carpenter, coming here from Marsh-field, Vermont, in 1833."
- He married a Mary L. Barnes, daughter of Joseph and Elizabeth (Putnam) Barnes, on January 7, 1830.
- Mary L[ouisa] was born in Litchfield on April 17, 1811 and died in Troy, New York, on May 6, 1893.
- Their children were:
  - Mary Elizabeth, born in Marshfield, Vermont, on August 27, 1830; married on January 4, 1848, to Milton Parker of Milford, and died on January 9, 1861.
  - Charles Carol, born October 9, 1833; married on November 9, 1858 to Elizabeth Shoup of Daven-port, Iowa, and was a merchant residing in Chicago at the time of publication of Colburn's Register (1901).
  - George Washington, twin of Charles C., born October 9, 1833; died in Milford, July 21, 1837.

16.
The 1840 federal census for Milford, New Hampshire, lists the members of Samuel Boyles' household as fol-lows:
- one male, aged 5–9.
- one male, aged 30–49.
- one female, aged 5–9.
- two females, aged 20–29.

The male and female aged 5–9 are most likely their children Mary Elizabeth and Charles Carol, with Charles's twin, George, already dead. No information has been found concerning the two females in their twenties, and so it is not known at this time whether they might or might not have been "Poor not on the [County] Farm." In any case, their ages do not match those of the spinsters listed in the federal census two decades later as residents in the Boyles' home.

THE W_____ , MASSACHUSETTS, PERIOD

17.   "Allida" reports that Mrs. Wilson, not yet married at the time, was brought to W_____, Massachusetts, by an "itinerant colored lecturer."

18.   W_____, Massachusetts, was an "ancient town" with a straw hat industry, according to "Allida."

19.   According to "Allida," Harriet E. Wilson:
- Became an "inmate" of Mrs. Walker's household in W_____, Massachusetts.
- Began immediately as a "straw-sewer."
- Soon her "constitution was greatly impaired."
- Became at that point Mrs. Walker's domestic help.

20.   The town histories of three W_____, Massachusetts, towns indicate the existence of a straw-sewing industry in the central part of Massachusetts.
- "A common household industry—the sewing of hats by hand," according to Herman DeForest's *The History of Westborough, Massachusetts* (p. 364), "was for a long time confined to this part of Massachusetts." DeForest reports that "a large number of sewers were required." Braid, brought to Westborough sewers by "stock-carts" from Upton—where the industry began in 1825—was "sewed into straw hats by women in this town."
- Arthur Chase's *History of Ware, Massachusetts* (1891) describes the "manufacture of straw goods" as "an important industry of the village in former times." (p. 224) He reports that this industry "was commenced in 1832" but "besides the work done in the shops, straw-sewing was done largely in the houses about town."
- Isaac Newton Lewis, in his *A History of Walpole, Massachusetts* (1905), refers only to the straw goods manufacturers of the town—this is in his section on the

industry of Walpole. The straw works were in operation in the 1840s and 50s. (p. 201)

- The other W———, Massachusetts, town in this part
of Massachusetts is the town of Worcester.

21. According to the Accelerated Indexing System's name
index to the 1850 federal census of Massachusetts,
there were approximately two dozen Walker families
living in W———, Massachusetts, towns in 1850. A large
proportion of these Walker families lived in Worcester.
There is no way of narrowing the list of Walker families,
based on available evidence.

22. "Allida" reports that "months passed." And then in the
"early Spring of 1842,"

- The "lecturer" returns, this time with a fugitive slave.
- The fugitive slave had been a house servant.
- "Suffice it to say," she says in a vague and discreet
tone, "an acquaintance was formed, which, in due
time, resulted in marriage."
- In a few days, she left W———, . . . and took up her
abode in New Hampshire."

23. Given that "Allida" attests in 1859 to knowing Mrs. Wilson only about eight years (i.e., c. 1851–52), this date
(of "1842") could not be a correct one from first-hand
knowledge. Most likely, this date is rather a typographical error for 1851 or 1852, considering that Thomas
Wilson married Harriet Adams in Fall 1851 (this marriage being reported in the Spring of 1852).

MARRIAGE OF THOMAS WILSON AND HARRIET ADAMS

24. A Thomas Wilson is reported to have married a Harriet
Adams on October 6, 1851, in Milford, New Hamp-

shire, according to the marriage records (v. 2, p. 3) of the Milford Town Clerk.

- This information was "returned by Rev. E. N. Hidden" in April of the following year (i.e., 1852), along with information about a dozen or so other marriages.
- No age or race is listed for any of the marriages.
- Thomas Wilson is said to be from "Virginia." It is not clear if this address is intended as a "residence," "birthplace," or "last known residence."
- Harriet Adams is said to be from "Milford." Again the status of this address is ambiguous.

25.   The 1850 federal census for New Hampshire lists Rev. Ephraim N. Hidden as a "Cong[regational] Clerg[yperson]" with property valued at $1,500. He has a wife and two children. He is white, and 38 years old as of the 1850 census. His place of birth is listed as "New Hampshire."

26.   Rev. David L. Clarke, the pastor of the First Congregational Church of Milford, New Hampshire, in 1982 reports that his church records show that Rev. Ephraim Nelson Hidden was the fifth pastor of the Church, for the years 1849–58. Church marriage records for the period were burned in a fire.

BIRTH OF GEORGE MASON WILSON

27.   George M. Wilson was born probably in late May or early June of 1852, according to his February 15, 1860, death record found at the New Hampshire Bureau of Vital Records.

- His age at time of death is listed as "7 years, 8 months."
- His race is listed as "Black."
- His parents were Thomas and Harriet Wilson, of Virginia and Milford, New Hampshire, respectively.

- This birth is approximately nine months after a Thomas Wilson, of Virginia, married a Harriet Adams of Milford.

28.　The birth occurred in Goffstown, New Hampshire—where the Hillsborough County Farm was located at the time. (The Goffstown, Hillsborough County House's records were burned in a fire, as were the Town Clerk's records for Goffstown.)
- Goffstown is only a few miles from Milford.
- Both Goffstown and Milford are located in Hillsborough County.
- Both towns are directly north of the Worcester area.

29.　The *Farmer's Cabinet* of February 29, 1860, confirms that George Mason Wilson was "7 years, 8 months" at the time of his death. (George Mason was a prominent Revolutionary-Era Virginia planter and statesperson, who opposed the institution of slavery. Also, "Mason" is the name of a town in Hillsborough County, not too far from Milford.)

30.　"Allida" reports that "for a while" things went well for the new couple. But then the husband ran away to sea. "Days passed; weeks passed," and then Mrs. Wilson felt she had to go to the "County House," where she gave birth to her child.

NEW HAMPSHIRE PERIOD AFTER BIRTH OF
GEORGE MASON WILSON

31.　"Allida" reports that "then" the husband returned. The family moves to "some town in New Hampshire, where, for a time, he supported her and his little son decently well."

32.　"But again he left her as before," and this time for good, reports "Allida."

33. Margaretta Thorn reports that the son was put on the "County Farm" while Mrs. Wilson was "in her sickness" and not able to "pay his board every week."

34. In his chapter, "Hillsborough County Farm," in *The History of the Town of Goffstown, 1733–1920,* Concord, New Hampshire: Published by the Town, c. 1922–24, pp. 424–27, George Plummer Hadley recounts that the Hillsborough County Farm was purchased in 1849 in order to house the "County poor, which at that time numbered eighty-eight. The buildings at the time of the purchase consisted of a large farm house and a farm barn, a small dwelling-house near the oak tree, and some smaller buildings." (p. 424.)

- "The paupers were scattered through different buildings, which were heated by wood fires." (p. 424.)
- One of the two "justices" who oversaw the operation of the County Farm at the time of its inception was removed in 1853. By 1855 the justices "were at a loss to understand" the actions of Mr. Whittemore, particularly with reference to "sales of property made by Mr. Whittemore and no account rendered." (p. 424.)
- "In 1853 some of the inmates were stricken with smallpox, and it was necessary to build a pest-house for the proper care and segregation of the smallpox patients." (p. 424.)
- He concludes: "What tales of sorrow could some of the unfortunates unfold." (p. 427.)

35. A "Harriet E. Wilson" appears on the February 1855 "Report of the Overseers of the Poor" listed under "Poor not at the Pauper Farm" and costing the town $45.45. The 1856 overseers' report lists a "Harriet E. Wilson and Child." (BAW)

36. Records of the Hillsborough County Farm show that George Wilson, age three, a "colored" resident of Mil-

ford, was admitted to the county poor farm for four weeks beginning August 19, 1855, and was discharged to his mother on September 11 of that year. "Paupers Received and Discharged, 1852–1855" Hillsborough County Nursing Home (formerly Hillsborough County Farm), Goffstown, New Hampshire. (BAW)

37. "At length," Margaretta Thorn reports, "a kindly gentleman and lady took her little boy into their own family." Mrs. Wilson had taken him "from *that* place [the 'County Farm'] and now he has a home." See Note 74.

38. While the reports compiled by the overseers of the poor for 1857, 1858, and 1859 do not list Harriet Wilson, close to $20 a year is listed for either "Harriet E. Wilson's child" or "Wilson boy." This evidence seems to support the claim that Wilson left her son in New Hampshire while she was living and working in Massachusetts. (BAW)

39. Mrs. Wilson, says Margaretta Thorn, "wishes to educate her son." Margaretta Thorn reports that as of her writing (1859), the child is accepted, well-adjusted, and shows promise.

40. "Allida" became acquainted with Mrs. Wilson "about eight years ago" (c. 1851).
   - She is aware of and mentions letters sent by Mrs. Wilson to Mrs. Wilson's friends in W——, Massachusetts.
   - 1851 was probably the year Mrs. Wilson lived in W——, Massachusetts, since she still was in New Hampshire in August of 1850 and she returned in October of 1851 to New Hampshire to marry Thomas Wilson, whom she met in W——, Massachusetts.

41. Margaretta Thorn has "known the writer . . . for a number of years." She is familiar with Mrs. Wilson's son— who died in Milford, New Hampshire, six months after

the book was published. She also speaks of "our dark-skinned brethren."

42.   "C.D.S." reports from Milford [New Hampshire?] on July 20, 1859, that he/she has been "acquainted with her [Mrs. Wilson] for several years." He/she has a "deep interest in the welfare of the writer" and testifies that "her complexion is a little darker than my own."

43.   "C.D.S." is a legal abbreviation denoting a "colored indentured servant." It is possible that the C.D.S. who wrote the letter in the Appendix was in fact a colored indentured servant, and used the abbreviation as a pseudonym.

44.   There are no persons with the initials "C. D. S." listed in the Milford tax records for 1860, the Milford federal census for that year, nor in Ramsdell's *The History of Milford.*

45.   The two persons with the initials "C. S." listed in those records are Catherine Shannahan and Charles Shepard.

SECOND MASSACHUSETTS PERIOD

46.   The 1855 *Boston Directory* lists a "Harriet Wilson" as a "widow, house, 7 Robinson Alley."

47.   The next year, 1856, a "Harriet Wilson, widow," is living in a "house, 4 Webster ave."

- Also, there is a listing for a "Harriet Wilson, dress-maker," who has a business (?) address at 19 Joy Street.
- Webster Avenue and Robinson Alley are in northeastern Boston, down near the commercial wharves. These two streets are only a few blocks from each other.

48.

49.

- Joy Street is a block north of the Boston Common, off Belknap Street on the western side of Boston.

Harriet Wilson is listed as a "widow" living in a "house, 4 Webster ave." from 1856–63. After that year, she disappears from the *Boston Directory*.

Allida reports that "the heart of a stranger was moved with compassion, and bestowed a recipe upon her for restoring gray hair to its former color. She availed herself of this great help, and has been quite successful; but her health is again failing" and she has decided to write her "autobiography" as "another method of procuring her bread." No dates or places are given in this section of Allida's account of Mrs. Wilson's life after her husband left her.

PUBLICATION OF *OUR NIG*

50.

51.

52.

Our Nig was copyrighted on August 18, 1859.

This novel was published by Mrs. Wilson on September 5, 1859.

- A copy was deposited at that time "by Mrs. H. E. Wilson, In the Clerk's office of the District Court of the District of Massachusetts."
- New Hampshire is not included within the boundaries of the District of Massachusetts. This seems to indicate that Mrs. Wilson was living in Massachusetts, not New Hampshire, in 1859.

The novel *Our Nig* was printed for the author by George C. Rand & Avery printing company of Boston, Massachusetts. Rand & Avery were not known as regular publishers of novels.

DEATH OF GEORGE MASON WILSON

53. A George Mason Wilson, aged "7 years, 8 months," died in Milford, New Hampshire, according to the February 15, 1860, death record from the New Hampshire Bureau of Vital Records. He was black, and his parents were Thomas and Harriet Wilson. He died of the "fever."

54. Because George Mason Wilson died in a census year, his death was recorded in the Mortality Schedule of the Federal Census for Milford. Revealing further details of his illness and death, the census lists George Mason's cause of death as "billious fever" following an illness of twelve days. His "color" is given as "mulatto." (The census choices were "white," "black," or "mulatto.") (BAW)

55. The February 29, 1860 (v. 58, no. 31), *Farmer's Cabinet*—which was the local paper for Milford, New Hampshire, and published in Amherst—reports in its death notice column (p. 3) that a George Mason Wilson died in Milford on February 13, at the age of "7 years, 8 months." He was the "only son of H. E. Wilson."

56. Mrs. Wilson's son, for whom she wrote *Our Nig*, hoping to realize enough money to be able to provide for him, thus died within six months after this book was published.

PERIOD AFTER THE DEATH OF MRS. WILSON'S SON

57. In the last chapter of the novel, the author, speaking in her own voice as she pleads for support for herself in her present destitute condition, tells how "Frado"

"passed into the various towns of the State she lived in, then into Massachusetts."

58. No blacks fitting the description of Harriet E. (Adams) Wilson appear in the 1860 federal census for Hillsborough County.

59. A name-by-name search for Harriet E. (Adams) Wilson, Margaretta Thorn, and C. D. S. through the 1860 federal census for Milford, Wilton, Amherst, and Sharon produced no results.

60. According to the 1860 federal census for Goffstown, there were 96 persons residing on the Hillsborough County Farm in that town. Only one black person appears on the list—the "infant Haskell." Harriet E. (Adams) Wilson does not appear on this list.

61. There is a listing in the Boston, Massachusetts, July 5, 1860, federal census for a "Harriet Wilson," who was described as a "Widow," a "B[lack]," and a resident of a household that also included Daniel and Susan Jacobs—both also "B[lack]." This "Harriet Wilson" appears to be the same person who was listed as "Harriet Wilson, widow" in the *Boston Directory* from 1855–1863. Her "birthplace" was listed in the 1860 census as "Fredericksburg, Va.," and her age was reported to be "52."

62. The 1860 federal census for Milford, New Hampshire, shows that Samuel Boyles (who had been head of the household where Harriet Adams was living in 1850) was a "52"-year-old carpenter born in Massachusetts, with $1,500 of real property.

• His wife Louisa was "49" years old, born in New Hampshire, and is listed in the census simply as his "wife."

• His son Charles is no longer living at the house.

• A John W. Stevens, who is a "26"-year-old physician born in New Hampshire and worth $200 in personal property, also resides with the Boyleses.

- The three other residents of the household in 1860 were Melinda, Rachel, and Harriet Hutchinson, "spinsters" born in New Hampshire and listed as being "61," "58," and "115" (?) years old respectively.
- As of this writing, we have not been able to establish any further information about Melinda, Rachel, and Harriet Hutchinson. We do not know if there is any family relationship between them and Rebecca Hayward, *née* Hutchinson, the apparent real-life counterpart to the "She-Devil" Mrs. Bellmont in Mrs. Wilson's thinly-veiled autobiographical novel. One might expect that these three spinster Hutchinsons were either "Poor not on the [County] Farm"—as Harriet Adams probably was a decade earlier and perhaps also the two females in their twenties listed in the 1840 federal census as residents in the Boyles' home—or, more likely, given the wealth and standing of many Milford Hutchinsons, simply senior-aged boarders. A possible connection between Mrs. Wilson and various Hutchinson family members is highly intriguing and calls for additional research, so that we may extend, even further, knowledge of the circumstances surrounding Mrs. Wilson's life in Milford, New Hampshire.

63. The discrepancies of birth dates and birthplaces between this widowed Harriet Wilson of Boston and the apparently younger Harriet E. Adams Wilson of Milford, New Hampshire—who would have moved to Massachusetts after she was abandoned and then widowed if the fictionalized autobiography is true-to-life at this point in Mrs. Wilson's life—suggest a number of intriguing possibilities, among which are the following:

- Either the 1850 Milford, New Hampshire, federal census or the 1860 Boston, Massachusetts, federal census is seriously erroneous or incomplete (for one

of several possible deliberate or unintentional reasons) concerning Mrs. Wilson's birthplace and birthdate; or

- Harriet E. Adams Wilson died sometime between the
  date her son died (February 13, 1860) and the time
  of the 1860 federal census-taking (Summer 1860),
  and thus she was not enumerated in that census.
  ("Harriet Wilson," "widow," of Culpepper County,
  Virginia, died on January 14, 1870, but there is no
  death record for a Harriet E. Wilson in the 1860 Massachusetts Bureau of Vital Statistics); point 64 below,
  which establishes that Mrs. Wilson was still alive in
  Milford, New Hampshire, three years later, militates,
  however, against this possibilty); or,

- In 1860, there were two black women named "Harriet Wilson" living in Massachusetts, one of whose
  names has not yet been located in the unindexed
  1860 federal census records; or

- The two "Harriet Wilson" entries in the 1856 *Boston
  Directory* refer to the same person. Either Mrs. Wilson, living in the shadow of the Fugitive Slave Act,
  altered significantly her vital statistics when she
  reported her age and birthplace to the census taker,
  or the fading ink of the census manuscripts has
  blurred the distinctions among the arabic numerals
  "22," "52," and "32"—the last being what her age
  "should" be if the 1850 census is correct.

64.   In 1863, Harriet Wilson is listed in the "Report of the
      Overseers of the Poor" under "Support of County Pau-
      pers" instead of "Support of Paupers not on the Farm."
      (BAW)

65.   After 1863, Mrs. Wilson's name does not appear in Mil-
      ford or Boston records. Researchers, including Barbara
      A. White, have found no trace of Mrs. Wilson after

1863, including in the (decidedly incomplete) admission or death records of the Hillsborough County Farm.

* This Chronology supersedes the Chronology by David Ames Curtis, published in the first Random House edition of *Our Nig* (1983), as well as the version of the Chronology published in earlier printings of the second Random House edition (2002). Research facts, hypotheses, and conclusions provided by Barbara A. White are indicated by "BAW" in the present Chronology. We wish to thank her here for her pioneering research that has significantly extended knowledge of Harriet E. Adams Wilson's life and circumstances, just as we thank, once again, all those researchers who first helped make it possible for us to establish the identity of the author of *Our Nig*. (See "Acknowledgments," above, pp. vii–viii, and our narrative account of these discoveries, "Establishing the Identity of the Author of *Our Nig*," Henry Louis Gates, Jr. and David Ames Curtis, in *Wild Women in the Whirlwind*, ed. Joan Braxton, Andrée Nicola McLaughlin, New Brunswick, New Jersey: Rutgers University Press, 1990, pp. 48–70, as well as White's "Afterword" in the present volume, pp. *iii–liv*.) We welcome all further research information bearing on this book and its author.

Select Bibliography

Bassard, Katherine Clay. "'Beyond Mortal Vision': Harriet E. Wilson's *Our Nig* and the American Racial Dream-Text," in *Female Subjects in Black and White: Race, Psychoanalysis, Feminism*, ed. Elizabeth Abel. Berkeley: University of California Press, 1997.

Baym, Nina. *Woman's Fiction: A Guide to Novels by and about Women in America, 1820–1870*. Ithaca and London: Cornell University Press, 1978.

Bell, Bernard W. "Harriet E. Wilson," in *The Afro-American Novel and Its Tradition*. Amherst: University of Massachusetts Press, 1987.

Bennetts, Leslie. "An 1859 Black Literary Landmark is Uncovered." *New York Times*, November 8, 1982.

Bergeaud, Emeric. *Stella*. Paris: E. Dentu, 1859.

Blackson, Lorenzo D. *The Rise and Progress of the Kingdoms of Light and Darkness*. Philadelphia: J. Nicholas, 1867.

Blake, Jane. *Memoirs of Margaret Jane Blake*. Philadelphia: Printed for the Authors, 1834.

Blassingame, John W. and Mae G. Henderson. *Antislavery Newspapers and Periodicals, Vol. I (1817–1845)*. Boston: G.K. Hall and Co., 1980; *Vol. II (1835–1865)*. Boston: G.K. Hall and Co., 1980; *Vol. III (1836–1854)*. Boston: G.K. Hall and Co., 1981.

Bloom, Harold. *Black American Prose Writers before the Harlem Renaissance*. Broomall: Chelsea House Publishers, 1994.

Bone, Robert A. *The Negro in America*. New Haven: Yale University Press, 1957.

Branch, E. Douglas. *The Sentimental Years, 1836–1860*. New York: D. Appleton-Century Company, 1934.

Breau, Elizabeth. "Identifying Satire: *Our Nig.*" *Callaloo: A Journal of African-American and African Arts and Letters*, Spring 1993, pp. 455–65.

Brent, Linda. [Jacobs, Harriet]. *Incidents in the Life of a Slave Girl. Written by Herself*. Boston: By the Author, 1861.

Brissenden, R. F. *Virtue In Distress. Studies in the Novel of Sentiment from Richardson to Sade.* London: The Macmillan Press, Ltd., 1974.

Brown, Herbert Ross. *The Sentimental Novel in America, 1789–1860.* Durham: Duke University Press, 1940.

Brown, Jane. *Narrative of the Life of Jane Brown and Her Two Children. Related to the Reverend G. W. Offley.* Hartford: Published for G. W. Offley, 1860.

Brown, Josephine. *Biography of an American Bondman by his Daughter.* Boston, R.F. Wallcut, 1856.

Brown, Sterling A. *The Negro in American Fiction.* Washington: Associates in Negro Folk Education, 1937.

Brown, William Wells. *Clotel; or, The President's Daughter: A Narrative of Slave Life in the United States.* London: Partridge and Oakley, 1853.

———. "Miralda; or, The Beautiful Quadroon." *The Weekly Anglo-African,* November 30, 1860–March 16, 1861.

———. *Clotelle: A Tale of the Southern States.* Boston: James Redpath, 1864.

———. *Clotelle; or, The Coloured Heroine, A Tale of the Southern States.* Boston: Lee and Shepard, 1867.

Carter, George E. and C. Peter Ripley. *Black Abolitionist Papers, 1830–1865.* Sanford, N.C.: Microfilming Corp. of America, 1981.

Child, L. Maria. "The Quadroons," in *Fact and Fiction: A Collection of Stories.* New York: C.S. Francis, 1846, pp. 61–77.

Christian, Barbara. *Black Women Novelists: The Development of a Tradition, 1892–1976.* Westport: Greenwood Press, 1980.

Cole, Phyllis. "Stowe, Jacobs, Wilson: White Plots and Black Counterplots," in *New Perspectives on Gender, Race, and Class in Society,* ed. Audrey T. McCluskey. Bloomington: Indiana University Press, 1990.

Cooper, Anna J. *A Voice from the South. By a Black Woman of the South.* Xenia, Ohio: Aldine Publishing House, 1892.

Creighton, Jane Margaret. "The Bordering Nation: Problems of American Identity in Selected Novels from Our Nig to George Washington Gomez." *Dissertation Abstracts International,* Section A: The Humanities and Social Sciences, September 1997.

Select Bibliography

Cutter, Martha J. "American Women's Fiction, 1850–1880: Domestic Discourses in Writings of Fanny Fern, Louisa May Alcott, and Harriet Wilson," in *Unruly Tongue: Identity and Virtue in American Women's Writing 1850–1930*. Jackson: University Press of Mississippi, 1999.

Davis, Cynthia J. *Nineteenth-Century American Women Writers*. Westport: Greenwood Press, 1997.

———. "Speaking the Body's Pain: Harriet Wilson's *Our Nig*." *African American Review*, Fall 1993, pp. 391–404.

Delany, Martin R. "Blake: or, The Huts of America." *The Anglo-African*, January 1859–July 1859; *The Weekly Anglo-African*, November 26, 1861–May 24 [?], 1862; Boston Beacon Press, 1970.

Detter, Thomas. *Nellie Brown, or the Jealous Wife*. San Francisco: Cuddy and Hughes, 1871.

Dinah. *The Story of Dinah, as Related to John Hawkins Simpson, after Her Escape from the Horrors of the Virginia Slave Trade, to London*. London: A.W. Bennett, 1863.

Doriani, Beth Maclay. "Black Womanhood in Nineteenth-Century America: Subversion and Self-Construction in Two Women's Autobiographies." *American Quarterly*, June 1991, pp. 199–222.

Douglass, Frederick. "The Heroic Fugitive," in *Autographs for Freedom*, ed. Julia Griffiths. Boston: John P. Jewett, 1853, pp. 174–240.

Elder, Arlene A. *The "Hindered Hand": Cultural Implications of Early African-American Fiction*. Westport: Greenwood Press, 1978.

Ellis, R. J. "Body Politics and the Body Politic in William Wells Brown's *Clotel* and Harriet Wilson's *Our Nig*," in *Soft Canons: American Women Writers and Masculine Tradition*, ed. Karen Kilcup. Iowa City: University of Iowa Press, 1999.

———. "Traps Slyly Laid: Professing Autobiography in Harriet Wilson's *Our Nig*," in *Representing Lives: Women and Auto/Biography*, ed. Alison Donnell. New York: Macmillian/St. Martin's Press, 2000.

Ernest, John. "Economics of Identity: Harriet E. Wilson's *Our Nig*." *PMLA: Publications of the Modern Language Association of America*, May 1994, pp. 424–38.

Foreman, P. Gabrielle. "The Spoken and the Silenced in *Incidents in the Life of a Slave Girl* and *Our Nig.*" *Callaloo: A Journal of African-American and African Arts and Letters,* Spring 1990, pp. 313–24.

Foster, Francis Smith. "Adding Color and Contour to Early American Self-Portraitures: Autobiographical Writings of Afro-American Women," in *Conjuring: Black Women, Fiction, and Literary Tradition,* ed. Marjorie Pryse. Bloomington: Indiana University Press, 1985.

Fox-Genovese, Elizabeth. "'To Weave It into the Literature of the Country': Epic and the Fictions of African American Women," in *Poetics of the Americas: Race, Founding, and Textuality,* ed. Bainard Cowan. Baton Rouge: Louisiana State University Press, 1997.

Gardner, Eric. "'This Attempt of Their Sister': Harriet Wilson's *Our Nig* from Printer to Readers." *The New England Quarterly: A Historical Review of New England Life and Letters,* June 1993, pp. 226–46.

Gates, Henry Louis. "Harriet E. Adams Wilson," in *Dictionary of Literary Biography, V50. Afro-American Writers Before The Harlem Renaissance.* Gale Group Publications, 1986.

————. "Parallel Discursive Universe: Fictions of the Self in Harriet E. Wilson's *Our Nig,*" in *Figures in Black: Words, Signs, and the "Racial" Self.* New York: Oxford University Press, 1987.

Gates, Henry Louis and David Ames Curtis. "Establishing the Identity of the Author of *Our Nig,*" in *Wild Women in the Whirlwind: Afra-American Culture and the Contemporary Literary Renaissance.* New Brunswick: Rutgers University Press, 1990.

Gregg D. Crane. "Resistance and Reformation in Nineteenth-Century African-American Literature: Brown, Wilson, Jacobs, Delany, Douglass, and Harper." *American Literature, Vol. 69, No. 1, Unnatural Formations,* March 1997, pp. 221–22.

[Griffiths, Mattie]. *Autobiography of a Female Slave.* New York: Redfield, 1857.

Harper, Frances Ellen Watkins. "The Two Offers." *The Anglo-African Magazine.* September 1859, pp. 288–291; October 1859, pp. 311–13.

————. *Iola Leroy, or, Shadows Uplifted.* Philadelphia: Garriguer Brothers, 1892.

Herndl, Diane Price. "The Invisible (Invalid) Woman: African-American Women, Illness, and Nineteen-Century Narrative." *Women's Studies: An Interdisciplinary Journal,* September 1995, pp. 553–72.

Holloway, Karla F. C. "Economies of Space: Markets and Marketability In *Our Nig and Iola Leroy,*" in *The (Other) American Traditions: Nineteenth Century Women Writers.* New Brunswick: Rutgers University Press, 1993.

Jackson, Rebecca. *Gifts of Power: The Writings of Rebecca Jackson, Black Visionary, Shaker Eldress,* ed. Jean McMahon Humez. Amherst: University of Massachusetts Press, 1981.

Jacobs, Harriet. See under "Brent, Linda."

Joanna. *Narrative of Joanna, an Emancipated Slave of Surinam (From Stedman's Narrative of Five Years' Expedition Against the Revoluted Negroes of Suriname).* Boston: I. Knapp, 1838.

Johnson, Amelia E. *Clarence and Corinne, or, God's Way.* Philadelphia: American Baptist Publication Society, 1890.

Johnson, Ronna C. "Said but Not Spoken: Elision and the Representation of Rape, Race, and Gender in Harriet E. Wilson's *Our Nig,*" in *Speaking the Other Self: American Women Writers,* ed. Jeane Campbell Reesman. Athens: University of Georgia Press, 1997.

Jones, Anne Goodwyn. *Tomorrow Is Another Day: The Woman Writer in the South, 1859–1936.* Baton Rouge: Louisiana State University Press, 1981.

Jones, Jill. "The Disappearing 'I' in *Our Nig.*" *Legacy,* 13, 1996, pp. 38–53.

Kelley, Emma Dunham. *Megda.* Boston: James H. Earle, 1891.

King, Debra Walker. "Harriet Wilson's *Our Nig*: The Demystification of Sentiment," in *Recovered Writers/Recovered Texts: Race, Class, and Gender in Black Women's Literature,* ed. Dolan Hubbard. Knoxville: University of Tennessee Press, 1997.

Kirkpatrick, David D. "On Long-Lost Pages, A Female Slave's Voice." *New York Times,* November 11, 2001.

Lee, Jarena. *The Life and Religious Experiences of Jarena Lee, A Coloured Lady, Giving an Account of Her Call to Preach the Gospel. Revised and*

Corrected from the Original Manuscript, Written by Herself. Philadelphia: Printed and Published for the Author, 1836. Cincinnati: Printed for the Author, 1839.

————. *Religious Experience and Journal of Mrs. Jarena Lee, Giving an Account of Her Call to Preach the Gospel. Revised and Corrected from the Original Manuscript, Written by Herself.* Philadelphia: Printed for the Author, 1849.

Leveen, Lois, "Dwelling in the House of Oppression: The Spatial, Racial, and Textual Dynamics of Harriet Wilson's *Our Nig.*" *African American Review,* Winter 2001, vol. 35, issue 4.

Lindberg-Seyersted B. "Skin Color as Social, Ethical, and Esthetic Sign in Writings By Black American Women." *English Studies,* February 1992, vol. 73, issue 1.

Lindgren, Margaret. "Harriet Jacobs, Harriet Wilson and the Redoubled Voice in Black Autobiography." *Obsidian II: Black Literature in Review,* Spring-Summer 1993, pp. 18–38.

Loggins, Vernon. *The Negro Author: His Development in America to 1900.* New York: Columbia University Press, 1931.

Lovell, Thomas B. "By Dint of Labor and Economy: Harriet Jacobs, Harriet Wilson, and the Salutary View of Wage Labor." *Arizona Quarterly: A Journal of American Literature, Culture, and Theory,* Autumn 1996, pp. 1–32.

Lowenburg, Bert James and Ruth Bogin, eds. *Black Women in Nineteenth-Century American Life: Their Words, Their Thoughts, Their Feelings.* University Park: The Pennsylvania State University Press, 1976.

MacDougall, Frances Harriet (Whipple) Green. *Memoirs of Eleanor Eldridge.* Providence: B. T. Albro, 1838.

————. *Eleanor's Second Book.* Providence: B. T. Albro, 1839.

McKinney, James Joseph. "The Theme of Miscegenation in the American Novel to World War II." Ph.D. dissertation, University of Tennessee, 1972.

Mitchell, Angelyn. "Her Side of His Story: A Feminist Analysis of Two Nineteenth-Century Antebellum Novels—William Wells Browns'

Clotel and Harriet E. Wilson's *Our Nig.*" *American Literary Realism,* Spring 1992, pp. 7–21.

Mullen, Harryette. "Runaway Tongue: Resistant Orality in *Uncle Tom's Cabin, Our Nig, Incidents In The Life Of A Slave Girl,* and *Beloved,*" in *The Culture of Sentiment: Race, Gender and Sentimentality in Nineteenth Century America,* ed. Shirley Samuels. New York: Oxford University Press, 1992.

Nelson, Emmanuel S. "Harriet E. Wilson (1827?–1863?)," in *African American Authors, 1745–1945: A Bio-Bibliographical Critical Sourcebook.* Westport: Greenwood, 2000.

Pattee, Fred Lewis. *The First Century of American Literature, 1770–1870.* New York: D. Appleton-Century Company, 1935.

Peterson, Carla L. "Forced To Some Experiment: Novelization In The Writings of Harriet A. Jacobs, Harriet E. Wilson, and Frances Ellen Watkins Harper," in *Doers of the Word.* New York: Oxford University Press, 1995.

Picquet, Louisa. *Louisa Picquet, the Octroon; or, Inside Views of Southern Domestic Life.* New York: By the Author, 1861.

Pierson, Emily. *Jamie Parker, the Fugitive. Related to Mrs. Emily Pierson.* Hartford: Brockett, Fuller and Company, 1851.

Plato, Ann. *Essays: Including Biographies and Miscellaneous Pieces in Prose and Poetry.* Hartford: Printed for the Author, 1841.

Prince, Mary. *The History of Mary Prince, a West Indian Slave, Related by Herself, With a Supplement by the Editor, to Which is Added the Narrative of Asa-Asa, a Captured African.* London: F. Westley and A.H. Davis, 1831.

Prince, Nancy. *A Narrative of the Life and Travels of Mrs. Nancy Prince, Written by Herself.* Boston: Published for the Author, 1850.

Ramsdell, George. *The History of Milford.* Concord, N.H.: Rumford, 1901.

Reid-Pharr, Robert Fitzgerald. *Conjugal Union: The Body, The House, and the Black American.* New York: Oxford University Press, 1999.

Shockley, Ann Allen. "Harriet E. Adams Wilson," in *Afro-American Women Writers, 1746–1933.* Boston: G.K. Hall, 1998.

Select Bibliography

Short, Gretchen. "Harriet Wilson's *Our Nig* and the Labor of Citizenship." *Arizona Quarterly: A Journal of American Literature, Culture, and Theory,* no. 3, Autumn 2001, pp. 1–27.

Smith, Jessie Carney. *Notable Black American Women.* Gale Group Publications, 1992.

Spear, Chloe. *Memoir of Chloe Spear, a Native of Africa, Who Was Enslaved in Childhood. By a "Lady of Boston,"* ed. James S. Loring. Boston: James Loring, 1832.

Stern, Julia. "Excavating Genre in *Our Nig*." *American Literature: A Journal of Literary History, Criticism, and Bibliography,* September 1995, pp. 439–66.

Stewart, Maria W. *Meditations.* Boston: Printed for the Author, 1832.

————. *Productions of Mrs. Maria W. Stewart.* Boston: Printed for the Author, 1835.

Still, Peter. *The Kidnapped and the Ransomed: Being the Personal Recollections of Peter Still and His Wife "Vina," after Forty Years of Slavery. Related to Kate Pickard.* Syracuse: W.T. Hamilton Press, 1856.

Stowe, Harriet Beecher. *Uncle Tom's Cabin; or, Life Among the Lowly.* Boston: J.P. Jewett, 1852.

Takaki, Ronald T. *Violence in the Black Imagination—Essays and Documents.* New York: Capricorn Books, 1972.

Tate, Claudia. "Allegories of Black Female Desire; Or, Rereading Nineteenth-Century Sentimental Narratives of the Black Female Authority," in *Changing Our Own Words: Essays on Criticism, Theory, and Writing by Black Women,* ed. Cheryl A. Wall. Brunswick: Rutgers University Press, 1989.

————. "Maternal Discourse as Antebellum Social Protest," in *Domestic Allegories Of Political Desire.* New York: Oxford University Press, 1992.

Truth, Sojourner. *Narrative of Sojourner Truth, a Northern Slave, Emancipated from Bodily Servitude by the State of New York in 1828. Narrated to Olive Gilbert, including Sojourner Truth's Book of Life, and a dialogue.* Boston: Printed for the Author, 1850.

Upham, T. O. *Narrative of Phebe Ann Jacobs.* London: Printed for the Author, 1866.

Warren, Joyce W. "Performativity and the Repositioning of American Literary Realism," in *Challenging Boundaries: Gender and Periodization*. Athens: University of Georgia Press, 2000.

Webb, Frank J. *The Garies and Their Friends*. London: G. Routledge, 1857.

West, Elizabeth J. "Reworking the Conversion Narrative: Race and Christianity in *Our Nig*." *MELUS: The Journal of the Society for the Study of the Multi-Ethnic Literature of the United States*, Summer 1999, pp. 3–27.

Wheatley, Phillis. *Letters of Phillis Wheatley, the Negro Slave Poet of Boston*. Boston: John Wilson & Son, 1864.

White, Barbara. "Harriet Wilson," in *American Women Prose Writers*. Gale Group Publications, 2001.

———. "*Our Nig* and the She-Devil: New Information about Harriet Wilson and the 'Bellmont' Family." *American Literature: A Journal of Literary History, Criticism, and Bibliography*, March 1993, pp. 19–52.

[Williams, Sally]. *Aunt Sally; or The Cross the Way to Freedom. Narrative of the Life and Purchase of the Mother Revered Issac Williams of Detroit, Michigan*. Cincinnati: American Reform Tract and Book Society, 1858.

Wilson, Harriet E. *Our Nig; or, Sketches from the Life of a Free Black, In A Two-Story White House, North. Showing That Slavery's Shadows Fall Even There*, ed. R. J. Ellis. Nottingham: Trent Editions, 1998.

[Wilson, Mrs. Harriet E.]. *Our Nig; or, Sketches from the Life of a Free Black, In A Two-Story White House, North. Showing That Slavery's Shadows Fall Even There. By "Our Nig."* Boston: Printed by George C. Rand & Avery [for the Author], 1859.

Yarborough, Richard Alan. "The Depiction of Blacks in the Early Afro-American Novel," Ph.D. dissertation, Stanford University, 1980.

Yellin, Jean Fagan. *The Intricate Knot: Black Figures in American Literature 1776–1863*. New York: New York University Press, 1972.

ALSO AVAILABLE FROM VINTAGE BOOKS

THREE CLASSIC AFRICAN-AMERICAN NOVELS
Edited and with an Introduction by Henry Louis Gates, Jr.

Three lost treasures from the African-American past—edited by one of the foremost authorities on black American literature. Originally published between 1853 and 1901, these novels represent the beginnings of the black literary tradition in the United States and portray three crucial periods in African-American history: slavery, Reconstruction, and the Jim Crow era. They are collected here in one volume for the first time.

Clotel, or *The President's Daughter* by William Wells Brown (1853). Written by an escaped slave, this novel is the gripping account of the ordeals of a mulatto woman purported to be the daughter of Thomas Jefferson.

Iola Leroy, or *Shadows Uplifted* by Frances E.W. Harper (1892). In this pioneering work of the black woman's literary movement, a light-skinned black woman is raised as a free white, only to be tricked into slavery.

The Marrow of Tradition by Charles W. Chesnutt (1901). This suspenseful masterpiece tells of a sensitive African-American doctor facing the realities of segregation and racial terror in the Reconstruction South.

Fiction/Literature/0-679-72742-6